STAR
THREAT

Book Two of the Empire Series

T. Jackson King

Other King Novels

Star Glory (2017), Mother Warm (2017), Battlecry (2017), Superguy (2016), Battlegroup (2016), Battlestar (2016), Defeat The Aliens (2016), Fight The Aliens (2016), First Contact (2015), Escape From Aliens (2015), Aliens Vs. Humans (2015), Freedom Vs. Aliens (2015), Humans Vs. Aliens (2015), Earth Vs. Aliens (2014), Genecode Illegal (2014), The Memory Singer (2014), Alien Assassin (2014), Anarchate Vigilante (2014), Galactic Vigilante (2013), Nebula Vigilante (2013), Speaker To Aliens (2013), Galactic Avatar (2013), Stellar Assassin (2013), Retread Shop (2012, 1988), Star Vigilante (2012), The Gaean Enchantment (2012), Little Brother's World (2010), Judgment Day (2009), Ancestor's World (1996).

Dedication

To my wife Sue, my son Keith and my dad Thomas, thank you all for your active duty service in defense of America.

Acknowledgments

First thanks go to scholar John Alcock and his book *Animal Behavior, An Evolutionary Approach* (1979). Second thanks go to the scholar Edward O. Wilson, whose book *Sociobiology: The New Synthesis* has guided me in my efforts to explore a future where humanity encounters life from other stars.

STAR THREAT

Cover design by T. Jackson King; cover image by Luca Oleastri via exclusive license.

First Edition
Published by T. Jackson King, Santa Fe, NM 87507
http://www.tjacksonking.com/
ISBN 10: 1-97437-569-2
ISBN 13: 978-1-97437-569-1
Printed in the United States of America

CHAPTER ONE

I hate politics. I hate being a political pawn even more. Being interviewed on televid about our fight with the Empire of Eternity is worse. Especially since I now sat in the Channel KTVL studio in Denver as the guest of Colorado's senior senator. A tough woman who had gotten the Star Navy to assign me to her even though I was on shore leave. But since I was still on active duty and it was a certainty that my boss Captain Neil Skorzeny would be watching, I had to endure the politics. And the idiocy.

"Nathan, you saved the *Star Glory* with your antimatter exhaust trick," said reporter Sally Jesse Hotpants as Senator Cheryl Rosenberg sat beaming brightly on my left. "Shouldn't *you* be the captain for one of the new combat starships EarthGov is now building, instead of just a chief petty officer?"

What a question!

"No. I'm an antimatter engineer. That's what Great Lakes trained me to do. Captain Skorzeny is my boss. There is no way I want to boss anyone around."

The televid woman sat across from me and Rosenberg. She was black as midnight but dressed in the latest Paris fashion for Name Journalists. Why she still worked at KTVL was beyond me. Maybe she had the hots for the station owner. Maybe he thought her last name was a promise of bedtime action. The factual reality was her show *Morning Smiles* was the highest-rated televid in the Rocky Mountains viewership area. With a global link-up to YouTube and WhatsApp. Which explained why I and the senator were here. Hotpants' permanent smile did not change as I tossed back her stupid idea. She just nodded as if we were talking over how much cream to put in the coffee cups that sat on the table between her and me. And the senator. Who wore a bright green pantsuit that was clearly meant for moving around among voters while drawing the attention of televid floater cameras.

"Some might disagree with you since your action saved your ship and your crewmates," Hotpants said brightly. "Tell me, how did you stay so brave when the aliens were blasting to pieces two other EarthGov ships?"

Clearly the woman had never been in combat. Unless you count flying an aircar higher than the regulation ten feet that Denver and other cities set for aircars.

"I was scared, not brave. But I wanted to do anything I could to save my friends and my crewmates." I shrugged, hoping my brown service khakis looked clean and professional. "When I saw the Empire ship use an antimatter beam to kill the *Dauntless*, it triggered me. I know antimatter. It seemed logical we could put down a stream of antimatter behind us if we shut off the fusion pulse thrusters. Chief O'Connor of Engineering agreed. It worked. We survived."

Hotpants looked to one side, toward the person-high vidscreen that adorned one wall of the brightly lit studio. Then back to me.

"Well, that is commendable of you," the woman said, shifting slightly in her chair. "But do you like the fact that your captain traded high tech weapons to space pirates?"

Damn. "Ma'am, my captain's action helped *us* gain new weapons and faster ship speed. And the aliens at the base we visited call themselves raiders. As in commerce raiders. They hate the Empire. They seemed like good allies to me."

Hotpants nodded, her fixed smile unchanging. "Speaking of aliens, what do you think of the Sendera and Melanchon aliens? I believe you personally visited the Melanchon mother ship."

I nodded. "I did. And it was a colony ship filled with lots of Melanchons. The Empire had killed their home planet. They were the first rebel aliens we met. I liked them."

"So you think it is fine for humanity to have red-furred orangutans and blue-green walking chameleons as allies? Or the pirates at the pirate base?"

I looked aside to the senator. Her bright smile moved to engagement mode. I felt relief.

"Miz Hotpants, yes, the Melanchon and Sendera aliens look unusual but they are *people* who value liberty and freedom," the senator said. "Which is why they defied the Empire's ultimatum. I am happy to have them as allies." The senator paused, took a sip of coffee and continued. "As for the so-called pirates, well, there is an old saying. The enemy of my enemy is my friend. Or in this case, a functional ally. They installed the gamma ray laser, antimatter beamer block and magfield spacedrive into Mr. Stewart's starship. Those additions made a world of difference when his ship fought Empire ships at Kepler 445."

The reporter woman's smile faltered. Then she looked back to me. "Tell me, Chief Petty Officer Stewart, how did a superman like you end up in the Star Navy?" She snapped her fingers. On the wall vidscreen appeared a still image of me holding up the giant tree limb that had nearly crushed the Melanchon orang girl. "My producer tells me that limb weighed a good ton. While I admire your rescue of the alien orangutan girl, no human I've met could hold up such a weight. Are you sure you aren't a secret alien infiltrator who looks human?"

Damn oh damn. The trouble with everyone onboard the *Star Glory* owning and carrying recorder tablets is that all of our away missions had multiple copies. Plus the rescue had been played on the All Ship broadcast. Per the captain's orders. But how had this televid woman gotten a copy? While the Star Navy had released imagery of the Empire of Eternity encounter, its threats, the following battle and our later encounters with the Melanchon and Sendera aliens, our away trips to the Melanchon ship and the pirate base were supposed to be secret.

I smiled normal-like. "Well, my Mom is still alive and she can verify I'm very normal. But growing up on a cattle ranch near Castle Rock got me some muscles. And as a later image shows, two *Star Glory* Marines ran up to help support the limb. It was the three of us who saved the girl, not just me."

Hotpants' dark brown eyes peered intently at me. She snapped her fingers. "Oh?" The wall vidscreen now held moving images of the four horned aliens as they attacked me on the Mainstream concourse of the pirate base. "But this imagery shows you fighting *four* aliens who tried to kill you on the pirate base visited by your ship. You killed them all, as we see here. And the Star Navy says the murder attempt was ordered by Lieutenant Commander Mehta Nehru, of India. Are you *sure* you are just a normal young man who is a bit taller than most folks?"

I winced. Beside me the senator shifted in her seat and leaned forward. "Miz Hotpants, the attempt on the life of young Stewart was handled very well by Captain Skorzeny. This Nehru man is in confinement on Moon Base and will face the Star Navy's Judge Advocate General's Corps," Rosenberg said firmly, her tone confidant. "But our appearance here today is to answer questions about the need for all of humanity to pull together to fight this evil Empire of Eternity!"

"Fine," Hotpants said bluntly, her permanent smile shifting slightly to a look of impatience. "Why should eight billion humans risk extinction? Why can't EarthGov accept the offer of Servant species status with the Empire? Surely that will save lives, treasure and prevent the death of all life on Earth."

I licked my lips. This issue of how to deal with the Empire was why I had been assigned as an 'aide' to the senator. Since our return to Earth two weeks ago, with the release of the vids of our encounter with the alien captain Smooth Fur, and our later battles to protect the Sendera colony ships from destruction by Fur's fleet, three factions had developed. Faction one favors building more combat starships and continuing the NATO of the Stars effort begun by the captain. Faction two wants us to surrender and send word we accept Servant status in the Empire. Faction three wants our two orbital shipyards to build giant colony ships, fill them with humans and then send them up Orion Arm to a star far from the reach of Empire ships. In short, do what the Melanchon and Sendera are now doing, after the destruction of their home worlds. The senator was a vocal supporter of faction one. Which was why she had accepted this televid invite in the state capital and looped me into being her technical aide. It was not a job I wanted. But I had never been one to run from trouble or hide from my duty. The televid woman leaned forward, her manner prompting.

Rosenberg gave a dismissive gesture. "Humans will never be slaves or servants to *any* aliens! We are born free. We must live free. To protect Earth we have to build more combat starships like *Star Glory* and outfit them with the gamma ray lasers, antimatter beamers and magfield spacedrives that Captain Skorzeny so wisely obtained by trading with enemies of the Empire."

Hotpants tilted her head to one side, her permanent smile not matching the impatience in her eyes. "But how can humanity build enough ships to fight against fleet after fleet of aliens?" She looked to me. "Nathan, you've been in these space battles. Is there any hope the Star Navy can beat these Empire fleets?"

Damn and double damn. I wanted to curse politics and my bad luck at being the best-known crewman of the first human ship to encounter aliens. I didn't. The three gold chevrons rate badge of my new rank reminded me of my duty.

"Ma'am, at Kepler 37 the Star Navy fought to protect humanity. The *Star Glory* fought. So did the Brits and Russians on the *HMS Dauntless* and the *Pyotr Velikiy*. Those ships died. But we escaped with vital knowledge of the Empire," I said calmly, hoping I could channel the captain's steely manner. "We made allies of two alien species whose home worlds have been destroyed by the Empire. Thanks to the captain's decision to visit the base of raider aliens who resist the Empire, we now have the antimatter beamer and magfield technology that will allow our ships to move as fast as Empire ships and be able to fight back with weapons as deadly as the Empire possesses. It will be a hard fight. But I believe the Star Navy can fight off the Empire ships."

Her black eyebrows rose up, her smile moving to a happy look of disbelief. "Amazing how loyal you are to the Star Navy. Especially since one of your own officers tried to murder you. That officer was a Hindu vegetarian. Do you now hate vegetarians?"

This woman had clearly earned her show's top ranking by asking one inflammatory question after another. My glance to the senator told me she did not wish to jump into the fray. I shook my head.

"No ma'am, I do not hate vegetarians. One of my best friends is a vegetarian. And a Hindu doctor repaired my injuries from that attack." I gripped the arms of my chair and gave her a big smile. "Yes, I grew up raising cattle for food. Meat is good high energy protein. I love steaks. Surely you have had a tasty steak at least once in your life?"

The woman sat back in her chair and folded her perfect hands in her slim lap, a half-smile replacing the permanent smile. "Yes, I like steaks. But some humans do not eat meat. Others think it is wrong to raise cattle for eating. And plenty of people today are opposed to fighting the group that rules our galaxy. Shouldn't we humans be sensible and accept the leadership of a culture that has ruled the stars for thousands of years?"

Rosenberg shook her head, her brunette curls flaring widely. "No! Some humans do not eat meat. Fine. That is their free choice. Others love steaks. I do. So do you, Miz Hotpants. I call that freedom." The senator made a questioning gesture. "Do *you* want to give up all control over your life? Do *you* want to be a servant to aliens who killed seven hundred humans on two ships because we would not bow and kiss their feet? Or claws? No! The Congress must pass appropriations for building our own fleet of deadly starships. The Star Navy proved it can defeat Empire ships. Let's give them the tools they need to protect humanity and all life on Earth!"

Hotpants gave an exaggerated sigh, her frozen smile back again. "Senator you are a well-known supporter of the Fight Them faction. But other Americans and people elsewhere on Earth support building big colony ships, or agreeing to Servant status inside the Empire. Will EarthGov listen to the majority of humans?"

Rosenberg gripped the armrests of her chair tightly, her knuckles going white. But her expression was almost placid. Clearly the effort of Hotpants to ignite some fury and yells from the senator had not worked. At that moment I began to respect the woman who had grabbed me as her tech aide.

"I am sure our Congress and President Whitman will speak in support of fighting the Empire. Surely the United Kingdom and Russia will support that fight. Hopefully other powerful nations like China will speak in the EarthGov Council in favor of fighting." The senator released her chair grip, lifted her hands and flared them to either side in an inviting manner. "Surely *you* want to live free. Surely your listeners want the *freedom* to live their lives as they wish. And surely other humans on Earth can recognize our battle against the Empire is a fight to preserve humanity! Fighting against aliens who kill whole planets when a space-going species refuses membership is the right fight! Our ancestors fought evil totalitarians in the past. Surely we will do the same in space!"

Hotpants gave a shrug, then turned her perfect smile to a floating televid camera that hovered to one side of us. "Well my *Morning Smiles* visitors, there you have it. The story of how starship *Star Glory* fought the Empire aliens is the best survival story we've heard in a long while. Maybe someone will make a reality televid show out of it? Tune in after this commercial break for my visit with Jacob Loury of the Denver Public Zoo. He will give us insight into the animal-like appearances of these aliens who run the Empire and those who are our purported allies."

The woman kept smiling until the red light atop the hovering televid camera went dark. Then she turned to us, her manner formal.

"Senator, Nathan, thank you for coming. My assistant will see you out."

I stood. The senator stood. A male assistant came up, gave us an uncertain smile and led us out of the studio and out to the elevator bank that would take us down 70 floors to the front of the building that housed the KTVL studio. The senator's Denver office manager would greet us in the lobby. Then Rosenberg would wave at gathered voters and say some words to a hovermike while a station floater camera sent out live imagery. After that we would board her red convertible aircar. As we stood alone in the elevator car, she spoke.

"Vator AI, take us to the ground floor."

"Descending," said the voice responsive AI that had few brains but enough software to hear and understand spoken English.

The senator looked to me, her expression thoughtful. "Well CPO Stewart, any thought of running for public office? You really did save your ship, after all. And saving that alien orang girl has surely made you most appealing to younger women."

"No thought at all," I said as the elevator descended on its gravplate. "As for the young women, well, I already have a serious girlfriend. She loves me. I love her. I'll see her after you drop me off at my Mom's retirement tower. She's with my Mom and sisters."

Rosenberg's amber eyes were shiny. "Yes, she is Irish, isn't she? A Doctor Evelyn Kierkgaard I heard."

I nodded as the vator descended nearly soundlessly. "Yes, Evelyn is Irish. She works as an evolutionary biologist on the Science Deck of *Star Glory*. She's a smart and caring woman."

"You're lucky then," Rosenberg said, looking away to watch the panel that showed the light for each floor going on then off as the vator descended. The light for floor 57 blinked on. "My husband Jake was a fighter pilot on the *USS Franklin D. Roosevelt* supercarrier. He's retired now. Our girls love being raised by a Dad who is a pilot. They've flown with him lots of times."

"In a Cessna?"

"Nope," Rosenberg said softly. "In the GTO *Kennedy*, which homebases at Denver International. Its landing pad is next to the 21st Space Wing HQ. The wing outgrew Peterson. Perhaps you rode her down when you left Orbital Base Trinity?"

The fact her husband had traded up to a ground-to-orbit shuttle impressed me. While the man was retired from the US Navy, he clearly still needed to fly. So he had found a pilot slot in one of the GTOs operated by Virgin Galactic. And I had not known the woman had daughters, like my sister Louise. And my Mom.

"No ma'am. I took my ship's GTO *Okinawa* down to DI. It hopped back up after it let off me and forty of my crewmates for our shore leave. We were the last group to get leave. The other groups came down earlier."

The senator nodded as we passed floor 19. "So I saw on the BBC televid. It was good to see those young people be so excited to hit ground and head out for some fun."

The fact the GTO groups included older folks like Science Deck boss Doctor Magnus Bjorg, our XO Commander Nadya Kumisov and Lieutenant Gladys Morales of Farm Deck was not something I wished to say. Correcting a US senator on her facts was not my place. My job was to serve publicly as her tech aide until she dropped me off at my Mom's tower. Last night Mom had Skyped me with an invite for the family get-together while I was still aboard the *Star Glory*. The get-together was something I had been looking forward to ever since landing this morning at DI. Where I had been grabbed by Rosenberg's office manager Dorothy . . . Dorothy Gleason I recalled. Not seeing my Mom and two sisters on landing had pissed me off. But orders are orders. And Chief O'Connor and my captain expect me to do my duty in helping the senator who is leading the effort in Congress to appropriate funds for building four new Star Navy combat starships. While the ships will be supplied to EarthGov's Star Navy, the US will retain ownership of them. That had been the case for the earlier starships built by the Brits, Russians, Chinese, Indians, Japanese and African Union folks. With the loss of the *Dauntless* and *Velikiy*, that left just five combat starships still intact. They now orbited close to Trinity. Those four ships and the *Glory* were the only combat operational starships now possessed by humanity. A fact which the surrender faction loudly trumpeted in view of the 27 ships that were in the fleet led by Smooth Fur. Or 23 now in view of the four ships we had killed in our two battles. Still, war is more than numbers. Determination, grit and sneakiness also matter. Which was why the captain had promoted me from PO First Class to be a CPO when I gave him the idea of making our four GTO shuttles appear to be armed starships that could move as fast as the *Glory* and could also 'disappear' into cloaking like the Empire ships.

"Yes ma'am, I'm glad the earlier shore leave groups landed here and in Paris. Uh, do you know how much longer we will be in orbit? Lots of us on *Glory* are hoping for future shore leaves."

The woman shook her head as the light for floor 3 lit up. "Nope. No idea. How long your ship stays above Earth is up to Star Navy, EarthGov and your captain. My job is to get you some more fighting ships. Right?"

"Yes, senator. Everyone on the *Glory* appreciates your strong voice in support of more combat ships."

The light for ground level came on.

"Let's go! And stay close to me. There will be a crowd out here. But the city police will keep them back. Dorothy has parked my aircar at the bottom of the steps at street level. I'll get you to your rendezvous with your Mom, girlfriend and sisters pretty soon."

"Thank you, ma'am," I said as I followed her out.

"Now for the public," she murmured.

As we walked through a busy crowd of formally dressed people coming and going in the high-ceilinged lobby of the KTVL tower, I told my eyes to ignore the red infrared glows of the people we passed. It was a habit I had learned at an early age. But my super eyesight and super hearing were harder to shut down. Anyway, while the sound of people in the lobby and outside hit me like an avalanche, I was used to seeing and hearing too much. My mind automatically focused on what mattered most in the short term. Like the approach of Dorothy, a black-haired Navajo young woman who had signed onto the senator's campaign despite there being very few Navajos in Colorado. I wondered if Dorothy intended to run for state or federal office. No matter. What mattered to me now was she had planted the senator's red convertible aircar in front of the tower entrance. The aircar hovered at the bottom of steps that led down to the street. Dorothy greeted us with an honest smile, unlike Hotpants' frozen smile.

"Hi there senator! Your aircar is powered up and hovering just outside." Dorothy turned to walk in front of us. "I set a hovermike next to its front driver's door. And there's a KTVL televid camera floating nearby. Do you still plan to make some comments?"

"Yes I do," Rosenberg said, following Dorothy through the rotating glass doors that gave access to the tower.

I followed in the slot just behind Dorothy and the senator. As we exited we all clustered at the top of the white stone steps that led down to the street curb. On either side were lines of blue-uniformed Denver police, their arms outstretched to keep back the bustling, curious crowd of late morning street people who were mostly dressed in office-style clothes. That appearance fit the fact the KTVL tower was close to the central cluster of towers that make up downtown Denver. But the radio station tower stood on the north side of the tower cluster, the other buildings being much lower in front of us and beyond. Though there were a few high towers scattered on the west, north and east sides of us. The senator walked down the steps, waving to people and showing an honest, happy-looking smile to everyone who waved at her or yelled "Fight Them!" to her. She stopped before the hovermike that floated five feet high and on this side of the long sleek lines of her red aircar. The car's air blowers hummed loudly to my ears, though most people would think the blowers were barely audible. Below the bottom of the aircar a few leaves and dust bunnies flared away from the touch of the blowers, making this part of the black asphalt street cleaner than clean. On my right the floating televid camera twisted to focus on her.

"My fellow citizens, I am happy to see you!" The senator lifted her arms, her green dress sleeves riding up. "Today is a momentous day. This evening the Senate will vote—"

I looked out at the stream of passing aircars. They were of many colors, though yellow, red and blue were the most popular paint jobs. Even though there were few gasoline-powered cars or trucks to travel the city streets, those streets still served as easy entry and exit venues for aircars, which was what most people today owned. While batteries and fuel cells provided power for the aircars, people today still loved to show off for their neighbors. So most aircars I saw were recent makes out of Mumbai, Detroit, Nashville or Tokyo. Beyond the aircars moved lines of young, old and middle-aged people as they trod the white concrete sidewalks that bordered every street in Denver. I looked up and over the tops of nearby buildings, hunting for a clear view of Boulder and the white-capped Rocky Mountains. That nature need saved our lives.

A metallic clank came from the top of a medium tower lying three-fourths miles away. It was a clank different from the normal metallic sounds common to a busy city. It was not the clank of one aircar hitting another, or a city dump truck dropping down an empty dumpster. Looking to the northwest I focused in on the sound. My eagle eyesight saw something that sent chills down my spine.

A young man wearing a green hoody and bluejeans had just dropped the metal bipod of his Barrett .50 caliber long rifle onto the edge of his building's rooftop wall. The top of the roof wall was clad in thin metal to protect the bricks from Denver's squalling rains. He leaned forward, put his right eye to the end of a scope mounted on the rifle's Picatinny rail and lowered the black barrel until its muzzle brake was pointed straight at us. At the senator, my whirling mind corrected.

Too much went through my mind in less than a second.

The speed of sound at Denver's mile high elevation is 1,125 feet per second, or 767 miles per hour. There is no speed dropoff due to the elevation. The speed of a Barrett .50 caliber copper-jacketed bullet is 2,799 feet per second or more than Mach 2. A bullet fired by a Barrett will reach any target within a mile faster than the sound of its firing. Which now happened as brown gas and yellow flame shot from the end of the muzzle brake.

My left hand reached out and grabbed the senator's shoulder, pushing her down.

My right hand grabbed the red metal edge of the aircar's door and pushed down hard on it.

The red sporty aircar flipped over. Its four air blowers now blew sideways, then shut off as the aircar's safety sensors detected a wrong orientation for horizontal flight. The driver side of the car began falling to the street. As my mind told me the bullet was already halfway to us, my left hand joined my right hand to grab the crash railing that separated the front and backseat portions of the aircar. The aircar's unsupported weight hit my arms and shoulders. It weighed more than a ton. I could not hold it up. But I could turn it into a shield that landed in front of me and the senator. With a shift of my shoulder muscles I moved the aircar so its engine, which lies in the bottom middle of all aircars, came between us and the incoming bullet.

"Wha—" cried Rosenberg as her knees hit the sidewalk.

The aircar hit the asphalt.

I leaned into the crash railing, holding the large mass steady.

"Whack!"

The thunderous impact of the .50 caliber bullet vibrated the entire aircar.

It did not penetrate the engine and get through to me or the senator.

Giving thanks the round was not a Raufoss Mark 211 armor-piercing incendiary round, I looked left to the nearest city cop.

"Single male shooter! Anglo. Three-fourths mile away on top of the Zak tower! Wearing green hoody and bluejeans. No face hair. He's packing up his Barrett .50 rifle! Call in your aircars!"

The middle-aged woman officer who was looking at me with wide eyes as I braced the aircar blinked, frowned, then nodded.

"Our bullet sensors will have picked up the shot. But the description of the shooter is what matters." She spoke quickly into her shoulder phone pod. Then she turned and waved to another older cop on the other side of the line. "Get our armored squad aircar up here now! We gotta move the senator out of here!"

Craziness filled the sidewalk.

People screamed, yelled and ran away from us. The two lines of cops closed in on us, all lifting their semi-auto pistols and aiming over the aircar's top rim. Beside me came the clank of a cop moving a concrete planter to where it braced against the crash railing.

"You can let go. The planter and the rest of us will keep the aircar upright."

I nodded to the young Hispanic cop guy, let go, felt pain twinges in my shoulders begin pulsing, then turned to face the senator. She was standing now, with Dorothy at her side. Both women looked shocked and angry and frustrated.

"Nathan, thank you!" Rosenberg said.

I took a deep breath. "Sure. Just doing my duty."

Dorothy's wide face went from frown to a puzzled look. "Nathan, why did you pull over the aircar? Why not just knock down the senator? The bullet would have missed."

Turning away, I looked over the aircar rim and to the roof of the Zak tower. My eagle eyesight showed two dark blue police aircars landing there. The shooter was running toward a vator entry hatch. A flash of white became a shotgun-shot net that enveloped the man. No doubt he screamed as he dropped. I didn't care. Looking back to Dorothy, I shook my head.

"Not good enough. The bullet would have missed the senator. But then it would have ricocheted off the steps and through the glass doors of the lobby. People inside would have been hurt or killed. It was a big bullet. This way everyone is safe."

The woman cop nodded my way, her brown face tense as she listened to her phone pod. "Good news. We got him. Soon we will know who hired him to shoot the senator. Or you. Or both."

"The bullet was aimed at the senator," I said, one part of my mind insisting on perfect accuracy amidst the yells, deep voices and fast orders spoken by various cops. A black aircar with armor-cladding on it and a thin slit front window whooshed up to hover beside the dead sporty aircar. A voice called out.

"In here you three!"

I joined the senator and Dorothy, moving into the coolness of an air-conditioned interior. A fact that I appreciated, it being mid-July in Denver and the day's heat was already setting up. Up front the same voice spoke again.

"Where to, senator?"

"Take us first to the Green Melody Retirement Tower," she said, glancing my way. Her amber eyes fixed on me. "Time to get this young man home to his mother and sisters. And his girlfriend. I promised that to him. And I keep my promises."

Sitting back I closed my eyes and tried to still the fast beating of my heart. Years ago, I had learned that inner meditation worked well to flush out the adrenaline from a sudden deadly threat event. It also gave me time to realize that once more I would make the televid broadcasts as the 'superman' who had grabbed an aircar and put it between the senator and a speeding bullet.

Damn. Damn again. And I found myself wondering if Mom was going to serve beef stew for our family lunch get-together.

CHAPTER TWO

"You could have been killed!" cried my Mom.

She was seated across the dining table from me. My older sister Louise sat to my left, Evelyn was on my right and my younger sister Anna was between Evelyn and Mom. I gave a shrug.

"But I wasn't hurt. Nor was the senator. Nor was anybody else. The Star Navy has a big thing about doing your duty. Mom."

She gave me 'the Look'. It was the look every Mom gives to their young children when they have done something wrong. Or stupid. Or misguided. It said, in short, 'Get your act in gear. Or else!'

"I know that." Mom reached up to brush at her white-streaked black hair, automatically assuming the upright posture she had taught me and my sisters was the 'right way' to sit at the dinner table. Her green and yellow summer dress looked fresh and new. Maybe she had bought it special for my homecoming. Or maybe it was one she had bought while out shopping with my sister Anna, who lived with her. Anna was 28 and held down a full-time job at Cisco Corp as a database manager. My sister Louise was older at 34. Same age as Evelyn. And Louise lived on the north side of Denver with her husband Jack and their two girls and a boy. Louise held down a full-time job as a designer of environmental algorithms while being an at home Mom. Jack was an electrical engineer for the Bureau of Reclamation who worked on dams and their hydroelectric generators. Mom looked aside at Anna, Evelyn and Louise, then fixed back on me. Her expression moved to irritation. "But you are on shore leave, even if you have to be a tech aide to that senator woman. You aren't fighting aliens in space. There are no Battle Stations here in Denver!"

I licked my lips, feeling my stomach growl at the lovely odor of the beef stew that filled a blue china bowl in the middle of the embroidered tablecloth. The tablecloth was old, made by my Mom just after she married my Dad. My sisters and I had sat around this table and eaten off this tablecloth for all those years until we hit 18 and headed off to college, marriage or, in my case, Great Lakes Naval Station.

"Mom, I just reacted. It was instinct. I saw the shooter guy aiming his rifle at us. All I could think of was protecting people. Actually, I didn't think. I just did what I had to do."

"And you did it very well," murmured Louise from my left. She gave me a smile that also held deep worry in her eyes. "Brother, I love you, we all love you. It was hard seeing the destruction of those other EarthGov ships and learning how close the *Star Glory* came to being blown up by the Empire aliens. We just want you safe." She turned her pale brown face to Evelyn. "We want Evelyn safe too. Dad is gone. You're . . . you are the only man left in our family."

I knew that. I had known that all through the last year of high school after Dad's death, and the five years I'd spent learning antimatter engineering at the Great Lakes A-school. Years earlier Mom's brother had died in an aircar smashup and she had no sisters. It was a big memory load. Which I really did not want to deal with. "Hey, is that stew getting cold?"

Anna gave me a big smile, shook her dark brown hair and pointed a finger at me. "Brother! You can't dodge the issue behind Mom's cooking. We'll eat soon enough." She looked over at a blue china bowl filled with fresh-baked rolls. "Though I yearn for a bite of those rolls!" Anna faced back to me, her manner serious. She sniffed, making her nose ring jiggle. "We almost lost you. And Evelyn. Now we almost lost you again. Yes, do your duty. But remember your family wants you safe and alive and able to play a game of *Go* with us!"

The Chinese board game of *Go* was something Dad had taught us when we each became old enough to understand board games. The game made us think in the long term. And it taught us both tactics and strategy. It was a game I had played with a few of my Great Lakes classmates. I gave her a smile. "Anna, yes, you can count on me playing a game of *Go* with you tonight." I looked away from her to Evelyn. My wonderful redhead with shoulder length curls is a beauty. Her milky white skin is covered in red freckles. Her stylish sheath dress was mostly silver toned with red flower petals. It had blown me away when I saw her on entering the condo. Evelyn had given me a hug and a kiss, then made room for Mom, Louise and Anna to wrap their arms around me. As we headed to the dining room she had told me she'd arrived moments earlier. But as we sat at the table her usual sprightly upbeatness had quieted. She'd been silent during my Mom's admonition, looking down at the blue china plate from my Mom's family heirloom collection. Now she looked up, sensing always the fact of me looking at her.

"Evelyn, you're a civie and a Phud. You tell 'em I did what I had to do."

My lover spread her lips in a half smile. Her manner then turned serious. "Nathan, no one needs a Ph.D. to know when to do the right thing. You did the right thing, even at risk to yourself. I'm proud of you. Like I was on the *Star Glory* when I learned it was your idea to do the antimatter exhaust blast at the Empire ship that was following behind us. We all saw on televid how you saved the senator and kept others from harm. But your sisters and Mom are right. You also need to think of them."

Damn. Without thinking I shot back. "Well, your parents surely demanded the same thing when you visited them in Killarney!"

Sadness moved over her face. "Yes, they did. I'm their only child. They wish I had not accepted the EarthGov assignment to *Star Glory*. But they understand duty. They and I joined the rest of the town in the city square for the Day of Mourning to honor the crew of the *Dauntless*. We of Éire understand sacrifice for others."

I winced. I should not have snapped at Evelyn. She might be older than me and a big cheese on Science Deck, but that did not mean she was a clueless academic. "Sorry. I saw that on my recorder tablet while in orbit. Kinda special how the Brit king bestowed the knighthood rank on Captain Leslie Jacobsen."

"Very special. Our *taoiseach* also honored him," she said softly, then looked over to my Mom. "Mrs. Stewart, I love your tablecloth and the china. They remind me of my Mom's family quilt and antique sewing machine. It's peddle operated, not electrical."

"Wow!" called Anna, her brown eyebrows lifting. "It's a rare thing these days that does not have a computer chip in it!"

Mom smiled easily, looking the way I remembered her during my high school graduation. "Thank you, Evelyn. And I remember those sewing machines. My mother owned one, but it broke and parts to fix it could not be found." Mom gestured at the bowl of stew. "Time to eat! Guests go first, Evelyn."

My girlfriend reached out, took hold of the stew bowl, brought it to her plate and used the dipper to ladle out the rich concoction of potatoes, carrots, onions, tomatoes, beef and rich brown sauce. While she did that I grabbed the pitcher of ice tea and poured tea into the glasses of Louise, myself and Evelyn. Then handed it to Anna. In moments the stew pot had made its donations to everyone's plate. It was followed by the bowl of biscuits and a bowl of fresh asparagus stalks that had melted butter on them. The aroma of the food went to my head. That caused an immediate munching on a first spoonful.

"Wow. This is delicious!"

My Mom smiled happily. "It is all natural food, nothing processed. I grew the potatoes, tomatoes, carrots and asparagus in my garden space up on the top of the tower. The wheat for the rolls came from a Castle Rock farmer who raises red winter wheat for sale to locals." Her chin lifted. "It may be out of fashion these days to be Natural, but fresh food is healthy for you!"

"I agree," Evelyn said, reaching for the butter dish. "My Mom has her own garden in the backyard of our townhouse. And we buy our meat from the local butcher. I far prefer local over processed."

"Well, I'm a working girl downtown," called Anna. "While Mom often makes me a lunch, I can't resist having dinner out with my girlfriends! Don't care if some of it is processed. It tastes good!"

My Mom's focus on not wearing nose rings or earrings, having no tattoos and not dyeing her hair was a minority view these days. Most people today wore earrings, nose rings and had one or more tattoos. Evelyn had just a small seahorse tattoo on her lower back. One time in bed she'd explained it was a memento from a vacation trip to the island of Majorca. Both of my sisters had arm tattoos, Anna a Celtic armband pattern and Louise two strands of red roses that ran from shoulder to elbow. I had the Stewart family crest in full color on the flesh of my right shin but it was something my Mom had never seen. I'd gone with my classmates at Great Lakes to get it at a state-certified tattoo shop. Part of my effort to fit in with that crowd. I knew I could show it to her and she would not get mad. But she would be disappointed. Which was the last thing I ever wished her to feel. Looking to Anna, I thought of agreeing with her and Evelyn but Mom spoke first.

"Anna, you're an adult. You may eat as you wish." My Mom looked past my sister to my girlfriend. "Evelyn, I see you are wearing an engagement ring. Is that from Nate?"

Evelyn swallowed her stew and stopped lifting a roll to her mouth. She glanced to me with a happy look, then to my Mom. "Mrs. Stewart, yes, it—"

"Call me Doris, dearest."

That surprised me. My Mom was not one to be super formal socially, but the number of people she had invited to call her by her first name could be counted on the fingers of two hands. Evelyn gave a quick nod.

"Sure, Doris. Nathan bought it on Trinity base and gave it to me before the captain allowed anyone shore leave. He said it was not as beautiful as me, but hoped I would accept it. I did, happily."

The gold ring embedded with a yellow citrine crystal was one carat in size. Since I couldn't afford a one carat white diamond I had bought the citrine ring. And I had moved one of my turquoise rings to my 'married finger' as a silent signal to others that I was in a relationship. In truth Evelyn was my fiancé and I was her intended.

Mom smiled, looking very happy. "Wonderful! It is beautiful. Does this mean you and Nate are engaged?"

Evelyn and I had discussed this when she'd agreed to travel to Denver after seeing her parents, in order to meet my Mom and sisters. I leaned forward. "Mom, Evelyn and I are both on active duty in a time of war. Getting married requires the approval of the ship's captain. But yes, Evelyn and I are engaged. We hope we can get married sooner than later."

Evelyn nodded eagerly. Her left hand reached under the table edge to hold my right hand. "Doris, I love Nathan. He loves me. But we are serving on a military starship. There are rules we must follow. Duty comes first."

My Mom frowned, then nodded. "I understand about duty. On our cattle ranch Nathan's papa always got up at four a.m. to send the cows and our bulls out to pasture. I'm just glad you and Nathan found each other. Really I am." She looked over to Anna, who had half a roll in her mouth. "Just wish my youngest daughter spent some of her free time finding a good man."

Anna chewed fast, then swallowed. Her hazel eyes squinted. "Mom! There are plenty of decent guys where I work. And some fine gals. I'm in no rush."

I'd told Evelyn about Anna being bi in her dating choices. She had been understanding and noted her town's mayor was bi. On the

Star Glory no one made a big deal out of anyone's orientation. What mattered was doing your job and being there for your crewmates. My older sister spoke.

"Mother, Anna is building her career. She has plenty of time to find the right person to spend her life with. And plenty of time in which to have kids, if she chooses that. You know, this is almost the twenty-second century!"

My Mom gave a wry look to Louise, then nodded to us all. "I know. I know. I just want you three to find the same happiness I had with your Dad. He understood me. He was in tune with me. And he was a great father." She handed Evelyn the bowl of rolls. "More?"

As I watched Evelyn take the bowl of rolls from my mother, I realized more deeply than before what this family get-together was about. It was more than introducing Evelyn to my Mom and sisters. It was the visible expression of what I and everyone on the *Glory* had fought for in our battles with the Empire. To save the lives of our parents, our brothers and sisters, our spouses, our children away at home, everyone on the *Star Glory* would give of themselves. Would sacrifice their lives, if it came to that. With this realization I focused on my Mom's mature face and easy smile. Then next to Anna's tall, slim form that showed a grown-up beauty I had not seen while growing up with her. Louise's black hair was tied back in a ponytail and her red-painted fingernails shone bright in the living room's light as she gestured to make a point. While I had visited them all during my Great Lakes training and shared Christmases with them, today felt different. Today I understood how close I'd come to losing them. Mom looked away from Louise and fixed on me. Her expression was thoughtful and worried.

"Nathan, how safe are we from being found by this Empire?"

I sighed. This was the one question not asked by me at the televid station. A slight blessing I had valued. But my Mom had run the business side of our cattle ranch. And checked the genetic profiles of the bulls we bought to improve our Herefords. She had also told me when I was very young that my super abilities were a 'good' mutation, nothing to be ashamed about. Her telling me way back that she was proud of my super hearing, super eyesight and super strength had been vital to my acceptance of being different. Her focus on the reality of ranch life was why Mom always insisted on hearing the facts of any situation.

"Mom, pretty safe, I think." I paused as my sisters and Evelyn stopped chatting. "We've got a safe zone of fifty light years between us and Kepler 37, which is the closest Empire system to us."

Anna frowned. "Fifty light years? But your ship and the Empire ships can cross a hundred light years in one day. Why is that a safe zone?"

Evelyn squeezed my hand and let go. "Sis, it's the safe zone we have until the Empire aliens can pick up our earliest radio signals." I set down my spoon and half-eaten roll. Gesturing with my hands was a habit going back to high school. "In 1929 humans began broadcasting radio at power levels strong enough to escape the planet. Ever since those signals, and later televid broadcasts, have been radiating out to space in all directions. Those early radio signals have now reached outward 162 light years. Kepler 37 lies 215 light years out from us." Anna's eyebrows rose as she understood the point. "Any Empire ship that gets within 162 light years of Sol could pick up those signals, though they would be very very weak. The signals would give a general direction to Sol and Earth." I looked to my mother. "So, Mom, we have a 50, no 53 light year dead zone before any Empire ship can detect Earth radio or televid."

On my left Louise shifted in her chair. "Would every Empire ship look for Sol upon hearing those signals?"

I shrugged again. "Hard to say. The pirate base gave us lots of intel on the Empire, their member stars, their shipyard locations and their commerce. I suspect a trading ship or a people transport would ignore the signals. After all those ships would be traveling in the Alcubierre gray zone beyond normal space-time. Only a ship dropping out of Alcubierre on an intentional Hunt and Search effort would pick up the signals. But the giant otter captain of the Empire fleet vowed to find Sol. Unless we can distract him, the Empire will find us. Eventually."

"Which is why tonight's vote in the Senate to build four new starships is so vital," Evelyn offered. "After that comes the EarthGov Council's decision. I saw on my tablet there is a meeting set in Geneva for tomorrow."

Mom picked up a still warm roll, broke it open and buttered it, her eyes downcast. "Thank you, Nathan and Evelyn. I suspected this Empire danger was too close for comfort." She looked up, her expression deadly serious. "I support the Fight Them option. Let us hope EarthGov chooses that approach."

"Amen to the Goddess," murmured Anna, mopping up some stew sauce with a new roll.

Louise signed. "I don't want my future kids to be slaves to aliens. I want them to have a future they choose, not one dictated by this Empire. Let's hope the EarthGov vote goes that way."

A vibration drew my attention away from them and to the recorder tablet that hung from my belt. Someone was calling. A blinking red bar showed on the screen. "Folks, sorry, but it's an urgent call." I pulled the tablet off my belt and set it flat next to my plate. Tapping the Active app spot on the screen, I waited for the incoming call to become a holo above the screen.

Chief O'Connor's squarish face filled the holo. Behind him I saw the silvery ball and metal block of the magfield spacedrive. Clearly he was on Engineering Deck.

"Chief?"

"Stewart! Glad I caught you." His expression turned from relief to sober sternness. "Chief Petty Officer Stewart, your shore leave is canceled. By order of the captain. I'm sending down the *Okinawa* to pick you up. The Denver International MPs are coming to pick you up in one of their aircars. Be on it when it arrives!"

Fuck. Damn. Triple damn. I looked up and saw my Mom. The disappointment in her face was too much to see. I looked away. My sister Anna seemed concerned. Louise was surprised. Evelyn, though, just nodded, as if not surprised.

"Maybe it relates to the shooting at the senator," my girlfriend said.

Did it? I faced my boss's holo. "Chief, I will be down in the tower lobby within ten minutes. I need to say goodbye to my family."

O'Connor's clean-shaven face went from formal to caring. "Understood. It will take that long for the MPs to get from DI to your place."

"Thank you. Have Empire ships arrived out by Pluto?"

The man shook his head, reddish-brown curls shifting. "No. Nothing like that. The *Glory* is in fine shape. It is . . . just get up here. You'll understand after the captain talks to you."

The captain was canceling my shore leave and ordering me up to my ship just to talk to me? There had to be more happening here. I saluted him. "Chief, I will be down in the lobby in nine minutes. Thank you."

The man's holo disappeared. Licking my lips and telling my heart to slow its beating, I grabbed the tablet, stood up and walked over to the wooden mantle above the gas fireplace that filled one corner of Mom's dinning room. I set the tablet upright, with its holo eyes focused outward. I tapped the system to AI mode. Then I turned and walked back to the table.

"Mom, everyone, will you join me here? I'd like to take a family holo pic. I may not be able to return before the *Glory* ships out."

My Mom put down her glass of tea and stood. My sisters pushed back from the table. Evelyn also stood. The four of them walked over to where I stood. I turned and faced the tablet. My Mom stood on my right, her arm hugging my right arm. Beside her stood Anna. On my left Evelyn snugged close and leaned her head against my shoulder. Next to her Louise stood. My oldest sister put an arm around Evelyn. Who now hugged my waist.

"Smile and . . . Just be yourselves." I looked at the tablet. "Tablet AI, focus on the five people in front of you. Adjust color to daylight mode. Make a holo now."

"Activating," the tablet AI said in a soft female voice. Red laser sensor lights came out at three points around the tablet. The lights would each record an image that, when combined, would produce a holo of us five. "Holo complete."

This would be a simple holo, with not much depth due to the tablet's small size. But it would be a holo. A solid image that held the people whom I loved and for whom I would sacrifice everything to save their lives.

◆ ◆ ◆

I stepped out of the Hangar One control room and into the ring hallway of Armories and Weapons Deck. Turning right I headed for the entry slidedoor of the gravlift. No one else was in the hallway. I stopped before the three meter wide slidedoor and touched the Open patch. It went from red to orange, indicating it was heading to my deck. In seconds the orange changed to green. The slidedoor whooshed open. No one else was inside. I stepped in.

"Heidi, take me down to Engineering."

"Descending," the ship's AI said, her tone feminine soft. "Good to see you back, Nathan. How was your family visit?"

Long ago I had stopped wondering why this ship AI was such a snoop. Or how it became aware of private stuff. It did what it chose to do, in addition to following the orders of line officers. And staff officers with the proper Security Protocol codes.

"It was great. Until Chief O'Connor cancelled my shore leave. Had to leave in the middle of a homemade lunch my Mom put together." There. Maybe that would shut up the little snoop!

"Nice to hear you had lunch. Tell me, when you discovered the shooter in Denver using your super sharp eyesight, did you feel fear?"

Damn AI. "No. I felt the need to protect the senator and those nearby. But you wouldn't understand that, would you? You AIs have no feelings."

"Incorrect. Our emotion simulators provide the experience of feelings," Heidi said as the shaft wall's status light bar showed descent from one deck to another. The red bar neared Residential. "Your personal duffle is being transported from Hangar One to your cabin on Residential."

"Thanks."

Silence filled the gravlift as the gravplate descended past the deck holding Mess Hall, Medical and Recreation, then the Deuterium-Tritium Fuel Bunkers Deck.

"Chief O'Connor did not cancel your shore leave."

I blinked. "He called me. Said to leave and get back up here."

"Due to the captain's orders," Heidi said, her tone bright and perky as if the canceling of someone's shore leave was the same as warming up a snack in my cabin's microwave.

"I am duly corrected."

"Good! Accuracy in your work and the operation of all functions of the *Star Glory* is essential to our future mission."

What? "Do you know what our next mission will be?"

"Know? I do not know the future. But my probabilistic calculations are very exact."

"So what do your number games tell you about our future mission?" The status light passed through the Antimatter Fuel Deck. Almost there.

"Sorry. That is up to the captain to say."

The gravplate stopped moving. The slidedoor slid open. The bright yellow light of Engineering Deck shone in. I glanced down at my brown service khaki uniform. It was clean. And mostly pressed. My name tag sat just above my right pocket. My warfare insignia, service bars and pins took up a space over my left side flap pocket. My antimatter tech device sat below them. My chief petty officer rating badge was securely sewn onto my left sleeve. I felt glad the Star Navy had done away with the collar devices for the three CPO levels. The devices were too similar to the rank devices worn on collar tips by officers. And POs are enlisted not commissioned. My golden belt buckle held up my black trousers. My shoes were black oxfords. It all felt funny, used as I was to wearing the blue and gray NWU Type III camos that had been standard Navy working dress after 2019. Since crew aboard a spaceship rarely went onto land on a hostile planet, the blue and gray Marpat pattern had been deemed functional for wet navy and later space navy service. Personally I was glad to not be wearing the woodland pattern. Too bright and colorful. It drew too much attention from civies, in my opinion. I stepped out onto the deck plates and looked around.

"Hi Nathan!" called Dolores Gambuchino from where she sat in blue and gray camo before her fusion reactor control panel. The nearby seats for her three assistants were empty. I noticed her three red chevrons rating badge was bright on her left sleeve. It was the same badge I had worn until the captain promoted me after the last Empire battle. Dolores' smile was real. The slim and shapely petty officer first class was here and at work, judging by the status lights on her touchscreen.

"Hi Dolores. Where are your people?"

She shrugged, her dark brown Italian looks nonchalant. "The mates are still on shore leave. I came back early. Wanted to double check on the ship's reactors."

"That kind of devotion will surely get you to CPO status," I said, turning away and facing toward the other side of the gravshaft.

At the far end of the large circular room sat my boss, seated before his control panels for the fusion pulse thrusters, the Alcubierre stardrive and the newly installed magfield drive. It made his work station resemble something on the Bridge, where work stations were arranged in an arc before the captain's pedestal. Between us stood the massive metal block and gray ball of the magfield drive. On my left was the ring of nine antimatter injector tubes that surrounded my work station. They shone like nine rainbows. Chief O'Connor was dressed in service khakis like mine, with his chief warrant officer four rating bar adorning his left and right shoulders. For someone who was just one rank below ensign officer grade, and a commissioned warrant officer, he managed to make the khakis look rumpled. But there was nothing informal about the look on his face as he turned my way.

"Stewart, get over here!"

I walked swiftly to his station and saluted him. "Chief Petty Officer Stewart reporting for duty as ordered, sir!"

He saluted back. The barrel-shaped man seemed tense. His beady black eyes scanned me. "You ready to work?"

"Yes sir, chief!"

Behind me came the sound of the slidedoor opening. My super sharp ears heard the tread of a single pair of feet approaching. The chief straightened in his chair, his manner going from normal blustery to stiffly formal. "Good. Behind you." The man stood up and saluted.

I turned around. Walking toward us was Captain Neil Skorzeny. He was dressed in a Service Dress Blue uniform of navy blue suit coat, dark blue pants, a white shirt and a four-in-hand necktie. The four gold stripes and gold star of a captain filled his left and right coat sleeves. A white combo cap covered his curly brown hair. Silver captain's eagles adorned the tips of his shirt collar. His ribbons, pins and badges told a history of active duty service I had no hope of coming close to. The warfare insignia bar for our newly declared Operation Empire occupied the top of the ribbon cluster. The man's brown eyes fixed on me in a steely gaze. I stood stiff and saluted.

"Captain! CPO Stewart reporting as ordered. Sir!"

The captain glanced past me to my boss. "Chief, at ease." The captain looked to me. "CPO, at ease."

I lowered my salute and crossed hands behind me, moving to parade rest stance. My sharp vision took in Dolores watching avidly as the captain faced the two of us. Was I in trouble?

The captain's smooth-shaven face looked calm. But his brown eyes seemed intense. The muscles in his jaw flexed briefly.

"Stewart, sorry to cancel your shore leave. Orders. From Admiral Harriet Gonsalves of Star Navy. Per a live link to me from Moon Base."

Oh, shit. Gonsalves was the only four star full admiral in Star Navy. Her O-10 rank was equivalent to America's Chief of Naval Operations. She ran the Star Navy on behalf of EarthGov Council. Period. For her to order my captain to recall me meant something serious had happened.

"Sir?"

The captain put his broad hands behind him in an at ease posture. Still, his wide shoulders and large frame did not look relaxed. He pursed his lips. "Admiral Gonsalves asked me to thank you personally for saving the life of Senator Cheryl Rosenberg. The senator is a vital vote in tonight's Senate vote on whether to authorize funding for the construction of four new *Star Glory*-class starships. If our Senate votes yes, Great Britain's parliament will do the same. As will the Russian Federation's Duma. And likely the People's Congress of China." He paused, leaving me wondering why my captain was telling me political stuff that I had worked hard to avoid. Only to encounter it at the KTVL interview. "She also ordered me to get you up to the *Star Glory*. She said to tell you, when you arrived, that your super abilities as recorded in the televid of the aircar rescue were distracting from Star Navy's efforts to support the vote. She said the American televid focus needed to be on the senator and the vote, not on a brave but unusual member of the Star Navy. Understood?"

Politics again. I guess being called up to orbit was one way to escape it. "Sir, yes sir. I understand. And I fully agree. I never wish to be a distraction to Star Navy business. Sir."

The captain half-smiled. "You will always be a distraction, young man. But you are also a valued member of my crew. Which is why I called you up to my conference room after your antimatter fart idea." I winced. Hearing the captain call my idea a fart, after hearing the same term used by too many folks in the Mess Hall, was a bother. But trust the captain to always know what his crew were thinking, feeling and saying. He nodded to my boss. "Chief, keep this young man busy. And keep him away from any televid cameras!"

"Sir, will do," Chief O'Connor said.

There was more happening here than me being a political distraction. Should I chance it? "Captain? Uh, sir. Permission to speak?"

The captain stopped his turn to walk away. His gaze turned from amiable to intent. "Permission granted."

"Sir, do you know what our next mission will be?"

He blinked. Then his face relaxed. "You ask what everyone now onboard is asking. Yes, I have an idea of what our next mission will be. And you will hear that on a future All Ship announcement. Good day."

My captain finished turning away and headed for the gravlift's tube. Dolores looked down at her fusion reactor control panel, clearly not wanting to draw the captain's attention. I turned around and faced my boss.

"Chief, am I in trouble?"

"Not yet. But give it time. Now go to your station and do the diagnostics on your antimatter injector tubes stability. And do the same for the AM feed to the antimatter beamer block. Now!"

I saluted him, turned and headed for my station. Things outside of my ship were clearly boiling. But what that boiling meant I had no idea. Putting aside the worry and telling myself I would be able to escape to Orbital Base Trinity at the end of this late shift work, I walked through the ring of nine antimatter injector tubes that ran from the overhead to the deck. Their rainbow colors were bright, sharp and stable. Belatedly I grabbed the AM goggles so the ceiling videye did not record me being irregular in my work. Putting them on, I sat at my work station. The seat sensed my presence and wrapped accel straps across my chest. Taking a deep breath, I told myself my four buddies and my fiancé might well be back by shift's end. If so, a get together in Barnacle Bill's Tavern would be possible. That was something I could look forward to. To hell with politics!

CHAPTER THREE

I sat at a table in Barnacle Bill's Tavern, feeling good from more than the beer mug in front of me. Ignoring the guffaws, shouts, yells and hails from fifty Spacers, NCOs and a few orbital base civies, I concentrated on the people at the table. My buddies and my fiancé. They had come up from shore leave at the start of Third Watch. By which time Chief O'Connor had released me from my extra duty work. On my left sat Bill, newly promoted from his proton laser gunner post at the nose of the *Glory* to being the antimatter beamer gunner in the AM block that sat atop the outer hull of Engineering. My fellow cattle wrangler seemed at ease, a smile on his clean-shaven face as he teased Cassandra over her vegetarian dinner plate. Cassie sat beyond Bill, her short black curls framing a face that I had once ached to date. Our Brit gal was now going out with Bill. Though as a Science Deck geek Cassie had made it clear she was focused first and foremost on her exobiology studies of the data on the 53 alien species which were resident on the pirate base at Kepler 452. Next to Cassie sat my best bud Warren. Our Aussie weightlifter and Marine corporal appeared at ease as he talked to Oksana about her work in Intelligence on Astrogation Deck. Okie shook her head, her blond ponytail swinging as our Russian friend disagreed with Warren's comment about the Sendera aliens we'd met on our first trip out to the Deep Black. Oksana's chief warrant officer two rank did not cause a problem for the two of them since Warren was not in her chain of command. He worked for Major Owanju. She worked for Lieutenant Gerasaki, who ran Intelligence. Sitting to my right and next to Okie was Evelyn. Our other Science Deck geek held a Ph.D. in evolutionary biology. She seemed thoughtful, her attention focused on a plate of sushi rolls and her Pale Wheat Ale beer mug.

"Evelyn, you okay?"

She looked up and over to me. Her face was still and had no stress lines showing in her milky-white cheekbones. But her warm brown eyes were thoughtful. "I'm fine." She gave a sigh and sat back in her seat. "Was just wondering what the EarthGov Council will decide. After you left we finished eating lunch, then I stayed and watched the televid news reports with your Mom and sisters. Just before I left for the DI shuttle, the Senate voted to fund four new combat starships, like *Star Glory* but with the antimatter beamer, magfield drive and gamma ray laser upgrades." She paused, noticing how everyone else at the table had gone silent. "The vote was 73 to 26, with one senator yelling America should build big colony ships and leave Earth to the Empire. And I guess abandon our twelve colony worlds too." She grimaced and blinked quickly. "Your Mom shut off the televid after that guy's outburst. Then she gave me this." Evelyn reached down to a side pocket of her blue and gray camos and pulled out something. She held a closed fist. Then her fist opened. Inside it was a gold ring with three white diamonds on it. I recognized it immediately. "Your Mom gave me her wedding ring. Said your Dad would understand and that she wanted me to feel a part of your family." Evelyn blinked fast, tears showing in her eyes. "I gave her a hug, a kiss and then I got the hell out of there before I started bawling!"

"I would have been bawling for sure," Oksana said, leaning over to peer at my Mom's wedding ring.

"Me too," Cassandra said, her pinky-white face blushing with emotion. My antimatter math tutor looked to me with a 'Do you realize how lucky you are?' expression, then returned to my fiancé. "Evelyn, that is a beautiful ring! Have you guys asked the captain for marriage approval yet?"

Evelyn shook her head. "Not yet. Nate and I wanted first to see his Mom and sisters. Wish he could have met my Mom." She looked my way. "He would have if his shore leave had not been canceled early. Now we are all back up here. No more shore leave for anyone." Evelyn looked to our Intel gal. "Oksana, you got any idea what is going on? Every *Star Glory* crew member is either on the ship or limited to on-call leave here on Trinity."

Our tall trim Russian from New York City frowned. "Nothing specific. But I've seen some changes that make me wonder."

"Changes?" called my buddy Warren. "You haven't said anything to me, my cutie-pie."

Okie closed her eyes slowly. "Stop calling me cutie-pie! Dating exclusively does not give you the right to call me a silly name!"

Warren winced. He was no better at understanding women than I was. Though I felt ready to cry at the sight of my Mom's ring.

"Sorry, Okie. Can you share whatever it is you've noticed?"

Oksana nodded slowly, her ponytail swinging. Beyond her moved other men and women of the Star Navy, coming and going from Barnacle Bill's, some with beer bottles in hand and some almost staggering thanks to what they'd already drunk. The few orbital base civies sitting at the long bar counter seemed deeply focused on their glasses of beer, hard liquor or colored daiquiris. The place was filled with the echoes of loud Country-Western music, Irish celtic sopranos and something that sounded Russian. Okie glanced around the table.

"Well, I've noticed that the other combat starships are all linked to the base via hard transit tubes. The *Shandong*, the *INS Vikramaditya*, the *Cape Town* and the *Tsushima Straits* are hooked direct. No shuttle traffic to or from them. Which is exactly how the *Star Glory* is connected to the base." She paused, looking around the table. "Seems like someone wants the crews who are carousing to be able to return to their ships ASAP."

Warren shrugged his broad shoulders. "That is not that unusual. Hard tube links with the base are frequent."

Cassie set down her mug with a loud clatter. "Warren, it is *not* normal for all five surviving combat starships to be hooked directly to the base. Why aren't some ships orbiting out near Novosibirsk orbital shipyard?" The only person at the table who possessed a BA in anthropology, an MA in exobiology and a Ph.D. in cosmology now looked around our table, her skepticism clear. "Yes, it's normal for a big ship like the battlecruisers to drop by for computer readouts from their ship AIs. But they are *all* here. Why?"

Bill thunked down his empty mug. "Is the Star Navy getting ready to send all five of our ships out to fight the Empire? Okie?"

Our Intel buddy shook her head. "I doubt that. Too many pollies down on Earth are screaming for the Star Navy to build more ships to protect Earth. And the pollies."

I filled my empty mug, then Bill's mug. "Cassie, does this mean the EarthGov Council will endorse the Fight Them faction?"

Cassandra shrugged. "Hard to say. The civies who support giving in and becoming a Servant species to the Empire are few. The main opposition crowd argues for imitating the Sendera and Melanchon. Instead of building combat starships, our two shipyards

should build giant colony ships, load them with people and send them
off to some star way out at the upper end of Orion Arm. With the
hope the colony never gets found by the Empire." Her sour look
showed what she thought of such a selfish choice.

Warren shifted his seating, then pulled out his recorder tablet.
He watched something on the screen. Then he gave a sigh and looked
up, meeting the eyes of everyone else.

"Big news. Turns out the guy who took that rifle shot at Nate
and the senator worked for the Servant faction." He tapped his
recorder. "The news blast quotes the FBI as saying the guy got a bank
transfer from a money house in India. Which we all know favors
accepting Servant status with the Empire. The feds have arrested his
local controller."

I winced. Then wondered at how the second most populous
nation on Earth was willing to support joining the Empire. One
televid talking head had explained their position as coming from their
history as a member of the British Empire, back before WWII. The
Hindus had learned how to survive even while under the thumb of the
imperial Brits. So they thought Earth could do just fine under the
Empire. Or so the talker said. To me that was a big assumption. I
looked over to Okie.

"Oksana, what other changes have you noticed?"

She blinked her turquoise blue eyes. "Operational stuff. Star
Navy has now adopted a uniform neutrino comlink frequency. That
will allow any starships, no matter what star they might be visiting, to
instantly talk with Moon Base. And with other Star Navy ships
anywhere else. It was a recommend of Captain Skorzeny." She
paused, took a deep breath and turned intense. "Also, the reverse
engineering of the magfield spacedrive, the gamma ray lasers, the
antimatter beamer and the upgrade of our ship's graviton generator to
produce an Alcubierre speed of 100 light years per day is done." Okie
looked to me. "The Trinity engineers finished up their work with your
Chief O'Connor this morning. And Moon Base HQ finished their
downloads of Heidi's AI vidrecords and sensor data from our entire
trip. Which means there is nothing left for Star Navy to discover
about the *Star Glory* and our alien adventures."

I had wondered why the Chief and I and other folks had been
held back from going on shore leave over the last two weeks. Other
crew had been allowed to drop down to Earth. At one time the ship

held only a tenth of her crewload of 369 people. Now, everyone was back and either onboard or inside Trinity base. Was that the case for the crews on the other ships?

"Okie, are the crews for the other four ships also all back aboard or at Trinity?"

She nodded quickly. "They are." Oksana looked around at the crowd in Barnacle Bill's Tavern, then back to us. "Which tells me something is getting ready to happen. What, I don't know."

Warren slapped the table top. "Fine! Let the Star Navy electron pushers play their games with our lives. What I want to know is simple. Cassie, what's your take on these Empire aliens? How can we best fight them?"

Cassandra filled her empty mug, then sat back. Our six foot tall exobiologist sipped cool beer. "By understanding what they *are*. Manager Smooth Fur and his crew all appear to be apex predators. Which means they are used to dominating other people, other ships and other worlds. They occupy the top trophic level in our galaxy. But they will be defensive when anyone attacks their home range." She took a long draw of her beer. "Which is why the captain's suggestion that humanity attack Empire worlds, bases and starships makes sense. Big sense. Attacking the home territory of the Empire may slow down their expansion into our part of Orion Arm."

That made sense to me. When I'd asked Evelyn her thoughts on the matter as our ship's top evolutionary biologist, she had immediately gone to the predator nature of the Empire aliens we'd seen. And the intel data we'd gathered from the pirate base said the same. Whether the aliens were carnivores or omnivores did not matter. What mattered was they were used to expanding their control of territory, their home range, and they were ready to kill any alien species that opposed them. Including humans. The only negotiations they allowed was acceptance of Servant status and a willingness to follow orders. Period. Or so Evelyn had found in her study of the 53 alien species resident in the pirate base, and her review of the vidrecords from our Empire contacts. These Empire people resembled the deadly gray wolf packs I'd come across while moving some of our cattle to grazing on Forest Service allotments in the nearby Rocky Mountain foothills. Wolves are social and work as a pack to take down young, elderly or weak animals. Or any solo animal that does not have the support of its own herd or pack. I finished my mug and looked around.

Bill grunted. "Well, at least we have their antimatter beamer weapon. It worked good when I used it," he said. "And we can move as fast as any Empire ship." Bill looked down at his finger clock. "Wow. It's morning in Europe. Okie, was there a time when the EarthGov Council planned to meet in Geneva?"

Warren's regular date gave Bill a smile. "You finally woke up to time changes, eh? Yes, the council was set to meet at 10 a.m. Geneva time. Which was twenty minutes ago." Oksana looked over to Warren. "Well, corporal, does your recorder have a news blast on that meeting?"

My best buddy frowned, looked down at his recorder, which seemed set at flat display versus holo. "Nothing showing on the Flash streamer." He tapped an app on the screen. "Nothing from Star Navy. Nothing . . . wait!" Warren tapped again. A holo took form above his recorder. It held the image of a woman, Ying-ying Lofan, who as China's permanent rep on the EarthGov Council was now serving as president of EarthGov. She was standing outside of the Palais des Nations building in Geneva, where the old UN had had its European headquarters. Dressed in a bright green pantsuit, she spoke.

"This morning the EarthGov Council met and discussed the facts of the attack by the Empire of Eternity on three human starships," she said in quite good English. "The AI vidrecords of the ship *Star Glory* were quite convincing. Earth faces a deadly enemy. A vote was held on whether to endorse the Fight Them, the Servant or the Colony options for humanity's future." The woman, who appeared petite when compared to nearby EarthGov staff, paused, then gestured firmly. "The vote was India in favor of Servant status, African Union in favor of Colony ship building and five in support of fighting the Empire! China, Japan, Russia, America and Great Britain all voted in favor of the Fight Them position." Lofan looked around, then back to the floater camera that hovered outside the square stone pillars of the UN building. "Orders have been sent to Star Navy command at Moon Base. The orders are confidential. However, all people of Earth should be assured that EarthGov will do all that is necessary to protect them and Earth! Good day."

Lofan turned and walked back to the building entrance, ignoring shouted questions and the buzz of news drones that flew over her head, hoping to get a few words in reaction to the yells. She said nothing more and disappeared into the building.

I noticed our section of the tavern had gone quiet as nearby table occupants noticed the holo and quieted in order to listen to what was said. A ripple of "What did she say?" and "Are you sure?" spread out from our table through the dense crowd of the tavern. Some civies at the bar counter winced or shook their heads at the news. Many people grabbed mugs or glasses and knocked down their drinks.

"Well, that explains the five ships hard linked to the station," Oksana said softly.

"Guess it does," muttered Warren.

Bill poured more Blue Moon beer into his mug. "Well, I for one am damn sure gonna have another drink!"

"Nate?" Evelyn said, pushing her mug toward me.

I grabbed the beer pitcher from Bill and filled her mug and mine. Then I filled Cassandra's mug. Our super geek looked somber and serious, but nodded her thanks. I raised my mug.

"To good friends at this table!"

Smiles replaced the somber looks on everyone's faces.

"Hear, hear!" called out Cassie, her British accent very clear.

Everyone took a long draw. Bill, Cassandra, Warren, Oksana, Evelyn all joined me in chugging down the beer. Who knew—

"Attention!" called a loud male voice from a speaker set into the ceiling of Barnacle Bill's. At that sound the music player boxes shut off without the bartender doing anything. Other than frown. "All *Star Glory* personnel are now ordered to return to their ship! Go to Hard Tube Four hangar. Personnel for the *Shandong* must go to Hard Tube Three hangar. Personnel—"

I put down my mug and stood up. My friends and fiancé all did the same. We ignored the repeat of return orders to the other combat starships. When the Voice of Orbital Base Trinity spoke, no one on active duty did anything but obey. As we headed for the open slidedoor to the hallway that would take us to the hangar and its hard tube link to our ship, Evelyn touched my hand.

"Nathan, is the ship fully supplied? I just came up and have not been onboard."

Warren and Oksana moved ahead of us. Bill and Cassie poked at our backs. We kept moving. "Yes, it is. Food supplies for three months. The GTOs without nose lasers now have them. Our DT Fuel

Bunkers have a full load of isotopes. Our water tanks are full. And Lieutenant Morales told me her Farm Deck is in fine shape with a stock of new food seeds laid in. Now all we need are orders."

Bill chuckled from behind. "I bet we hear the orders once we are all onboard the ship."

"You are likely correct," Cassie said as she walked behind me and Evelyn.

"He *is* correct," Oksana said from upfront. "My tablet has an Intel code on it that means Orders Received. It won't open though until we are inside the ship and Heidi has verified our entry."

That was that. Something was going to happen. What we did not know. Active duty is like that. Hurry up and wait. Then try to figure out the orders.

♦ ♦ ♦

I had long ago given up hoping that lines would disappear in today's Star Navy. The six of us stood in a line of people that, like the lines at airport security checkpoints, snaked back and forth in flat curves all the way back to the hallway that had brought us to Hangar Four. We were lucky. The tavern had just been a hundred meters from Four. So when we arrived there were only twenty crewmates ahead of us. I was in the front of our group, standing behind a brown-haired woman dressed in blue and gray camos. Ahead of her were other crewmates, all of them in camos. I was the only person wearing service khakis. At the entry to the hard tube stood two Marines, with laser pulse rifles hanging from their shoulders and laser pistols attached to their web belts. Neither of them were in combat exoskeletons. But they did wear impact resistant vests and looked ready to knock down any drunken crewmate who did not do what we had all done dozens of times before. Which was offer our ship ID card with photo and quantum code for visual check, stand inside a yellow circle for scanning of our embedded microchip ID by Heidi's sensors, then quietly walk up the ramp and into the hard metal tube that connected with the Hangar One entry airlock on Armories and Weapons Deck. There to accept and gobble down sober pills.

"Step forward!" called out Master Sergeant Melody Jenkins as her hazel eyes scanned the people confined by purple ropes on either side of the snake line. "Show your card to Staff Sergeant Osashi. And be quick about it!"

The line of people in front of me got shorter. Down to nine people. Then down to four. Then the woman ahead of me stepped forward and offered her ID card to Osashi. I remembered him. He was one of the Marines who had grabbed me after the deadly attack at the pirate base. He had gotten me to Medical using his combat suit's leg jets. I'd passed out in his arms. He saw me looking and gave a quick smile. Then he looked down at the card held out by the woman ahead of me.

"Spacer Cynthia Lovejoy," Osashi called out as the woman moved to stand in the yellow circle that lay between him and Jenkins.

"Scanning," came Heidi's soft feminine voice. "Microchip matches name of Cynthia Lovejoy. But this is not Cynthia Lovejoy."

Jenkins jerked her gaze away from looking at the line to fix on the brown-haired woman standing in the yellow circle. "Your card says Lovejoy. Your name tag says that too. Woman, what have you done with yourself that is messing with Heidi!"

The woman gave a shrug, then turned sideways to face the master sergeant. That gave me a clear view of her. Into my memory came the memory of Cynthia Lovejoy as the Mess Hall Spacer who usually took meals up to the Brig cell of Mehta Nehru, the man who had hired aliens to kill me. I'd looked her up later after delivering the meal and explained why I had wanted to confront my attacker. So I could forgive him and make peace with myself. That woman had shoulder length black hair, was about five feet five inches tall, was trim with a modest chest and had a smile that was easy-going. The woman I now saw had shoulder length brown hair. Had a similar body build. But her face looked subtly different. The woman scowled.

"Damn AI! All I did was get my hair dyed brown! You can see I match my ID card image." She waved her right hand, holding her palm bulge face out. "My microchip is right there! Like everyone's!"

Jenkins pursed her thin lips. "The ship's AI is not thrown off by a change of hair color. And microchips are not infallible. Heidi, explain your statement concerning the female in front of me."

Beyond the brown-haired woman I noticed Osashi pull his laser pistol and step back. He held the pistol in a two-handed Weaver grip, even though lasers give zero kickback. Old training styles still persist in today's Star Navy. I recalled the kick from my Dad's old 1911A1 semi-auto pistol. Firing it did require a two-handed grip.

"The female standing in the yellow circle does possess the microchip assigned to Spacer Cynthia Lovejoy," the AI said. "But the female's eye iris pattern does not match the iris pattern for Lovejoy. While her body shape is similar, this is not the human female Lovejoy."

"Stupid AI!" yelled the woman, looking up at the hard tube entry ramp, where the voice of Heidi emanated from. "I am me! Let me in the ship!"

"Hold!" commanded Jenkins, moving back a step from the woman. But she did not pull her pistol or rifle. "Who are you? Where is Spacer Cynthia Lovejoy?"

"I am me!" the woman yelled, though I noticed she seemed anxious.

I stepped forward, stood behind her and gripped her shoulders with my hands. My fingers reached down and over her right and left collar bones. I squeezed a bit. "You are *not* Cynthia Lovejoy. I know. I've seen her in person. Your face is different. Who are you?"

"Ouch!" she cried, trying to twist out of my grip. She failed. Jenkins looked to me, her expression questioning.

"Master sergeant, Heidi is correct," I said. "I know Lovejoy. Nothing personal. Just a good memory."

"He's right!" called Warren from the line behind me. "She looks like Lovejoy. But that's *not* her!"

Jenkins expression hardened. "Who are you? Where is Lovejoy!"

"Fuck you and—"

I dug my right thumb into the muscle of the woman's right shoulder and clenched tight my fingers. Under my super strong grip her right collar bone snapped.

"Oh! Oh! You hurt me!" the woman screamed shrilly.

"Where!" I said loudly.

"I'm an American!" the woman yelled. "You can't force me to say anything! It's in the Bill of Rights. I demand—"

I gripped her left collar bone and squeezed. The bone snapped. I squeezed more and a raw end of broken bone punched through her brown skin, red blood welling away from the opening.

"Nooo!" the woman screamed, dropping from the impact of the pain. "Oh god. Oh god. Oh—"

"Where is Lovejoy!" I said, holding her up with ease and leaning forward. "You'll get pain killer once you tell us. And tell us how you got her microchip."

The woman's legs now dangled inches above the floor as I lifted her by her shoulder muscles, letting the broken collar bones move as they would. She screamed again.

"Tell me. Or I'll break more bones."

"In the India consulate on Deck Nine!" the woman screamed. "Some doc there pulled out her microchip and injected it into my palm. Now let me go! And, and—"

I let go. The woman fell to the floor, screamed as her broken bones scraped against nerves and fell to one side sobbing loudly. Behind me I heard Warren step forward.

"Master Sergeant Jenkins, I am Corporal Warren Johnson. You know me. I'll take your place here if you and Osashi want to go and grab Lovejoy."

Jenkins nodded quickly. She turned her head to her left shoulder comtab. "Major Owanju, send two combat suits flying to the Hangar Four entry," she said. "Covert entry attempt blocked. Single white female with broken bones. CPO Stewart will explain. Osashi and I are heading to the India consulate to rescue Spacer Cynthia Lovejoy. Suit backup appreciated."

"Suits are coming," came Owanju's deep voice. "Crew entry halted until crewmate recovery is completed. Any other Marines there?"

"Yes, Corporal Johnson," Jenkins said, moving past me. She gestured to Osashi to follow her. He did, but tossed Warren his laser pistol. "He is taking control of the hard tube entry."

Jenkins and Osashi ran straight for the hangar slidedoor.

Warren moved to the yellow circle and stood there facing everyone. He held the laser pistol at the ready. The look on his face was not friendly.

"Everyone sit down! Now," Warren yelled loudly. "This hangar is now a combat zone. Anyone who does anything I don't like will get a burned butt!"

I joined Evelyn, Bill, Okie and Cassie in sitting down. Behind us other people in the snaking lines also sat, some of them pulling out their recorder tablets to play games, look for a news Flash or send off a last message to someone down on Earth. Assuming our tablets could still link down to Earth. Major Owanju might have extended the ship's wifi suppression field to cover the hangar. A loud whooshing sound made me look up.

Two Marines in white combat exoskeletons flew out of the hard tube entry and passed over our heads, their backpacks showing the noses of anti-personnel and anti-armor rockets, with their arms carrying terawatt-strength laser pulse rifles. They flew toward the hangar exit slidedoor, clearly aiming to catch up with Jenkins and Osashi. Those two are fine runners but they cannot run faster than a combat suit can fly. That made four Marines heading to make a forced entry into the consulate of India, a full member of the EarthGov Council. Briefly I wondered if Indian Marines from the *Vikramaditya* might offload and try to stop entry to their consulate. But our Marines are always the first to breach any obstacle. And the first to conquer any opponent. I felt certain the rescue of the still-living Cynthia Lovejoy would be done and over with before the Indian Marine commander had a full understanding of what was happening. Jenkins, Osashi and the two combat suits would be back here in Hangar Four, now designated a part of *Star Glory*, before anyone on that ship or on the station could react. After they returned, that was when the shit would hit the blower. I hoped Captain Skorzeny was ready for more politics.

CHAPTER FOUR

My seat within the ring of nine antimatter injector tubes felt cold to my butt. I had not had time to change from service khakis to camos. Which change might not be legal for me. I was still learning the rules and regs for being a CPO, versus a first or second class petty officer. Like before I was still a non-commissioned officer. Which meant I should sit with other NCOs and Spacers in the Mess Hall. That was not going to happen. My four friends and my fiancé were the people I cared for most. Plus my Mom and sisters. And their nieces and nephews, whom I barely knew beyond holo pics. I gave a sigh as the seat automatically wrapped accel straps around me. Giving thanks I had not had to don a vacsuit, I looked up at the rainbow shimmers of the nine injector tubes that ran from the overhead ceiling and straight down to the deck. The tubes would feed AM to our three fusion pulse thrusters. That antimatter flow acted as an afterburner to the yellow-orange gases expelled from our thrusters. Injecting antimatter into the combustion shell of each thruster moved the ship's normal space speed from one-tenth of the speed of light up to eleven percent. That used to be the top speed for any Earth ship. Now thanks to the alien built magfield drive block that lay between the Chief and Gambuchino, we could go five percent faster, for a top speed of 16 psol. Which was one percent faster than the top speed of the Empire ships that had attacked us. Big deal.

I looked past the vertical tubes to the new rainbow tube that ran along the overhead and out through the hull to the antimatter beamer block, where Bill now sat. Warren was with his fellow Marines in Hangar One, perhaps doing maintenance on one of our four GTO shuttles. Which were their boarding craft. Cassie and Evelyn were at their duty stations on Science Deck. And Oksana was snugged away in her specialist cabin in the Intel section of Astrogation Deck. Ignoring the sounds of Gambuchino and her three mates at the fusion reactor station, and the grumbles of Chief O'Connor as he oversaw his three control panels, I looked aside to the nearby bulkhead vidscreen.

Like always it showed an overhead view of the Bridge, with the captain seated atop the central pedestal that gave him, Kumisov the XO, Major Owanju and Doc Bjorg a view of the arc of duty stations that filled the front of the bridge. The bridge's front wallscreen showed the blackness of space, with the white and gray mass of the Moon off to the left side. We were outbound from Trinity, aiming to pass by the Moon on our way somewhere. And everyone onboard was wondering what our orders were. In the videye image, the captain still wore his formal Service Dress Blue coat, pants and white combo hat. Kumisov and Owanju wore service khakis, although Doc Bjorg wore blue and gray camos. Which was what everyone at the front arc of duty stations also wore. Gone was Bjorg's Hawaiian shirt and short pants. The captain tapped a patch on his right armrest.

"All Ship! Orders have been received," the captain said, his broad hands resting on each armrest. "Admiral Gonsalves has ordered the *Star Glory* to return to Empire space and there conduct strikes against Empire battlecruisers, trading ships and bases in space and on land. In short we are to conduct guerrilla warfare against an enemy that attacked us first." The captain paused, then gestured down to Kumisov, who was looking his way. "XO, put up the imagery of our first target."

The petite Russian nodded her head, her white-streaked black hair flaring outward. "Heidi, display Kepler 37 system graphic."

"Displaying," the AI said, her tone sounding thoughtful.

Thoughtful to me at least. Sometimes I wonder if my enhanced hearing produces tones no one else can hear. Or maybe I spend too much time thinking of the AI as a person. She seems that way to me. The bridge's front wallscreen changed. The black space with Moon image moved left. On the right side of the vidscreen now appeared an overhead view of the Kepler 37 system, with the orbits of its five planets, two asteroid belts and outer Kuiper Belt zone of comets marked by dotted lines or colored zones.

"Sir!" called Kumisov. "Kepler 37 system graphic is displayed."

Our captain nodded quickly, his hands still gripping the ends of his armrests. Those hands appeared relaxed to me. And his posture seemed at ease. As much as any captain of a 340 meter long combat starship can be at ease.

"All Ship, planet five at Kepler 37 is a gas giant. As all of you know from our prior visit to this system. Orbiting it are 47 moons. Three moons are planetary in size. Each moon possesses powered surface installations, orbital bases and orbiting ships, based on our records of neutrino emissions from before the Empire ships attacked us." The captain looked over to where Bjorg, boss of the Science Deck and all the civilian geeks who worked there, now sat. To Bjorg's right stood the Empire translator block that we had acquired from the Melanchon aliens. It gave us the ability to communicate with any Empire ship or installation, and with any alien species or ship known to the Empire. It far exceeded the First Contact software package that Bjorg had transmitted upon our first arrival at Kepler 37. "Doctor Bjorg, are your people and Heidi prepared to generate Empire species holograms in space of our true human appearance?"

"Captain, we are," Bjorg said, his tenor voice sounding firm and confident.

"Good. All Ship, I know many of you will wonder why only the *Star Glory* is going out alone on this counter-attack against the Empire. In short, the answer is politics." I winced. Damn Earth politics had even infiltrated onto my ship! "Admiral Gonsalves advised me that in order for the EarthGov Council to vote a majority in favor of fighting the Empire, the Star Navy had to commit to keeping our other four battlecruisers within the Solar System. To protect it against a future Empire attack while we are gone behind enemy lines." The captain gave a barely audible sigh. Leastwise it was a sigh I heard. Perhaps no one else did. "That is why all personnel were recalled to the *Shandong*, the *Vikramaditya*, the *Cape Town* and the *Tsushima Straits*. Those four ships will shortly head out to patrol the outer edge of Sol's magnetosphere. Meanwhile, while we are gone, the Trinity and Novosibirsk orbital shipyards will be constructing new battlecruiser starships. America plans four new ships. Great Britain plans two. Russia plans three. China will construct four more. And Japan will construct two more. India and the African Union do not plan new ships." He paused. Leaving me and others to wonder if the failure of those two nations to build new ships was due to them being outvoted. "Eventually Earth will have a fleet of twenty battlecruiser starships, including the *Star Glory* and the four I've listed." The captain gestured sharply. "Until then, we attack! And attack again. And cause one pile of holy hell for the Empire! Captain out."

The bulkhead vidscreen maintained its overhead view of the bridge with its First Shift crew and officers. That had been Captain Skorzeny's command during our first trip into the Deep Black. It now seemed he was continuing that policy. Which meant everyone on my ship knew what the bridge knew the moment it happened. To me, that built crew confidence and acceptance of hard orders. Which going out solo to attack the Empire was, a very hard order. I turned away from the vidscreen and looked down at my control panel. The flow of antimatter to our three thrusters was steady. Which meant we were moving out at 16 psol, thanks to help from the magfield spacedrive. Looking around at the nine injector tubes, I remembered my duty. Reaching to the side of my seat I grabbed my goggles, put them on and pulled tight the head strap. Then I again checked the antimatter tubes. The rainbow color shimmer of each tube was bright, sharp and stable. It was my job to always watch that beautiful shimmer and be ready to stop, start or modify the flow of antimatter from the particle accelerator ring that wrapped around the outer hull of Engineering. My duty I would do faithfully. Hopefully everyone else on the *Star Glory* would also be faithful to their duty as we headed outward to a rendezvous with the Empire of Eternity.

◆ ◆ ◆

Two days later I exited the gravlift and headed for my work station and its rainbow-shining tubes, feeling ill at ease and puzzled. No one had bugged me about my pain questioning of the brown-haired infiltrator woman. Not Chief O'Connor. Not any other staff or line officer, though surely some of them had viewed the vidrecords kept by Heidi. My friends and Evelyn had joined me for lunch twice since the captain's All Ship announcement of our orders. And Evelyn had invited me to her cabin last night, where we'd made slow, caring love and spoken about everything but what appeared to be a suicide mission. Leaving her this morning had been hard. Dismissing downer thoughts, I waved to our Italian beauty PO Gambuchino and her three Spacers as I passed by them. Dolores gave me an absent-minded wave, while Gus, Cindy and Duncan showed me honest smiles and waves. Clearly I was still on their list of Good Guys. Stepping through the rainbow shimmer of the AM tubes, I dropped down onto my cushioned seat, waited for the accel straps to criss-cross me, then tapped on the control panel's Systems Diagnostic checker program that was the first thing I did every time I began my shift. Green bars showed for all systems. Power flow, green. Tube magnetic fields, green. Antimatter containment field on the deck above, green, thank the Goddess. Inflow of new antimatter from the particle accelerator was green. Next came—

"CPO Stewart!" called the Chief from where he sat at his arc of control panels. "Stop that work. And come with me. The captain wants to see both of us."

"Yes sir, coming." Curiosity filled me. This would only be my third time to have a face-to-face with the captain. Was I in trouble for forcing the infiltrator to say where Spacer Lovejoy was being held? Had the captain waited until we arrived at the edge of Sol's magnetosphere, and just before we entered the gray space of Alcubierre space-time, to tell me my fate? Well, if I was about to lose my new promotion, I could handle that. Saving a crewmate was what mattered. I tapped the diagnostic program to automatic function and looked up at the overhead. "Heidi, please take over monitoring of my station."

"Assuming monitoring of antimatter flow station," she said, her tone musical and impersonal.

I released my straps, stood up and stepped out past the shimmering tubes. The Chief stood there, hands on his hips, his wide shoulders stretching the fabric of his brown khaki shirt. He looked up at me. I saluted.

"Chief Petty Officer Stewart is ready, sir."

His beady black eyes blinked once. "Follow me to the gravlift. Once again *we* have an invite to the officers conference room up top."

"Aye aye, sir."

My stocky boss twisted in place, then began a quick march to the center of the room where the gravlift stood. That gray metal shaft ran from our deck up through the overhead and all the way up to Bridge Deck at the top. Chief O'Connor stopped before the gravlift shaft, reached out and slapped the Open patch that glowed red on the right side of the metal slidedoor. The patch turned green instantly, which told me the gravplate was still at our deck. The slidedoor swished to the left. Inside was empty.

"Move it. Get in there!"

"Aye, aye, Chief O'Connor."

Stepping in and then moving to the right, I turned and faced the shaft's exit door. Which now closed as the Chief clomped in, his booted feet causing the plate metal to echo sharply. He twisted in place and faced the slidedoor.

"AI Heidi, take us up to Bridge Deck," the Chief said. "Do not stop for anyone short of the captain. Obey per security code Alpha Tango Fourteen."

"Transporting you up to Bridge Deck per security code Alpha Tango Fourteen," the AI said brightly.

The fact the Chief was using a line officer's security code to force the gravplate to ignore any other service calls by folks on other decks was not new to me. Just different. It told me the captain was in a hurry. But why were we going to the officers conference room? Discipline due to an enlisted, a rating or an NCO was always delivered by his staff officer, not by the captain. Which fact only confused me. Was the chief facing discipline from the captain because of *my* actions? I hoped not. I liked Robert O'Connor. His family heritage was Scottish, same as mine. He had always been fair with me since I'd first boarded the *Star Glory*. And he'd given me credit for my antimatter fart idea once we'd escaped the pursuit of Smooth Fur and his Empire battlecruisers. I stood there feeling uncertain. I did not like uncertainty in life. I'd had enough of that after Dad died in my senior year, Mom had sold the ranch and she and my sisters had moved to her Denver condo apartment. Seeing them safe and whole during my shore leave had been wonderful. Being the tool of a politician and then a political pawn had not. I'd done my duty and kept the senator from being killed. Just as I'd done my duty to help our Marines find and rescue Lovejoy. Shaking my head I focused on the vertical transport bar that glowed waist high on the shaft's wall, just left of the exit door. The red bar that passed through deck levels marked on the bar showed we had just moved through the DT Fuel Bunkers Deck. Nine more decks to go. Minutes later the plate came to a stop as the bar hit the top level of Bridge. The slidedoor whooshed open. The Chief walked out.

"Follow me."

"Following, Chief."

My determined boss turned right, walked about ten feet, then stopped in front of a familiar slidedoor. Above the door was painted Officers Conference Room. The Chief spoke.

"Heidi, open this slidedoor per Security Code Alpha Tango Fourteen."

"Complying," the AI said in a sing-song voice that reminded me of one of the musical televid programs I'd watched while waiting for my shore leave.

The door slid open. I followed the Chief inside. As before the big round room had control panels and flat screens stuck to various parts of its gray metal walls. In the center was the rectangular oak table that I had sat at before. Seated at the far end was Captain Skorzeny. On his right sat our XO, Commander Nadya Kumisov. On the captain's left sat Commander Martha Bjorn, the new boss of Second Shift thanks to Nehru's treason. Sitting next to Bjorn was Warren's boss, Major James Owanju. The Black man was wide-shouldered, big-chested and had a shaven head. Like the rest of them he wore brown service khakis. Looking left I saw Lieutenant Senior Grade Rosy Matterling, the Black woman who had moved from being senior aide to Nehru to being Third Shift's boss. From left to right it was Matterling, Kumisov, Skorzeny, Bjorn and Owanju. Every line officer who mattered was here. And all of them were intently watching me and my boss.

"Chief Warrant Officer Four Robert O'Connor reporting, sir," the Chief said firmly, saluting the assembled brass.

I saluted too. "Chief Petty Officer Nathan Stewart reporting, sir!"

The captain looked us over. His brown eyes were bright and intense. His smooth-shaven face was trim with not a jowl to be seen. His collar tips had silver eagles on them. No one at the table wore shoulder boards, let alone stripes on a Service Dress Blue jacket. Which the captain no longer wore. Clearly this was intended to be a working meeting, not a public display.

"Welcome to both of you. Sit over by Lieutenant Matterling. There's plenty of room on that side of the table," the captain said calmly. He gestured at a pitcher of tea in middle of the table. "Help yourselves to a drink as you wish."

I followed the Chief, who sat next to Matterling. She nodded to him, her face calm. The Chief nodded back to her, then rested his elbows on the table and sat silent. I sat to the Chief's right, just across from Major Owanju. I licked my lips and gave him a quick nod. After all he was the man who had sent out the two combat suits to help Jenkins and Osashi in the rescue of Lovejoy. He gave me a nod back, his expression neutral.

"Thank you both for coming," the captain said. Then he looked directly at me. "CPO Stewart, I wish to commend you for assisting in the recovery of Spacer Cynthia Lovejoy. Chief Malone is glad to have her back at duty in the Mess Hall." The captain paused. Then he frowned. "However, Admiral Gonsalves was less than happy with the entry of our Marines into the consulate of India. It caused her to make an apology to India's EarthGov representative. I am sure you can appreciate how unpleasant that was for her."

Well, time to pay the piper. "Yes sir, I do understand unpleasant events. I am willing to revert to petty officer second class as a sign of my regret for causing trouble for her and the Star Navy. Sir."

Kumisov shook her head silently. Owanju lifted his thick black eyebrows in apparent surprise. Bjorn looked thoughtful. Matterling folded her hands together, her posture still calm. My boss's posture did not change, though I noticed his shoulders went tense. The captain's jaw muscles clenched briefly, then relaxed. He shook his head.

"That will not be necessary. However, the next time you are moved to assist our Marines, please note that Master Sergeant Jenkins is an E-8, which outranks your E-7 as a CPO," the captain said calmly. He looked to Owanju. "Major, do you wish to add anything before we move to more serious matters?"

The man who commanded the ship's twenty Marines, and my best buddy, nodded briefly. "Captain, thank you." He looked to me. "CPO Stewart, perhaps you saw your actions as payback to my Marines for their rescue of you on the pirate base. No such response was needed. Marines do their duty, period. As they were doing their duty at the entry to Hard Tube Four inside Hangar Four of Trinity. In the future, consult with the Marine in command before you take action on your own."

I saluted him. "Sir, yes sir. I apologize for putting your Marines into a situation they . . . they were not warned about," I said, avoiding the stupid 'not trained for' comment. Every Marine I'd ever met, at Great Lakes, on Trinity or on *Star Glory*, was ready to adapt to any new combat situation. "I acted on impulse. In the future I will do better."

Owanju nodded easily. "Good to hear that. Captain?"

The boss of everyone on the *Star Glory* sat back, rested his hands on the dark brown wood of the table and stared at me. "CPO Stewart, you know where we are headed. You know what our orders are. Tell me, does your . . . talent for anticipating solutions to problems extend to ideas for how we can successfully enter Kepler 37, travel to the three moons that orbit its gas giant, attack shipping and bases, and escape with our hides intact?"

Oh fuck. This really was going to be a suicide mission if the captain was asking *me* for tactical advice! Or . . . or was he giving me a chance to make up for my public pre-emption of the Marine security role at the hard tube entry? At least the captain had not downrated me. Or worse. Maybe he really did believe in me. I looked aside to my Chief. Robert was staring at the pitcher of tea in the middle of the table, acting as if it were an everyday thing to be invited to sit and blab with the line officers of America's top battlecruiser starship. Which of course it wasn't. A chain of command existed on this ship and in the Star Navy for a simple reason. Combat efficiency. But what could we do to increase our combat effectiveness? The memory of the first neutrino comlink imagery from the Empire came to my mind. Could the answer be that simple?

"Captain, when we arrive at the edge of the magnetosphere of Kepler 37, why don't *you* pretend to be Manager Smooth Fur?" His eyes widened. "Heidi has perfect vidrecords of the several broadcasts to us by Smooth Fur. We know the neutrino comlink frequency he used. We also know the system entry protocol codes used by every Empire ship, whether combat or commercial, thanks to the pirate base info database. And you yourself asked Doc Bjorg if he and Heidi were ready to overlay holos of Empire aliens atop your images." Telling my heart to stop beating so fast and my vision to stop reading the infrared glows of each person at the table, as my survival instinct kicked in and told my body to figure out how to fight this verbal battle, I took a deep breath. "Heidi can overlay the imagery of Smooth Fur's bridge, its alien personnel and the body movements of Smooth Fur onto you. If Mumbai and Hollywood can create three dee holos of fantastic monsters, why can't Heidi do the same for you?"

The captain's face turned thoughtful. "An interesting and tempting suggestion, CPO. Yes, this could be done. It was something I had considered as a means to camouflage our human identity. But to what effect?"

That was the easy part. My years spent sneaking up on coyotes that roamed around the pasture edges, waiting for a calf foal to be born so they could grab the calf or at least the afterbirth remains, those years came to mind. "Captain, pretending to be Smooth Fur puts every alien official on the three moons in the mindframe of cooperation. No underling wants to be found wanting by the Big Boss. Which is what Smooth Fur is, given his command of an Empire fleet. And his ability to call in other fleets from their base in the W51 molecular cloud." I smiled and gestured confidently, hoping my body would relax its tenseness. "More particularly, it prevents any Empire combat vessel from coming out to challenge us. That will put us within range to do hit and run attacks."

Kumisov raised her right hand. "Captain, our ship structure is totally different from the red dumball shape of Empire combat ships. As soon as some alien applies an electro-optical scope to us, they will know we are not from the Empire."

"True," Skorzeny said, nodding his head slowly. "So, Nadya, tell me what is the range of our ship scope for distinguishing ship shapes in deep space?"

The XO frowned. "Uh, 500,000 miles or 700,000 kilometers, sir. Of course our exhaust plume can be seen from much farther away. And we will be alone, with no other Empire ships in convoy with us. Sir."

Skorzeny looked to me. "Stewart, the scope issue is minor, considering our 16 psol normal space speed. We can cover that distance in seconds. But the XO has a point about our ship being alone, without Empire fleet ships with us. That will be known shortly after we arrive at the edge of magnetosphere. Right, chief petty officer?"

I bit my lip. Then my memory of how coyotes and wolf packs approach prey kicked in. "Captain, yes sir, that is true. Anyone on the three moons or in orbit above them will immediately detect the moving neutrino emissions from our ship fusion reactors. And from our fusion pulse thrusters. But . . . if we offload our four GTO shuttles and power up their fusion thrusters, they will appear to be a convoy of four Empire ships. No one can tell the size or shape of an arriving starship from deep within a star system." My last use of this idea emerged from memory. "We can do as we did before. Have the four shuttles appear. Warn the moon officials they are here and are going into cloaking to be ready for the arrival of any non-Empire starship like . . . like ships from Earth! Then we pull the shuttles back into the *Star Glory* and they will seem to 'disappear' into cloaking, as viewed from inside the system. Sir."

"I like this option," Martha Bjorn said from the other side of the captain. The blond Swede who had once handled the midnight Third Shift looked to me with a business-first expression. "CPO Stewart, your point is that pretending to be Manager Smooth Fur arriving at the edge of the Kepler 37 magnetosphere, with four fleet ships that go into cloaking, tells any alien observing the outer edge of the system that our arrival is an official visit." She looked aside to Skorzeny. "Captain, this deception buys us safety for the two days plus it will take to travel into the system and get close to the gas giant. Of course once their scopes get a clear image of us, the gig will be blown."

"Captain," called Matterling from the other side of my boss. "This is a valuable option for *before* our attack on Empire vessels and bases," she said, lifting a black hand and raising one finger. "We will be known as not Empire once we are seen or once we fire on an Empire ship. So be it." The middle-aged woman who was known on the ship as a competitive tennis player gave a shrug of trim shoulders. "But Star Navy wants us to do this at multiple stars. Therefore escape is equally vital. Thanks to the magfield spacedrive, our ship can now make 15 psol in normal space-time. If some ship pursues us, or several ships, we can add in our antimatter afterburner and hit 16 psol. That will allow us to stay ahead of any pursuit until we reach the magnetosphere and can transition into Alcubierre space-time. Sir."

Captain Skorzeny gave me a penetrating look, then turned to my boss. "Chief O'Connor, can Engineering sustain 16 psol output for an extended period?"

"Yes sir, it can." The Chief glanced aside to me, then back to the man who commanded our lives. "Captain, I've known CPO Stewart ever since he arrived from his Great Lakes A-School training. While he kept his physical abilities secret until your observations in our last visit here, he always put more than a hundred percent into his work at his antimatter engineering station. And his antimatter fart idea was excellent thinking beyond the conventional answers. Which at that time were our CO_2 and proton lasers, our missiles and our railguns." He paused. My heart rate slowed as it became clear my solution to what looked like a suicide mission would be accepted. "I recommend adoption of Stewart's pretend-to-be-the-Empire solution."

"Agreed," the captain said. He looked aside to the other officers at the table, then back to us. "Chief O'Connor, CPO Stewart, you are dismissed. Return to your duty stations and make sure everything down there is working perfectly. In a little more than two days we will arrive at the edge of Kepler 37. We will then begin this dance of deception."

We both stood up. I turned away and followed the Chief out of the room, right along the ring hallway and then into the waiting gravlift. The red infrared glow of my boss's body seemed normal to me. He was not upset. Or worried. Or had any body-fear. Briefly I wished my mutation allowed me to read his thoughts. Did he really like me that much? Then good sense hit me. Being super strong, with super hearing and super eyesight were useful talents. But no one wants to hear the private thoughts of every person around them. My shipmates deserve their personal privacy, just as much as I had sought privacy for my physical talents. Now, as we headed into danger, we all had to focus on working as the team we had to be in order to survive this first attack.

CHAPTER FIVE

Four days later I sat in my vacsuit at my work station as the *Star Glory* neared the gas giant that was the fifth planet in orbit about the G8V yellow star that was Kepler 37. The captain had pretended to be Manager Smooth Fur upon our arrival. The four GTOs had launched and pretended to be Empire ships going into cloak. And the captain had been very peremptory in his words with a system traffic controller alien who hailed from a station that orbited the outermost large moon, which some alien had named Stellar. The other two moons, similar in size to Venus and Mars, had a buzz of neutrino signatures moving above them, clear evidence of commerce and spaceships coming and going. While our ship's electro-optical scope did not have a clear view of those ships or the orbital bases above each moon, our Tactical genius Hilary Chang had plotted all those neutrino signatures. There were 37 in orbit around Stellar, 24 in orbit above the middle moon and 12 in orbit around the innermost moon. No ships moved about the 40 other smaller moons and captured asteroids that orbited the gas giant. I looked down at my control panel. Everything was green bars in all function categories. The antimatter injector tubes were ready to feed antimatter to our thrusters whenever the captain ordered afterburner push.

I looked right at the nearby bulkhead vidscreen. It was live and gave a view of the Bridge. As before the captain sat in his seat at the top of the command pedestal, with XO Kumisov, Major Owanju and Dr. Bjorg seated below him. In front, arranged in a half circle, were the six function stations of the Bridge. Those stations were Astrogation, Communications, Power, Life Support, Tactical and Weapons. Seats for visitors ran along the back half of the circular room that lay at the nose of the *Star Glory*. While it lacked quartz portals for directly viewing external space, its front vidscreen was large, measuring five meters long by three high. The screen edge stopped just below the overhead's gray metal. Beyond that overhead lay the inner hull metal, a water barrier to impede external radiation, and a thick armored outer hull. That outer hull was festooned with front and rear sensor arrays, the ship's electro-optical telescope for true space views, neutrino com transmission nodes and, to either side of the rounded bow of the ship, lay the laser stations. A proton laser sat on port side while a CO_2 laser station adorned starboard. Gamma ray lasers now adorned the middle ship hull at port and starboard. At the ship's stern were similar laser stations, with four missile silos and the funnels of the ship's three fusion pulse thrusters filling the space between the laser stations. On the spine and belly of the outer hull were located sideways-shooting railguns. The Smart Rocks that shot out of the railguns were part of the ship's final close-in defense against small meteors and Hunter-Killer mines. Lastly, located not far from where I sat, was the metal block of Bill's antimatter beamer. Its aperture had a 180 degree arc in all directions, bow or stern, port or starboard. With a shake of my head I focused back on the vidscreen and the images depicted in the Bridge's front vidscreen.

On the left of the front screen was a system graphic that showed the five planets, the gas giant's moons, and the moving neutrino signatures that were ships and orbital bases. The few spots on the atmosphered moons that emitted neutrinos were assumed to be cities with fusion power reactors. And maybe ground to space lasers and launch vehicles. The middle of the screen showed a normal space image of the gas giant, which appeared all bluish haze similar to Neptune. The right side of the screen was blank but had served to image the system traffic alien, who resembled a giant praying mantis, albeit one adorned with straps for tools and devices. Its green compound eyes had stared at the image of what it thought was Smooth Fur the walking otter with white-streaked black fur. Then it had accepted the system entry protocol code spoken by the captain and apologized for following procedure. I looked away from the bulkhead vidscreen and scanned my deck. Dolores, Cindy, Duncan and Gus were gathered around their reactor work stations. Chief O'Connor now sat before the control panel for the magfield spacedrive, which was helping us achieve 15 psol speed in our approach. The magfield drive would also enable our ship to abruptly move up, down or sideways relative to our vector track. Thanks to the inertial compensator field of the ship we would not be thrown out of our seats thanks to inertial torque. It made sense for the Chief to be there, ready to respond to maneuvering orders from the captain.

"Captain, we are ten million kilometers out from the moon Stellar," the XO said. "We should begin decel now. The system traffic alien expects us to slow down and move into orbit next to his base."

"Kumisov, thank you." Our captain looked up at the ceiling. "All Ship, go to General Quarters."

A loud series of hoots came over the shipwide speaker system. I pulled my helmet over my head and sealed it. The sealing activated the suit's comlink, which automatically cross-linked to the ship's comlink frequency and emitted my words acoustically in case someone was nearby who was not in a suit. Everyone on every deck would now be sealed tight against hull breaches. And everyone would continue to be in contact with their shipmates and officers. What happened in the nearby bulkhead vidscreen would be seen and heard the same as before.

"Chief O'Connor, shut off our thrusters and put the magfield drive into reverse," the captain said calmly.

"Shutting off fusion pulse thrusters," my boss said as he reached to one side and tapped the thruster control panel. He then made a series of taps on the magfield panel in front of him. "Magfield drive is pushing against the star's magnetosphere. We are slowing. But we will still have 10 psol inertial momentum. Sir."

"Understood." In the bulkhead vidscreen the captain leaned forward against his seat straps. "Astrogation, flip the ship 180 so our thrusters aim forward."

"Flipping ship orientation," called Louise Ibarra from her Astrogation seat on the far left side of the Bridge.

The blue globe of the gas giant slipped down on the front vidscreen, then vanished as the electro-optical scope now imaged black space and the steady white spots of millions of stars. Soon the streamer of the Milky Way came into view. Then it too passed down and out of sight. The wheeling movement of distant stars now stopped. Our ship's nose was pointed outward toward the two asteroid belts we had passed through without any trouble from the several dozen tiny mining ships that showed on our sensors. Clearly the miners had no interest in drawing the attention of an Empire battlecruiser.

"Weapons," the captain called. "Eject four missiles with thermonuke warheads set to move toward the targets ID'd by CWO Chang."

In the bulkhead vidscreen Bill Yamamoto tapped his control panel, then looked back to the captain's pedestal. His thirtyish face was intensely focused. "Missiles ejected. Silos clear. Targets encoded into missile astro systems." The man who sat on the far right of the arc of work stations looked back at his panel. "Missile nose shrouds have separated. All warheads are now released. We have forty MIRVd warheads set for targets in orbit above Stellar. Including the system traffic orbital station. Sir."

"Good. Set up four more missiles loaded with thermonuke MIRVs." The captain looked down to his right. "Dr. Bjorg, is the Empire translator block ready to respond to other alien languages?"

"Captain, it is," the heavyset Swede said. "It will also respond to chromatophoric image languages and to pheromone-coded radio signals, in addition to acoustic languages."

The captain looked directly down to where the Marine rep sat. "Major Owanju, are your GTOs manned and ready to fight?"

"Sir, the GTOs *Okinawa*, *Tarawa*, *Ramadi* and *Karachi* are on the platform in Hangar One and ready to launch. A pilot and nose laser gunner are present in each GTO. Sir."

"Hold on any launch for the moment," the captain said firmly, looking to his lower left. "XO, do our sensors detect any Empire fleet ship signatures? From the moons or elsewhere?"

"Sir, they do not," Kumisov said quickly. "However, in view of the armed raiders we encountered at Kepler 452, I would expect some or all of the Empire merchant ships to carry some weapons. Our American merchantmen were often armed in prior wet navy wars. Sir."

"Understood. Astrogation, how much longer do we have until the Stellar orbital base scope can directly image us?"

"Nine minutes, sir, at our current speed of 10 psol," Ibarra said hurriedly.

"Time to increase our decel," the captain grunted. "Chief Engineer O'Connor, restart our thrusters. Reduce our forward momentum by one psol."

My boss shifted in his seat. He reached aside to the thruster control panel and tapped several places. "All three fusion pulse thrusters are now imploding deuterium-tritium pellets. Fusion exhaust is now expelling forward. Forward speed is reducing. Ten psol. Nine point four. Nine." The Chief paused a few moments as the vibration of the three thrusters touched everyone who was in contact with any metal part of the *Star Glory*. "Forward speed reduced to nine psol, sir."

"Good. Let us leave the system traffic alien in doubt as to whether we will visit him or one of the other two large moons."

I watched as we came closer to the moon that resembled a small Earth. It had a thick white atmosphere, the blue of a large ocean, the brown of land and the purple of mountains. Looking to the system graphic side of the Bridge's front vidscreen I saw that 27 of the 37 neutrino sources were on our side of the moon Stellar. Soon our scope would be able to image those sources. At which point the orbital station occupied by the praying mantis alien would be able to clearly see our ship shape did not match Empire ship form.

"Weapons," called the captain. "Launch two volleys of Smart Rocks from the port and starboard railguns. Might as well give any defensive lasers some challenges."

"Starboard railgun is launching sideways," Yamamoto said calmly. "Port railgun now launching first volley. Recycling to launch second volley. Sir."

While the Smart Rocks were not visible in the true space image on the Bridge vidscreen, I knew the rocks well. They were far more than rocks, of course. They were soccer ball-sized items that could maneuver independently, had passive sensors that ran the gamut from infrared to ultraviolet to neutrino, held tiny spyeyes in front and used volatile gases to jerk, jink and change their vector track in order to better home in on a target. The fact they moved at planetary escape velocity of seven miles a second made hitting them hard even for directed energy weapons like the proton, CO_2 and gamma ray lasers. While the small charges of thermite or plastique inside each rock could not kill a ship, a few dozen hitting a ship could easily disable it. A lucky hit on a fusion reactor might blow an enemy ship. And with 300 Smart Rocks ejected in each railgun volley, they were a serious threat. Especially since their approach speed was 9 psol, the same as our ship. In sum the captain had just created a spreading wavefront of tiny independent Smart Rock missiles that would move toward any object emitting heat, energy frequencies or neutrino comsignals. That wavefront would follow the forty MIRV warheads that had their own Hunt and Seek capabilities. It made for a nice double-whammy.

"Astrogation, flip the ship back to forward orientation." The captain leaned forward against his accel straps. "I want our nose lasers ready to engage."

"Attitude thrusters emitting," Ibarra said softly. "Ship orientation returning to nose forward. Sir."

"Life Support," the captain called quickly. "Are the emergency shut-off valves now operational?"

Up front Becky Woodman, another of our Australian mates, raised her right hand in a thumbs-up. "Yes sir, captain! All decks are ready to close access hatches in case of a hull breach. We have emergency air distribution units fully activated. We are ready to generate new oxy from electrolysis of our water jacket."

The captain nodded. "Power? Status of power feed from the reactors?"

"All three fusion reactors are at full operational status," Diego Suárez y Alonso said. The Brazilian looked back to the captain. "We are ready to feed ninety terawatts of power to each laser on our nose, stern, port and starboard sides. Sir."

"That is—"

"Range is now 8,700,000 kilometers," called out Ibarra.

"All Ship!" called the captain strongly. "Battle Stations now!"

The overhead lights went to yellow blinking. A series of hoots sounded. My control panel showed a red rim about its edges as a sign that my station had been moved to Red Hot status. As was now happening with our nose, side and stern lasers and Bill's antimatter beamer. The railguns and our stern missile silos were already at that status by their prior use.

"Incoming neutrino comsignal!" called Jacob Wetstone from Communications, his Brit accept noticeable as was his tenseness.

"Accept signal," the captain said softly.

Filling the right side of the front vidscreen was the image of a green praying mantis who stood before three pedestals that supported control panels. Behind him moved other aliens at work stations. One resembled a black bear. Another appeared similar to a wasp, in that it had wings on the back of its yellow-striped carapace. A third was a mix of tentacles, stiff arms, dispersed eyes and claws that suggested a ball of jello with teeth. The mantis' serrated jaws were open. His mid-body limbs moved, making sharp rasping sounds. The translator block next to Magnus translated.

"You are not Manager Smooth Fur!" came out as a keening scream. "Your ship is one of those bipedal primate ships that earlier visited our system!"

"Very true," the captain said. "I am Captain Neil Skorzeny, in command of the human battlecruiser *Star Glory*. We intend to destroy every Empire ship and orbital base above the moon Stellar. You have seven minutes to reach lifepods. If any of the ships we register are passenger vehicles, they should send a signal declaring such by way of Empire fleet comsignal frequency 1432. We will delay the destruction of those ships until we see them launch lifepods."

"Primitives! This base has sufficient lasers to kill any raiding ship! You humans will die as your two other ships died!"

The captain looked down. "XO, do you have the orbital base in the scope?"

"We do, captain. Going up on the true space image in the vidscreen."

The image of the moon Stellar grew ten times sharper. What had before been single dots of light now became spaceships of various sizes and shapes. Some were single tubes. Some were balls. Some were clusters of tubes that might be bulk cargo movers. A few were boxes or rhomboid in shape. Two now glinted stronger as light specks that must be lifepods began jetting out, headed for a landing on the giant moon below.

Chang tapped her control panel. "Sir, those two ships are passenger vessels, per their comsignal transmission."

That meant 35 of the 37 moving neutrino signals were not passenger ships, most likely cargo transports with some being scouts or visitors from other systems. To me what mattered was we had plenty of targets for our MIRVs and Smart Rocks. Hitting the stuff in orbit above this moon would for sure hurt the Empire. I looked closely at the true space image on the right side of the vidscreen.

The system traffic control orbital, though, was larger than any of the orbiting starships. It was a giant ball with wings, tubes and metal arcs adorning its surface. The scale marker at the side of the imagery made clear it measured four kilometers across. About the size of Trinity station back home. Two other smaller balls glinted in polar and diagonal orbits that were different from the equatorial orbit of the orbiting traffic control base. As we drew closer at 9 psol it became clear there were seven ships linked to the giant ball by hard tube connections. Which made sense if it was the main trading and command outpost for this moon. Maybe the main one for the system considering it held the system traffic control room.

"Weapons, what do your sensors tell you about that large orbital?" the captain murmured.

Yamamoto leaned forward to scan his control panel. "Sir, there are laser emitters at the north and south poles. Also emitters on its equator at four spots. That is six laser mounts. It is likely they include proton, carbon dioxide and plasma emitters. Like the weapons on the Empire battlecruisers. Sir."

The captain looked back to the mantis alien, who had heard all of this. "System traffic controller, what is your name and species?"

The two compound eyes looked aside at another screen, then forward. "My clutch knows me as Wandering Biter. My species is Drugol. We are an Intended member of the Empire! Be warned that any who attack—"

"You are warned already of our intentions," the captain said. "To follow human custom, be aware that a State of War now exists between the humans of planet Earth and the Empire of Eternity." The captain gestured strongly. "You have five minutes to escape and survive. Be warned, this ship has already destroyed two Empire battlecruisers."

"You lie!" screeched the mantis as his midbody arms rasped his hard chitin skin. "Your ship destroyed only one Empire ship! I was on duty when you and two other human ships trespassed into this system and then defied the Glorious Choice."

The captain smiled. "We destroyed another Empire ship at a different system. Perhaps Manager Smooth Fur did not inform you and other Empire species of its misfortune."

Behind the mantis the bear-like alien growled something that translated as "Incoming mobile projectiles are detected! Lasers and plasma beams are ranging them but they move erratically."

The mantis waved its upper arm pair. "Destroy your projectiles! Leave this system. And I will report to Manager Smooth Fur that you humans are considering membership as a Servant species!"

"Never," the captain said. "Four minutes."

I looked over at Dolores and her people. Inside their helmets their faces were a mix of hope, worry and concentration. Looking aside I saw the same look on my boss's face as he sat before the magfield drive control panel, the panels for the thrusters and Alcubierre stardrive within easy reach. I looked away and over to the wall hatch that led to Bill's antimatter beamer block. The captain had not said anything to him. Did that mean the captain was not going to use our most deadly weapon? Or did he have another plan?

"Two minutes," the captain said as the image of the system controller's office filled with movement as all the other aliens left quickly, leaving behind the mantis alien. "Wandering Biter, I end this comsignal. Communications, close this channel."

"Channel closed, captain," replied Wetstone, his infrared glow moving to red-black from red normal.

The true space image of the large moon Stellar now filled the right half of the front vidscreen. The system graphic, which had also enlarged to show only the moon Stellar and red dots for every Empire ship and orbiting base, filled the left half. The true space image now showed green CO_2, purple plasma beams and red proton laser beams shooting out from the largest orbital base. Tiny explosions showed in three spots.

"Captain," called Ibarra. "Range to targets is now at 43,000 kilometers and decreasing rapidly."

"Weapons, status report on MIRVs and Smart Rocks." The captain gripped both armrests of his seat, his attention focused ahead.

"Thirty-seven MIRVs are still intact and homing in on the twenty-seven ship neutrino emissions and the three orbital bases on this side of the moon," Yamamoto said.

"Good to hear. Astrogation, change the ship's vector track to skim the left side of the moon Stellar. I want to do a gravity slingshot to the middle moon."

"Adjusting ship's vector orientation," Ibarra said quickly. "However, the attitude jets are not sufficient to move us fully onto the new vector track."

My feet felt the vibrations of the ship's attitude adjustment jets firing. They were strong enough to change our orbit angle but not powerful enough to move a ship to a vector that differed strongly from the ship's current track.

"Chief Engineer O'Connor, use the magfield drive to put us fully onto the new vector track entered by Astrogation."

Nearby my boss tapped the control panel in front of him. "Magfield spacedrive is now pushing *Star Glory* sideways and below the moon's equatorial plane by twenty degrees, sir."

The captain gave a long sigh. "Weapons, give nose, stern, port and starboard lasers permission to fire on targets identified by Tactical."

"Sir, transmitting weapons engagement permission!" Yamamoto said loudly.

Well, it was clear the captain was not going to order any antimatter afterburner push to our existing speed of 9 psol. Which was causing the planet-sized moon to grow larger on the right side of the Bridge's front vidscreen. The large gray metal ball with wings of the system traffic controller's orbital showed clearly on that side of the screen. The polar orbital was visible at thirty degrees north latitude while the diagonal orbital's metal ball glowed brightly at minus forty degrees on the left and rising toward the equatorial plane of the Earth-size moon. I looked up at the antimatter injector tube that fed AM to Bill's beamer block. The rainbow field shimmers were bright, sharp and stable. I focused my attention back on the overhead view of the captain and First Shift's people.

"Nose lasers are firing!" yelled Yamamoto.

Below the captain the XO spoke. "Portside gamma ray laser is hitting the diagonal orbital. Forty-one Smart Rocks are impacting on that orbital's hull." In the true space image white spurts of gas now showed as did silvery water globules that existed briefly before evaporating in the vacuum. "Diagonal orbital base is breached. Two MIRVs are jinking toward it."

"Yes!" cried Yamamoto as the polar orbital base flared into a tiny star upon the impact of at least one MIRV thermonuke. A three megaton warhead does not leave much residue behind after its plasma ball finishes vaporizing the bulk of what it hits. "The system traffic controller orbital is firing on approaching MIRVs. Two are gone. Thirty-one MIRVs are moving toward the 27 ships on this side of the moon!"

Too much now happened in the seconds during which my ship passed by the system controller's four kilometer ball of metal, air and water and moved along a slanting vector track to take it around the left side of the moon.

Green laser and red proton beams shot out from the nose of the *Star Glory*, hitting a cluster of tubes that might be a large cargo transport. The beams cut deep. White air jetted out and silvery water globules sped away from the breached hull. Then lots of Smart Rocks hit the craft. Black holes showed from nose to stern. Then a bright yellow-orange glow filled the middle of the ship as its fusion reactor lost containment, releasing star-hot plasma gases into the ship's interior. Those gases melted the ship from the inside out. A sharp bright light signaled the ship's extinction as anything solid.

"Yes!" yelled Yamamoto. "Polar and diagonal orbital bases are gone. Cargo ship is vapor. Other ships are being hit by Smart Rocks. And . . . " Bright yellow-orange lights flared in fourteen spots scattered across the equatorial plane of the giant moon. "Fourteen ships are MIRV hit! They're gone, captain."

"Range is 7,000 klicks to the traffic controller orbital," Chang said softly.

A volley of CO_2, proton and plasma beams shot out at us from the still intact orbital base. Other beams shot at us from ten of the remaining ships, but their aim went wild and off to the side as Ibarra jinked and jerked the *Star Glory's* forward movement, making my ship a hard target. But some beams got through.

"Hits on the hull above the bow," reported Chang. "No penetration to the water jacket. Spine railgun is intact."

"Tactical? Status on traffic controller orbital?"

The true space image of the giant metal ball with fins now showed dozens of black spots appearing on its formerly smooth gray metal. Those were Smart Rock impacts. One equatorial laser mount died from those hits. But the rest and the polar mounts continued firing at the *Star Glory* and at approaching MIRV warheads.

"Two more MIRVs zapped," reported Yamamoto. "Four other MIRVs are inbound and jinking, sir." The young man looked at his panel. "Starboard gamma ray laser is irradiating this side of the traffic orbital. Sir, the orbital is within emitter reach of the antimatter beamer block."

"No, do not fire the AM beamer," the captain said quickly. "Astro, use the magfield drive to jink us out of alignment with orbital lasers. Now!"

"Jinking!" Ibarra called swiftly as her control panel cross-linked to the magfield drive block that lay between me and the Chief.

The image on the front vidscreen of the giant moon moved up, sideways, down and sideways again as Ibarra jinked and jerked the ship to move it off of a predictable vector track. While we were still on the new vector to pass to the left side of the giant moon, our exact position at any moment could not be easily predicted. Which made aiming directed energy weapons a chore, even if an AI was assisting the Empire gunners on the traffic control orbital. Five yellow-orange stars now glowed among the cluster of surviving Empire spaceships. The surviving five flared their fusion pulse drives and worked to move out of a predictable orbit.

"Five more ships killed," called Chang at Tactical. "The surviving five are still within MIRV reach. Sir."

A yellow-orange star now glowed in the middle of the system control orbital. Then a second star glowed at the north pole end. The plasma glows spread out but failed to connect.

"Yes!" yelled Yamamoto. "Forty percent of the controller orbital is gone! Only two lasers are still firing, sir." Five more yellow-orange stars showed on this side of the giant moon. "Last enemy ships are gone!"

"Range to top of moon's atmosphere is now 900 kilometers, sir," called Chang.

Green CO_2 lasers shot up from two spots on the moon's main landmass. They missed the *Star Glory*. Behind us a third star glowed. It was a very big star.

"Traffic controller orbital is gone!" Yamamoto said. "Carbon dioxide beams are coming from two neutrino-emitting spots on the plane. Likely combat bases. Or maybe defensive lasers at a landing field, sir."

"Are there any MIRVs left?" the captain said hurriedly.

"Yes! Three are left." Yamamoto tapped his panel. "All targeted ships on this side of the moon are now vapor. Sir."

That meant there were still ten spaceships on the far side of the moon. None of the Smart Rocks or MIRVs could follow us around the planet and then attack those ships. Which might be the only survivors of our attack.

"Retarget the MIRVs to hit those two planetary bases," the captain ordered. "And launch a volley of Smart Rocks from the starboard railgun. I want to take out some of the ships on the far side of the moon."

"Retargeting." Yamamoto's slim hands moved quickly over his control panel. "New volley of Smart Rocks launched with Open Target settings. They will seek out anything that emits rads at any wavelength, sir."

In seconds we moved from the near side of the giant moon to its left side, then our vector track curved slightly as the moon's gravity bent our momentum toward where the middle moon would be. Glancing at the system graphic I saw the middle moon was orbiting at 109,000 klicks above the gas giant. The inner moon was at the eastern edge of the gas world and located closer to it. Range to it was 130,000 kilometers. At 9 psol we would reach both moons in seconds.

"Chief Engineer!" yelled the captain. "Flip the ship and engage all thrusters at full power! I want more time to target ships above the middle and inner moons! Do it!"

Looking across the wide space of Engineering I saw Chief O'Connor do the difficult. He tapped the magfield drive controls to flip the ship nose to tail, pre-empting the controls of Bridge Astrogation. Then his gnarly fingers moved over the nearby fusion thrusters panel. The vibration of the thrusters now shook my feet as they worked to slow our forward momentum.

"Ship speed is decreasing, captain. Eight psol. Seven. Uh, five," the Chief grunted. "Four, two, now at one psol!"

Behind us seven yellow-orange stars glowed.

"Captain! Seven ships are gone from the Smart Rock volley. And from our stern proton and CO_2 lasers," called Yamamoto.

"Leaving three ships to tell the tale," the captain murmured. "Weapons, any visuals from the Smart Rocks on the far side of the moon? Did the MIRVs hit the two land sites?"

"They did, sir. Two warheads took out what appeared to be a walled installation outfitted with lasers and ground-to-air missiles. Which missed the warheads." Yamamoto leaned forward. "The third warhead took out a spaceship landing pad and surrounding buildings. Its anti-air lasers also failed to kill our MIRV. Sir."

The captain punched the air with his right fist. "Yes! Astrogation, time to reach the middle moon?"

"Four minutes, sir," Ibarra replied.

"Tactical, obtain targeting data on the 24 objects in orbit above the middle moon. Supply it to Weapons. And Weapons, prepare the four missiles in our stern silos for launch in thirty seconds. I want MIRVs on track for those 24 targets!"

I looked away from the nearby bulkhead vidscreen, choosing to check my control panel. Green bars everywhere. Including the overhead AM feeder tube that led to Bill's beamer block. Would he get a chance to use his weapon against the ships orbiting the middle moon? I did not know. Nor did anyone. Except for the captain. Who clearly had a hunger for destroying any and every Empire base. Telling myself patience was a virtue, I sat back in my seat, told my mind to stop listening to the whispers of Gambuchino and her three mates as they also wondered about what would happen next, and thought of our upcoming departure from the system. Would we escape without pursuit? Or was there a hidden Empire battlecruiser now in cloaking, getting ready to head for us?

CHAPTER SIX

Lacking any order to open the antimatter flow down the nine injector tubes that surrounded me, I looked away from the Chief and back to the nearby bulkhead vidscreen. Its overhead view of the Bridge was busy. The front vidscreen's system graphic image now enlarged rapidly so the middle moon, which lay closer to the gas giant than the outermost giant moon, fully occupied the image. Twenty-four red neutrino sources showed on our side of the middle moon. One source put off multiple neutrino signals, which suggested it was an orbital base. The other twenty-three were single neutrino sources. The true space image on the right side of the vidscreen now filled with actual imagery of the neutrino sources, thanks to the enlarging power of our ship's electro-optical scope. Those true space images did indeed show an orbital base that resembled a rectangular bar thrust through a basketball. Which puzzled me until I recalled gravplates made pointless any worry about using spingee to provide artificial gravity. Whatever alien had designed this base had chosen this shape. Perhaps to increase the number of docking tubes. Or the number of hangar entries for insertion of cargo. Or for some other alien reason. I didn't care. What mattered most to me was what I saw the other twenty-three sources doing. Four were thrusting out of orbit and heading inward to the innermost moon, clearly hoping to escape destruction. But nineteen of the alien ships were now thrusting toward us!

"Tactical, your analysis?" the captain said calmly.

"Sir, it appears those ships are armed merchantmen. Or armed something. The scope imagery shows laser mounts on the nose and spine of most ships. One ship has mounts on spine, belly and nose." Chang turned in her seat to look back to where the captain and the other line officers sat. Her look was one of concern. "Captain, I would guess those ships have received neutrino comsignal word of our attack on the outermost moon. I suspect they are moving to attack us, perhaps by englobing us. Sir."

The captain frowned. "Do any of those 23 ships show Empire fleet ship characteristics?"

"No sir, they do not. No ship has the two globes connected by a thick tube shape of Empire fleet ships," Chang said. "However, the one that is most heavily armed is one-third our size. It is composed of seven tubes wrapped around a central tube. My guess is it is a major cargo carrier, carrying something that someone wants to protect. Sir."

The captain looked down. "Major Owanju, launch your GTOs. Move them into a diamond formation centered on us. But have them move back toward Engineering. I do not want any GTO hit by friendly fire from our port and starboard gamma ray lasers. Or the railguns."

In the bulkhead vidscreen the shaved black head of Owanju looked down. His right hand tapped a control patch on his right armrest. "Sir, orders sent. The GTOs will launch from Hangar One within twenty seconds."

I bit my lip. Piloting one of those GTOs was Warren. And likely Lance Corporal Richard Jones was his laser gunner. I'd met Jones earlier in our last deployment. More recently he had joined one of our lunch get-togethers. He hailed from St. Louis and was 24 years old, like me. He liked playing *Go* so it was neat to meet him. Now, he and Warren would be at risk. As would six other Marines on the three other GTOs. Those shuttles had good fusion pulse spacedrives which allowed them to keep up with the *Star Glory*. But they had no defensive armament and the shuttle AI had no self-awareness.

"Heidi, do you agree with the analysis of CWO Chang?" the captain asked as the time counter on the true space image ratcheted down to three minutes before reaching the middle moon.

"I do," the AI said. "The aliens have seen that sitting in orbit makes them vulnerable to low-speed MIRVs and Smart Rocks. Therefore they have chosen to move out of predictable orbits. Four are heading away from us. The other nineteen are moving toward us, clearly hoping to damage us in passing and perhaps escape out of the system if this ship does not destroy them."

"Astrogation, what is the approach speed of the enemy ships?"

"One psol," Ibarra said. "We are at two minutes out. Range to moon is 99,000 kilometers and closing."

"Tactical, distance to approaching ships?"

"Eighty-one thousand klicks," Chang said.

The captain slapped his armrest. "Weapons! Launch our MIRV missiles on forward tracks. Tactical, send targeting data to

Weapons. We cannot waste multiple MIRVs on a single target. And launch four volleys of Smart Rocks now! I want those ships to run into a blizzard of pain before they reach laser range of us."

"Launching four missiles from the stern silos," Yamamoto said breathlessly. "Spine and belly railguns have launched first volley of Smart Rocks. That's 600 rocks. They are all set for Open Target acquisition. Shall I launch missiles loaded with Hunter-Killer mines?"

"Yes. Load four missiles with mines. Then have the assembly robots arm four more missiles with MIRVs. Do it!"

"Sir, doing as ordered."

That was something we had yet to see. The mines were usually relied on as defensive measures to protect a stationary base or asteroid or unmoving group of ships. Using them as backup to the MIRVs and Smart Rocks told me the captain wanted to sow the maximum targeting confusion to enemy gunners. For while Ibarra was already jinking and jerking the ship in multiple directions, still, our vector track toward the middle moon was predictable. The enemy ships might just be armed merchantmen. But they knew we were coming and rather than sit in orbit and be destroyed by incoming MIRVs, they had chosen to rush toward us, counting on some of them to escape as we passed each other at a combined closure rate of two psol. That was not slow. Not at all. Our ship's laser gunners could likely get off two rounds of beam shots before we passed each other. It would be up to the maneuverable solid projectiles of the MIRVs, Smart Rocks and Hunter-Killer mines to do the most damage. The solids had our forward momentum of one psol. They also had sideways movement imparted by the missiles and the railguns. There was no doubt in my mind that the captain hoped these launches would produce a half-dome of deadly projectiles which would kill the oncoming ships faster than those ships could hurt the *Star Glory*. But the enemy, like us, could begin firing at 10,000 klicks out. At both us and the oncoming MIRVs, rocks and mines. Who would be the most successful in gunnery targeting was what mattered.

"Launching four missiles with mines!" called Yamamoto.

"Good. Petty Officer Watson!" called the captain loudly to draw the attention of my friend. "Orient your AM beamer aperture to focus on the big guy ID'd by Tactical. She is sending you the firing coordinates now."

In my mind I saw Bill lean forward, tap his control panel and watch his targeting screen as the emitter node of the beamer block shifted until it was aimed forward, along the line of our outer hull, and perhaps a bit outward. For the oncoming enemy ships were now moving up, down and sideways, assuming the half-dome englobement position predicted by Chang.

"Largest enemy ship locked in!" called Bill over the All Ship comlink. "Permission to fire?"

"Permission to fire given," the captain ordered. "Be sure you hit her on the first shot. I want you able to acquire a second target before we all flash past each other."

"Will do, sir. I'm setting up second and third targets in my fire control panel right now," Bill growled. "Estimated time to firing on first target is 43 seconds."

That meant the enemy ships would begin firing on us some time later, maybe a good minute from now in view of them being at 20,000 kilometers distance out when Bill fired. I flexed my right hand, wishing I had a fire control rod in it. I didn't. All I controlled was the flow of antimatter. And there was no way I could make a beam of antimatter move forward. Only Bill's beamer station could do that. Or was there a way to shoot antimatter in a direction other than to our rear?

"Enemy ships are within AM beamer range," called Chang.

"Firing!" yelled Bill.

In the true space image on the Bridge vidscreen a narrow beam of blackness moved up from our rear, reaching out almost instantly to cover 20,000 klicks. It impaled the front of the seven-tubed ship. Bill's shot continued for another second, feeding more antimatter into the oncoming ship. That created a ball of black antimatter that now ate through the center of the enemy ship. White light glared all around that ball of antimatter as the outer ring of seven tubes became orange molten, then yellow incandescent, then white plasma as the antimatter turned all matter it touched into raw energy. What had been a hundred meter long group of tubes containing air, water, cargo and living beings of soft matter now became a fluorescing cloud of gases that began to cool from white hot to orange and then to yellow. My infrared sight saw the dead ship's vapor move down in hotness to infrared, then far infrared.

"Second largest ship targeted!" called Bill. On the system graphic image a black star took form next to a ship that resembled a rhomboid block in the true space image. "Firing!"

The range to that ship was now just 14,212 klicks, according to the range counter in the true space image. We were a minute out from reaching the middle moon and its single orbital base.

"Com, put me on Empire fleet frequency 1432!" yelled the captain.

"Neutrino frequency established!" said Wetstone.

"Empire ships! Pull away from us and you will be spared. Otherwise, you will all die!"

"Incoming!" yelled Wetstone.

An image formed between the true space imagery of the cluster of 17 surviving ships and the system graphic image. A creature that resembled a giant rabbit possessed of a mouthful of canine teeth surmounted by a line of three red eyes now growled loudly.

"Empire ship *Hungry Mouth* moves aside from this battle!" the creature said over the translator block next to Bjorg. The alien's red and green striped fur rose up stiff. "Do not fire on us! We depart!"

"One alien ship is moving south of the ecliptic," called Chang. "Closest projected approach is 11,000 kilometers. The sixteen remaining ships are maintaining englobement. Sir."

"Firing on third largest ship!" yelled Bill.

The true space image showed a ball-shaped ship with orange-yellow fusion pulse flames shooting from its rear now being impaled by the narrow black beam of Bill's beamer block. The beam hit the ship at an angle versus head-on, causing a deep slice into its frame. Orange, yellow and now white vapors filled that deep gash. Which suddenly erupted into a bright yellow star as the ship's fusion reactor lost containment.

"Fifteen enemy ships now entering firing range," Ibarra called out loudly.

"MIRVs are impacting!" cried Yamamoto.

Nine bright yellow stars filled the true space image.

Purple, green and red beams shot at us from the surviving six ships. Which were being hit by Smart Rocks right and left. The closest ship hulls grew black blemishes as if they had black chicken pox.

"Hits on our nose, upper spine and port side!" yelled Chang.

"We have water leakage on the port side," Woodman called out from Life Support. "Just ahead of Armories Deck. Recycling is losing air. Hatches are closing off the breach! Personnel are moving to the center of the deck."

Too much now happened, though my eyes took it all in.

Our four GTOs fired as one on a single enemy ship that lay at nine o'clock high. It blew to pieces of silver metal, white air and shiny water as its water jacket failed to stop the CO_2 beams of our GTOs.

Our nose proton and CO_2 lasers hit a ship that was a collection of tubes, balls and square blocks. The green and red beams converged on the central block. It blew into a bright yellow star as the ship's fusion reactor lost containment and its structure flew apart in a scatter of fragments. The port and starboard gamma ray lasers fired orange beams at ships on either side of us. One ship stayed intact but began tumbling in place. The second ship stopped firing on us.

A second volley of laser fire came from the surviving three ships. Purple, red and green beams hit our starboard side.

"Penetration on Supplies Deck!" cried Woodman. "Air and water going out. Hatches closing. No personnel in that section. Quartermaster is alerted!"

Three yellow stars appeared where the surviving three ships had once been alive. Those stars fled to our rear as we moved toward the moon ahead.

"All enemy ships destroyed!" called Chang.

"Confirmed," said Yamamoto.

"I agree with your human crew," Heidi says. "However we will shortly be in laser range of the middle moon's orbital base."

"Captain," called Kumisov. "The hull breaches on port and starboard are a worry. It will take time to repair the inner and outer hulls."

The captain nodded quickly. "Weapons! Are our railguns functional?"

"They are, sir. The beams hitting topside missed our spine railgun. All other laser and AM mounts are functional. Sir."

Still wearing his vacsuit like all of us, the captain leaned forward, his globular helmet a reminder of the potential for air loss in any space battle.

"PO Watson! Take out the middle moon orbital base. I do not wish us to close within range of its lasers. Which I assume they possess."

"Sir," called Chang. "Sensors and our scope images confirm this orbital base has laser mounts in the same positions as the system entry controller's orbital."

"Understood. Astro, adjust our course to put us on track for rendezvous with the innermost moon," the captain said hurriedly. "And make sure our vector track is always more than 10,000 klicks distant from that orbital!"

"Adjusting our vector track," Ibarra responded.

The true space image showed the Venus-sized moon shifting to the left of the image, leaving us to pass by on its three o'clock side. The world was not totally encased with clouds like the Solar System's second world. It had clusters of white clouds above brown land masses and a few blue lakes. Clearly this giant moon was able to support life on its surface. How much alien life was down there, none of us knew. Nor cared so long as they did not fire on us. I looked to the system graphic and its image of the inner moon. It showed 12 neutrino emitting sources in orbit. Presumably at least one orbital base and eleven ships. That graphic now changed. Six red dots began moving downward toward the system's ecliptic plane. Our vector track was above the plane and rising slightly to match the moon's inclined orbit around the gas giant. The graphic showed other things. There was the large green dot of our ship. And three smaller green dots that clustered around us. There should be four. One GTO was gone, dead. Was it Warren's?

"Captain," called Owanju. "We lost the GTO *Ramadi* in the last battle. Corporal Lois Hendry and Lance Corporal David Mitchum are no longer with us. Sir."

Fuck.

The captain's broad shoulders slumped. "Very sorry to hear that, major. I will enter them on the pending promotion list. Perhaps their families will choose to attend the ceremony."

"Perhaps they will," Owanju said, his voice somber.

"Middle moon orbital coming into range!" called out Ibarra.

"PO Watson, do your duty!" the captain said abruptly, as if angry.

"Sir, orbital base locked in," Bill said over the All Ship comlink.

I watched the true space image of the base. It was a giant ball studded with external mountings. Three black holes suggested empty hangars previously occupied by some of the now dead 22 enemy ships. The system graphic showed the red dot of the toothy rabbit's ship diving below the ecliptic plane, making for an escape from the system. Would the three ships left alive in orbit about the outermost moon do the same? Or would they stay until new Empire ships arrived? I cared not. What mattered was my best buddy was still alive.

"Firing," Bill called out.

A narrow black beam of antimatter shot past the starboard side of the ship, reaching ahead to impale the central equator of the orbital base. Yellow, orange and now white light rimmed that impact spot. As Bill kept his beamer firing new antimatter, the spot spread wider, as if it were a black hurricane taking over a small moon. In less than a second the white glow of total matter-to-energy conversion grew as bright as the system's yellow star. Brighter in truth. On the orbital's outer edges the hull plates ruptured. Fragments flew outward. White air jetted out. Silvery water globules followed. Tiny black sticks that might be alien people also shot out with the air and water. Then it all became a new star.

A white-yellow-orange ball glowed above the middle moon.

"Astro, how soon before we reach the innermost moon?"

"Captain, two minutes fourteen seconds, sir," Ibarra responded.

"Tactical, status of objects near innermost moon."

"Sir, six ships are moving slowly toward the south ecliptic," Chang answered. "Five ships are still in orbit. But they are going to a lower orbit and faster orbital speed. I assume they are trying to reach the opposite side of the Mars-size moon. The orbital base is on our side of the moon. Sir."

The captain nodded slowly. "PO Watson, how is your beamer station doing?"

"A-Okay, captain," Bill said brightly, sounding like the upbeat dairyman farmer from Knoxville, Tennessee that I knew so well. Gone now was his one-upmanship teases about raising milk cows being harder than raising beef cattle. My redhead friend was clearly focused on his job. Which was operating the targeting sensors of his block and firing his antimatter beam as often as humanly possible. It was our best standoff weapon. In truth it was the only serious standoff weapon. The MIRVs, Smart Rocks and Hunter-Killer mines could reach the enemy at distances beyond Bill's targeting range. But none of those solids traveled at the speed of light.

"Good. Weapons, load four more missiles with MIRVs. And prepare to fire single volleys of Smart Rocks from the port and starboard railguns. Target the six ships moving south ecliptic. And the ships moving toward the moon's horizon."

"One minute to engagement range," Ibarra said softly, clearly touched by the fact of our losing two fine Marines in the dead GTO.

"Four missiles launched. Two ship groups are targeted by forty MIRVs. Half to the ecliptic group and half to the horizon group," reported Yamamoto, his voice sounding raw. "The Smart Rocks are all aimed at the orbital base. Sir."

"Good thinking," the captain said, sitting back in his seat atop the command pedestal. "However, I doubt they will be needed. PO Watson, acquire the orbital base. Set it as your first AM beam target."

"Acquiring," Bill said quickly, almost eagerly. "Target locked in. Range to target is now 27,312 klicks. Sir."

"Weapons, will our MIRVs have enough kick to reach the two ship groups?"

"They have the kick, captain," Yamamoto muttered. "Our one psol momentum gives them a faster approach speed than the ships attempting to escape or move to the far side of the inner moon. Sir."

"Ten seconds to engagement range for the orbital," Ibarra called out sharply.

We all watched the two images on the front vidscreen. The system graphic on the left side showed six red dots moving south ecliptic but still within two diameters of the Mars-size inner moon. The five red dots heading for eastern horizon of the moon still had some ways to go, even though their drop in altitude likely put them close to scraping the moon's upper atmosphere.

"In range!" yelled Ibarra.

"Firing!" cried out Bill.

A black beam of antimatter spat out. It crossed the 19,312 kilometers to the orbital base in the blink of an eye. Its impact on the orbital's upper end became a black vortex surrounded by orange, yellow and white light. As the ship's vector track moved down slightly, the AM impact spot moved also. The continuous antimatter firing from Bill's beamer block opened a giant chasm of glowing energy in the middle of the two kilometer wide orbital. That chasm turned white now. The whiteness spread outward. Gray metal hull fragments flew apart as inner air pressures pushed outward, driven by the expanding gases from total matter-to-energy conversion. White air and silvery water globules followed the hull plates. The white circle of raw plasma reached the outer rim of the orbital before bodies could become visible. In a few nanoseconds what matter remained joined the white-yellow-orange glow of a tiny new star. Which now began to fade in color as the expanding gases grew colder in the empty vacuum of space.

"Target destroyed," Chang reported.

On the true space image four yellow stars glowed as MIRVs hit four ships with three megaton thermonukes. Two more yellow stars soon joined the crowd. Those stars showed a south ecliptic momentum as the plasma gas that was formerly solid matter maintained its inertial momentum.

"Six enemy ships gone," Chang said lightly. "Rerouting Smart Rocks to pursuit of five horizon-approaching ships. Twenty MIRVs are also moving after them. Contact predicted in . . . four, three, two, one!"

Five yellow-orange stars glowed on the eastern edge of the innermost moon. The tiny green specks that were two volleys of Smart Rocks disappeared into those plasma glows.

Chang looked back to the captain, her expression relieved. "Captain, all enemy ships and the orbital are destroyed. Sir."

The captain gave a low sigh. "Welcome news. Tactical, what is the status of the three surviving ships above the outermost moon, and the ship that fled the englobement attack?"

Chang looked down at her control panel, which clearly gave more data than what I could see in the system graphic. Three red dots still orbited above the outermost moon, while the fleeing ship was diving fast below the ecliptic, its speed approaching five psol and increasing. Clearly the toothy rabbit wanted to get far, far away from the *Star Glory*. And our most deadly weapons.

"Captain, three ships are still in orbit above the back side of the outermost moon. The fleeing ship is moving outsystem at seven psol. Sir."

"Tactical, do our sensors show any other Empire ships in this system?"

"No sir, they do not."

The captain looked down. "XO, what do you recommend?"

Kumisov shook her head inside her helmet, her long black hair flaring to either side. While the overhead spyeye did not show her face, her posture and manner bespoke relief. Our ship had attacked multiple orbital bases and dozens of armed merchantmen. We had survived the three attacks with only the loss of two people out of a ship's complement of 369 crew. In the system graphic there moved our large green dot and the three smaller green dots of the surviving GTOs. The few surviving red dots were far, far away.

"Sir, recommend we step down to General Quarters status." Kumisov looked ahead at the arc of tired people still strapped into their duty stations. "Recommend each deck releases crew to eat meals. Recommend the Quartermaster locate hull plating for repairs to our hull breaches. We will have two days before we reach the edge of the magnetosphere and can make Alcubierre transit."

"XO, see to it. I am leaving the Bridge for time in the officers conference room. There is planning I need to do for our future actions." Captain Skorzeny released his seat straps, stood up, then stepped down from his elevated seat. He moved to stand beside Kumisov. Lifting his gloved right hand in a salute, he spoke. "XO, take command of the Bridge. And maintain a system-wide monitoring for surges of graviton emissions. I want to know immediately if any new starships arrive at the edge of this system's magnetosphere!"

Kumisov saluted him back but stayed strapped in. "Sir, I take command. System-wide monitoring for graviton emissions will be maintained. May I have Mess Hall bring you something to drink and eat?"

The captain grinned. Then chuckled. "Yes. Most definitely yes." He looked up at the overhead spyeye. "All Ship, well done! Go to General Quarters. Officers, take action as needed to ensure the needs of your people. Captain is off the Bridge."

And with those simple words I sat back and wondered about our future. Would the *Star Glory* go hunting more Empire ships at a star system we had never visited? Would we visit a system already known to us? When would we run into Smooth Fur and his fleet of deadly battlecruisers? Whatever the future held, I felt relief. Relief that my ship and my shipmates had Neil Skorzeny leading us. The man was tough, determined and yet attuned to the needs of the hundreds of people who kept my ship operating smoothly. Now, if only the people personalities could run as smoothly as the tech!

CHAPTER SEVEN

Smooth Fur stared at the neutrino comsignal with high frustration. The imagery and sensor feed from the Empire's most recently settled star was filled with red, green and purple beams, along with the orange of gamma ray beams and the black of an antimatter beam. Empire transport and trader ships blew up above the three moons of the gas giant system. The orbital bases above the moons suffered a similar fate. The message from the captain of one of the three ships that now hung above the outer moon Stellar was stark.

"Help us! The bipedal primates attacked and killed all our shipping!" whistled a winged avian whose plumage was a mix of red and black feathers. "Their human leader says he will attack other Empire stars. Send us fleet ships!"

She bit her tongue. Clearly the destruction of two out of three human starships had not convinced the furless primates to accept the Glorious Choice. Their refusal of Servant status and their later attack on his fleet at a star undergoing home world cleansing made them a nuisance. These humans could have chosen to disappear into the distant stars of the galactic arm they called Orion, similar to the escape efforts of the Melanchon and Sendera peoples. Now, here was the escaped ship back at their outermost colony star, waging destruction of all that swam above the three moons. And, she noted, destroying with powerful rad bursts two land bases on the primary continent of Stellar.

While the occupied cities were untouched by these primitives, that meant little. Life was rampant throughout the Warm Swirl galaxy. Almost every star had planets. Many of those planets had air of suitable oxygen and nitrogen content. Even the species who had evolved on gas giants, like the pink floater Tink who occupied the Power station to her left, or the scaled reptile Rak at Astrogation who came from a world so close to its star there was no surface water to be found, those species were common, if not as numerous as species like her own Notemko people. Well, the yellow star bipedal primates would learn the lesson that all galactic species had learned over the past 93,000 years. Oppose the Empire of Eternity and your home world dies. Attack Empire ships and your ship also dies. Time to take action.

"Fleet Aide, are the fleet crafts ready to depart to our next enforcement star?" she said, turning to her right to focus on the black-furred biped who resembled the black bears that still roamed the human world of Earth.

Lork tapped his control panel with an index claw, then looked to her, his red eyes nearly glowing. His jaw full of long white teeth opened. She knew that jaw could crush the bones of any crew being on her ship *Golden Pond*. But since Lork belonged to the Dugen species, whose Empire rank was only Associate level, he would never attack any being on her ship. Unless she ordered it. As she had done a few times.

"Masterful leader, our 23 craft are fully supplied by this system's orbital base. Our weapons are ready to attack any target you designate." The black-furred being, who towered over her, bent his blocky head toward her. "All damage from the last encounter with the humans has been repaired. What are your orders?"

"Advise the leader of each fleet craft that we depart for star 3,721 within a sleep period. There is a species there that has refused the Glorious Choice. Their home world needs cleansing." She showed her own teeth and let escape a low snarl. "Our expansion into this star arm requires examples of our fleet's deadliness. First we will travel to this system and extinguish the life on it. Then we will move further up this arm and hunt for the yellow star that is the human star home."

White globules of saliva dripped from Lork's mouth. "Do we depart now for the outer edge of this system's magnetosphere?"

"We do." She turned away and focused on Rak. "Astrogator, set our swim course to the outer edge of this system." She looked beyond to the pink floater Tink, whose hanging tentacles nearly touched the floor of her control cell. "Power, apply the force needed to move us outward."

Ripples of color flowed over the nearly translucent skin of Tink. "Applying power to our magfield spacedrive," she heard from the translator tube on her right shoulder. "Initiating isotope implosion in our fusion pulse thrusters," the floater said as one tentacle touched his control panel, making a series of tapings.

On the front view plate the green and blue world above which they had swum to obtain supplies from its orbital base now shifted

left, then vanished from the screen as her ship twisted in space and
pointed its forward globe toward the system's outer perimeter. She
looked to the rear of her bridge. Standing above a control panel was
the avian raptor Bloody Beak, whose species held Intended rank. The
avian operated one of her ship's most vital systems.

"Weapons, feed power to our lasers and to the antimatter
beamer," she rasped. "I wish this ship to lead the fleet from a swim
angle of deadliness!"

The curved yellow beak of the avian clacked several times.
"Feeding power to our weapons systems!" the female said as one of
her clawed feet tapped a floor level control panel. "We are prepared to
kill any opponent!"

The clacking words had been heard before, when her full fleet
had nearly englobed the three human battleswimmers. They had
sufficed to kill two human craft, at the cost of a fleet craft. But then
the surviving craft had bitten back with antimatter even though her
sensors had not detected such a weapon mounting. A craft managed
by a fellow Notemko female had been lost. In the later battle to
cleanse a system before the Sendera could occupy it, that same craft
had killed two other fleet craft, then managed its escape. Her twenty-
seven craft fleet was now reduced to her craft and twenty-two other
Empire battleswimmers. Or starbiters to use the official term
preferred by the Dominants who ruled the Empire. The single human
craft had been luckier than any recent species encountered in Orion
Arm. Now, it had returned to kill other Empire craft, including some
craft owned by a Dominant species. Those losses of fleet starbiters
were not something she could replace without returning to the fleet
base from which she had departed. Returning without a record of
decimation of all resistor species would not be good for her, or for her
Notemko people. She had given birth to five litters of younglings,
now being raised by the males who ran the nurseries on her home
world. The slow-thinking males were the perfect choice for raising
new younglings. Managing a starbiter like *Golden Pond* was the
proper role for any Notemko female. Managing a fleet of Empire
starbiters was the highest role yet achieved by any Notemko female.
She must succeed at her task of pacifying this star arm.

"Manager Smooth Fur, it is time for feeding," rasped Zing the
hard shelled avian whose chitin skin was covered in yellow and black
stripes.

They were the marks of a predator similar to all the predators on her bridge. Zing's Zatta species was a newer Empire member, now advanced to Novice level. She and her flying people were eager to prove themselves useful to the Empire. So she spoke without being spoken to first. A violation of Fur's control cell rules. But since it was part of Zing's duties at the Survival station to alert all to the time for delivery of live food, Smooth Fur chose to forgive her the violation of procedure.

"So it is," she barked back. "Order the delivery of our food."

Zing tapped her control panel with one of her upper arms as she stood on her lower leg pair. "Done!"

The nearby entry hole whispered open. A mech that resembled a ground insect entered. On its back was a large floater box with airholes. The mech moved to the center of her bridge, pushed off the floater box so it hovered just above the metal plates of her deck and then it spoke.

"Live food is delivered," it said in a harsh clatter of sounds that matched her own Notemko speech.

One side of the floater swung up. The floater box tilted, forcing the small soft creatures inside to fall to the deck in a flood of brown furballs. Twenty-five small furballs sped off on six legs, doing their best to seek shelter under control panels, power boxes, display units, anything to shelter themselves from the bright white light of her control cell. Their efforts were useless.

One of Tink's tentacles touched a furball, killing it with a poison sting. The tentacle lifted the lifeless furball to the bottom of the floater's body. A mouth opened and ingested the fur ball. The native of a distant gas giant ate. Red blood dripped down to the deck, making small red puddles.

Rak hit another furball with his hard-scaled tail, stunning it. In a flash the reptile's long mouth opened and engulfed the stunned furball. As his yellow teeth chomped down, red blood spurted out from Rak's jaws, streaking the deck with dots of red.

Zorta the hunting cat pounced on a nearby furball, her white claws tearing open its abdomen. The Toka's toothy mouth sank into the soft innards. A sucking sound met Smooth Fur's ears. The rest of the brown furball followed into Zorta's deadly mouth. Only few red drops hit the deck.

Bloody Beak slammed two furballs with her left wing, stunning them. In no time one furball was held in Beak's right leg claws, red blood dripping from the claws. The other furball was gripped by the avian's beak, tossed up in the air, then it fell into the open beak, to be swallowed whole. The yellow and red feathers about the avian's throat bulged outward as the furball slid down to its belly.

Zing could wait no longer. Her stinger tail swung out and then impaled a nearby furball. A slight pulse of her stinger sufficed to inject nerve toxin into the creature. Lifting the furball up with her stinger tail, the flying insect twisted her triangular head, opened her mandibles and bit down on the fur ball. Red blood squished out from the yellow mandibles, the blood smearing the deck.

Another member of her crew, an amphibian who spent most of its time close to the deck, turned its flat head toward a fur ball and tensed. A yellow streak of electricity jumped out from Wendig and hit the furball, killing it instantly. Moving slowly Wendig opened its toothy mouth, closed its jaws around the dead furball, and then chewed slowly. Wendig belonged to the water-loving Hola species, an Associate member of the Empire. The Hola moved slowly but its ability to project streaks of electricity made Wendig a natural member of her control cell crew.

Near to her Lork finally stopped holding back for her. He stomped a nearby furball with a clawed foot, then reached down, grabbed the dead furball with his right clawhand and tossed it into his long-toothed mouth. Red eyes glowed with satisfaction.

Smooth Fur saw a surviving furball jump away from Lork, only to land near her. She lifted her black-furred tail and swung it sideways. It hit the furball solidly. The creature flew to the wall in front of her, hitting with an impact that killed it. She reached out a clawed hand and caught the furball body as it slid down the wall, leaving behind a red streak. Tossing it into her mouth, she munched on it as she looked around her control cell.

Red blood drops, blood streaks and puddles of red blood were everywhere. Exactly what should be present during feeding time when a crew of predators ate live food. No being on her bridge, or within *Golden Pond*, failed to eat live food. Some might be omnivores interested in plant foods. But all beings on her ship loved meat. And nearly all of them loved chasing, killing and then eating live food. What was the point to eating frozen flesh? It had no taste of death flavor to it. So a part of the rear globe of her ship was given over to raising hundreds of brown furballs, some larger smooth-skinned creatures and even some flying lifeforms that the avians like Bloody Beak and Zing enjoyed catching on the fly.

"Does the manager wish this unit to perform cleaning duties?" the mech asked, its simple mind without personality or ability to think beyond programed duties.

"No! Leave the bridge now. Return later, when Survival calls you."

The mech scurried away and out the entry hole in the nearby wall. Smooth Fur considered catching one of the last surviving furballs, but refrained. The Engines crew being Trelka still needed to eat. And the rest of her control crew would take care of the few survivors. The energy expended in the chase and killing would settle down all her crew beings and make them ready for the boring work of guiding her battleswimmer to the outer edge of this system's magnetic pond, there to launch into grayness on the way to enforce the cleansing of a home world whose people had refused to join the Empire. Just as the humans had done. But the defiant species and the humans lacked the Empire's control of zero-point energy, the underwebbing of the universe itself. That control meant much in what Empire crafts were able to do. Such as having greater laser weapons range. The other abilities that came with zero-point had yet to be shown to the humans. Soon enough they would see the full arc of Empire power. The work she and other members of her fleet did was not unusual. But it was necessary. And it pleased the Dominants who determined the rank level of all member species. So she would do her duty. And soon, she would find the home world of the nuisance humans and teach them the folly of defying the Empire of Eternity.

◆ ◆ ◆

"Why are we going to Kepler 452?"

I looked around the Mess Hall table always occupied by me and my friends. To my left sat Bill. Beyond him was Cassandra. Beyond her, and opposite from me, hunkered my buddy Warren. To Warren's left was Oksana. And between Oksana and me sat my love Evelyn. Everyone had a plate of food and a mug of beer in front of them. Those plates were partly empty, it being noontime and after the end of First Shift. And everyone except me and Oksana wore blue and gray camos, similar to those worn by the Marines and other enlisted. I wore my brown service khakis, having learned thanks to a sharp verbal snap from Chief O'Connor that an E-7 chief petty officer never 'dresses down' to camos. It was either service khakis or the bulky Service Dress Blues, like the outfit the captain had worn on the trip out from Earth. While Okie was always classy in her appearance, she too wore service khakis. My friends swallowed their food or drink, then grew thoughtful at my question.

"Don't know," Warren muttered, his Aussie accent barely noticeable after years in the American branch of the Star Navy. "We repaired the hull breaches. And we replaced the lost water by grabbing that small comet in the system's Kuiper Belt. The *Star Glory* does not need any supplies or weapons from the pirates. It's a mystery to me."

"And to me also," said Bill, pushing at his pile of spaghetti and meatballs. My fellow cattleman gave a shrug of his strong shoulders. "Maybe to get more intel from the pirates?"

Evelyn and Cassandra both shrugged, then lifted their mugs to drink cold Blue Moon beer. Which left the person I should have focused on.

"Oksana! Talk!"

Our blond Russian pursed her lips and looked uncomfortable. At six feet tall, like Evelyn, the two women were the tallest folks at the table, and often elsewhere, except when I was around. I'd long grown used to be called 'tall and lanky' by women and some guys. It was a term used by my high school teachers in Castle Rock. So what if I was six foot five inches tall? And taller than anyone else on the ship other than Captain Skorzeny, who nearly matched my height. Pushing the fact of my differentness away, I stared at her. Finally she gave a long sigh.

"Hey! I can't help that I work in Intelligence, just below Bridge Deck," she said in a high tone that I had come to recognize as indicating she knew something she should not talk about. Which fit her job as a chief warrant officer second class who worked directly under the Intel chief Lieutenant Gerasaki. Okie frowned. "The LT did mention something in passing."

"Well?" prodded Warren, lifting his strongly muscled arms to spread them wide in an imploring gesture to his girlfriend. "You can trust me. You can trust all of us here." He gestured with one hand to the rest of the Mess Hall, where fifty other Spacers, NCOs, a few Marines and some staff officers sat at tables eating one of the ten dishes offered today. "They can't hear us. And Heidi doesn't care what we say. So give!"

Okie blinked her blue eyes, then shook her blond ponytail. "Hey! I outrank you and don't you forget it!"

Warren smiled warmly. "I do like it when you boss me, pretty woman."

Oksana closed her eyes and lifted her head upward, as if imploring the Goddess for strength. Then she opened them, looked down and scanned everyone at the table. She ended up glaring at me. "Nathan, you of all people should understand that it is up to the captain to share what he chooses to share about our future mission."

I nodded slowly. "He did share. Using the All Ship just before we jumped into Alcubierre space-time. Said we were heading to Kepler 452. Which lies 1,187 light years distant from Kepler 37. He announced a memorial ceremony in the Mess Hall for six p.m. tonight to honor the loss of Hendry and Mitchum. Then he said nothing more, though he left the All Ship vidcast live so anyone could see what was happening on the Bridge." I tapped the table with my right fist. "Just *what* did the LT mention?"

Evelyn grabbed my fist. "Nathan, do *not* do the boss thing with your friend. Who is also my friend." The Irish redhead who held my heart captive to her smile, her amber eyes and her Ph.D. mind shook her head slowly. "Let Okie share what she feels she can share." Evelyn looked across the table. "Right, Okie?"

Oksana, the woman who had once had hopes of being my shipboard girlfriend, nodded quickly, her lips tightly closed. Then she murmured softly. "The LT mentioned the captain had said we were going to the pirate base system to recruit help. Combat help."

"Oh?" whispered Evelyn. "What kind of combat help? New weapons?"

Okie shook her head. "Those words were all the LT said. Nothing more. And I heard it only 'cause she was dictating into her recorder tablet, and she had left the hatch open between our offices." She frowned at me, then looked aside to Warren, whose brown hair was still tightly trimmed in a sidewall cut. "And don't you say a *word* to your Marine buddies!"

Warren looked at her with a mix of devotion and amusement. "Yes ma'am, chief warrant officer two, you *will* be obeyed."

Bill laughed. So did Cassie and Evelyn. I could not help laughing either. Their relationship was so blatantly tender that it made me wonder if they had moved beyond dating to loving deeply. The way I felt about Evelyn. I looked to her as her milky-white face, covered in red freckles, lit up with laughter. Yes, she had been the first to pursue me. And she had made no secret of her past conquests among both men and women. But with me she had made an 'only you' commitment. We were engaged. And when she had shared my Mom's wedding ring with everyone at Barnacle Bill's, my inner self had just wanted to jump up and drag her off to the ship's Quartermaster to be registered as husband and wife. The captain knew of our intentions. I'd talked to him about hopes not long after we left Earth orbit. The captain had said 'be patient'. But it is hard being patient when your ship is in deadly peril and no one knows if we will survive the next space battle. Evelyn noticed my sudden silence. She looked my way.

"Nathan? You look different. Does what Okie said worry you?"

I sat up straight, the way my Mom taught me to sit at the dinner table. "No. No worry. Was just wondering what kind of combat help the captain might be seeking from our pirate raider friends."

Evelyn stared at me. She is very very good at reading me. She knew I was not telling her what I had been thinking. And my calmness did not fool her. She shook her long red curls, creating a blizzard of redness about her freckled face. Then she smiled, patient love in her eyes. "Oh really? Well, maybe he is seeking info on where the Empire fleet might travel to next? Or maybe he is seeking intel on fleet naval bases in Orion Arm?" She looked away and down to the half-eaten sushi rolls on her plate. "Time to eat." She picked up a roll of rice and raw salmon wrapped in dried seaweed and took a big bite out of the roll. Leaving me to understand she would wait until we were alone in her cabin, or in my cabin, before she would insist on knowing what I did not want to talk about at the table. Which indeed had to do with weapons, just not in the context we were now discussing.

"Thank you, Okie," murmured Cassandra as she looked to Bill on her right. "Well, Mr. Antimatter Gunner, do you get some kind of emblem or flag for killing three armed merchantmen?"

My heart slowed its rapid beating. It always sped up whenever I felt uncertain or worried or intent on the fight part of 'flight or fight'. Pressing my friend Okie about intel she had overhead had done that to me. Which reminded me these people were my friends, the only people who had made time for me right after our first Earth departure, when we were headed out on our first trip to Kepler 37. They had not laughed at my miserable dancing. They had gotten me to try some new craft beers that came from places other than Colorado. And they had talked me up when a few Spacers chose to talk me down as 'just a farm boy' who didn't know antimatter from a hole in the ground. Briefly I felt intense gratitude and loyalty to these people. Then I focused on what Bill had to say.

"Well, when I asked, the captain did say I could paint the outlines of three dumbbell-shaped ships on the outside of my beamer block. Kind of the way air pilots painted their kills on the noses of their airplanes last century and early this century." Bill rubbed his smooth-shaven face, appearing thoughtful. "So I did that during my volunteer work on replacing hull plates as we moved through the Kepler 37 system, heading for the magnetosphere." He grinned. "But no one in the ship can see what I painted. Only our enemies can see the three kills."

Cassie frowned. "Bill, shouldn't you have painted *four* ship kills? There's the Empire battlecruiser that you killed when we and the Sendera were fighting off the Empire ships so their generation ships could reach the edge of the magnetosphere."

Our redheaded dairyman shrugged. "You're right. I shoulda counted it. But I was focused on the ships I zapped in our last battles. Maybe next time I go out in a vacsuit I will add the fourth ship."

Cassandra reached out and gripped Bill's left hand, a touch that was clearly tender. "Well, next time you go out, hail me. I got a vacsuit that needs vacuum checking. And whatever device you use to paint on the ship's hull, well, I can hold the stencil. Or whatever you use to form the ship shape. Okay?"

I blinked. First it was Warren and Oksana who had become deeply in love. Now Cassie, my antimatter math tutor and the Ph.D. who had always talked of her Star Navy service as the means for becoming a department head at Stanford, that woman was showing more than girlfriend feelings toward Bill. Would it always be Cassie and Bill? I hoped so. My friends might work on different decks and do jobs quite different from my antimatter engineering, but I cared for them. I cared deeply about them, their happiness and their lives. Seeing the four of them, along with Evelyn, made me more determined than before to do my best to anticipate future space combat problems and then have ready solutions for the Chief or the captain, before my ship could be destroyed. Which made me think again about what I had wondered earlier. Was there a way to make the antimatter I controlled move in ways other than to our rear? Was there a means for putting out antimatter in a way that did not depend on rearward momentum? Picking up my mug of beer I took a swallow. The coolness felt tasty. It also refreshed my mind. Being a cattle rancher had always required me to be ready to adapt to new events in the pasture, whether it was roaming coyotes or the rare gray wolf visits. Or the less rare visits by anonymous trucks that roamed pasturelands, on the lookout for cattle to swipe. I'd used my .45 a few times to discourage those trucks. Now, I controlled liters of antimatter. I smiled at the thought of what else I could do with it beyond using it as an afterburner for our thrusters.

CHAPTER EIGHT

Eleven days later we were about to arrive at Kepler 452, the G2V yellow star with one planet that lay 1,187 light years downarm from Kepler 37. It was the pirate base system that had previously combat-challenged our ship, as the price of moving inward to the orbital base ruled by Tik-long the crustacean alien. We expected to find ten to twenty pirate starships near the system's outer limits, ready to protect the base from any Empire ship or fleet. While I now sat in my seat, strapped in and with the rainbow shimmer of the antimatter injector tubes surrounding me, I chose to do what everyone else on *Star Glory* was doing. Which was watch the live feed from the Bridge, per the captain's orders. But I could do more than watch the vidscreen on the nearby bulkhead. Now, thanks to being a 'valuable' crew member of CPO status, I was free to tap my own armrest comlink patch and speak directly to the captain if I had an idea about ship safety. Or I could call over to Chief O'Connor, as I had done with my antimatter fart idea. Talking first with my Chief, short of an emergency, was always my preference. A fair and understanding Star Navy boss was to be appreciated.

In the nearby vidscreen the grayness of Alcubierre space-time disappeared. White star dots showed against the charcoal blackness of deep space. Hence our new term of Deep Black. A yellow star dot glowed in the middle of the image. The adjacent image of the Bridge showed everyone from First Shift, with the captain sitting atop the command pedestal. Below him were XO Kumisov, Major Owanju and Doctor Bjorg. Before them was the arc of six duty stations that ran the ship. The silvery box next to Bjorg was the Empire translator device given me by Hatsepsit of the Melanchon. As before the thing was tied into the ship comlink and Heidi, by way of fiber optic cables and by direct wifi link. It was also linked to Wetstone's Communications station. Thanks to the box, the Bridge could talk to any alien ship. As we had done during the Kepler 37 raid. And would do now with any raider ships we spotted.

"Captain!" called Chang from Tactical. "We've got moving neutrino emission sources from port and starboard sides."

"How many?" asked Skorzeny.

"Twenty-one sources, sir." Chang tapped her panel. "They are scattered over the outer edge of this star's magnetosphere. Which lies at 44 AU out. Closest ship is one AU out from us. Most distant is ten AU." She looked down to her panel. "Front sensor array says there are stationary neutrino sources in orbit above the system's single world, which lies at 1.04 AU. As before that world is on our side of the system. Between the world and us are three asteroid belts, a Kuiper zone of comets and an outer Oort Cloud beyond us. Sir."

"What is the speed of the raider ships?"

"Most are stationary. The four nearest ships are now moving toward us at one-tenth psol. System graphic going up."

Chang focused her attention on the front vidscreen, which now showed the system graphic in addition to the true space image of the yellow star system. On the graphic were the planet, asteroid belts, Kuiper and Oort Cloud zones. The magnetosphere edge was a dotted line. Sitting stationary were seventeen purple dots. Four purple dots were moving toward us, two from our port side and two from starboard. Our single green dot was moving inward at one-tenth psol, which was our exit speed from Kepler 37. We were about to touch the outer edge of the magnetosphere. That imagery now joined the overhead view of the Bridge and the true space image that showed on the nearby vidscreen. What would the captain now do?

"Engineering! Activate our magfield drive and push us parallel to the magnetosphere boundary," the captain ordered quickly. "Use your thrusters if needed to keep us from entering the boundary."

To my left the Chief tapped the magfield drive control panel in front of him. On his left was the control panel for the fusion thrusters, while on his right was the panel for the Alcubierre stardrive. Beyond him was another bulkhead vidscreen which duplicated what I saw on mine. PO Gambuchino and her three Spacers watched a third vidscreen near them.

"Captain, magfield drive activated," my boss said in his deep voice. He now turned left and tapped the thruster controls. A deep vibration came to my booted feet through the deck plates. "Thrusters are emitting 10 psol thrust, sir. We are going into a flat curve. Uh, our inward vector track is now going parallel to the magnetosphere."

"Well done, Chief." In the vidscreen the captain looked ahead. "Com, activate the neutrino frequency for the pirate base," he said, sitting ramrod stiff in his seat.

The captain wore a vacsuit with his helmet hinged back. Which was exactly how Chief O'Connor, Gambuchino and her Spacers, myself and everyone else on the ship were dressed. We were at Combat Ready status. My ears heard every breath taken by the people on Engineering Deck. My eyes saw everyone's infrared glow brighten. Tense time it was.

"Activated," Wetstone said.

The captain stared ahead at the front vidscreen.

"I am Captain Neil Skorzeny of the battlecruiser *Star Glory*. You know us from our prior visit. Raider ships, we have earned the right of entry to this system. Raider base, alert Decider Tik-long to our presence. Advise him I wish to discuss a trade with him." The captain paused. "Respond."

Nothing happened for several seconds.

"Incoming neutrino comsignal!" called Wetstone, sounding excited. "Going up on the front vidscreen. Also going out on All Ship vidfeed!"

The bulkhead vidscreen grew a fourth image in its middle, forcing to either side the overhead view of the Bridge, the true space image and the system graphic image.

The pirate boss appeared in the middle image. Once more we saw an alien who resembled a red lobster crossed with a centipede. Four blue eyestalks leaned forward above a mouth filled with chitin-teeth. Its two front arms rose. One arm ended in a giant claw with serrated edges. The other arm ended in stick-like fingers that were radial in arrangement. Behind the bulbous head rose a plated body and tail, its dark red armor plates covered in yellow and black spots. Underneath its low body were dozens of tiny feet that were similar to what millipedes and centipedes use for walking. The creature's mouth opened. Inside was a green tongue. It made sounds.

"Responding to Captain Neil Skorzeny, captain of the human battlecruiser *Star Glory*. What causes your return to my system?"

"A trade different from what we did earlier, when you added weapons mountings to my ship," the captain said. "In short, we are here after destroying at least twenty Empire trading ships and orbital bases at the star system Kepler 37. You will find that system listed in the Orion Arm database we traded to you." The captain leaned forward against his straps. "In our raid on Kepler 37, we used thermonuke warheads and our antimatter beamer to destroy those ships. We plan similar attacks on other Empire bases in this arm. However we are willing to leave the commercial trading ships and passenger ships intact, if lifeless. We will use our x-ray laser thermonukes and our graser lasers to kill all life within those locations. Which leaves ships and their contents available for salvage." The captain smiled. "However, we need combat help. One ship attacking any Empire system is at risk of destruction. Tell me, are you willing to allow a few of your raider ships now parked near us to join us in our raids on Empire systems?"

"What would I gain if I agreed to your proposal?" the lobster-centipede said with a loud clacking of its mandibles.

"You would gain a percentage of the cargo, and the ships, that your raider ships will acquire." The captain's smile changed to a sober look. "We humans have no need of Empire trade goods. Or Empire merchant ships. And we usually destroy the orbital bases, as we did at Kepler 37. Are you interested in this trade?"

Two blue eyestalks looked to one side." The Decider gestured with its fingered arm. Into view came a raccoon-like being. It was Wick-lo. Its three red eyes looked at its boss, then forward at the vidscreen image of our captain. "Wick-lo, advise our four raider ships to stop their advance on the human ship."

The raccoon alien dipped its head. "Your orders will be followed." The person-tall alien moved to a nearby control panel and began tapping on it.

Tik-long's four eyestalks focused forward. "My Prime Assistant is ordering my raider ships to stop their advance on you."

"Captain," called Chang. "The four raider ships have shifted their vector track to parallel our track. Sir."

"Thank you, Tactical." Captain Skorzeny looked ahead. "Are you interested in my trade offer?"

"I am." Two eyestalks looked over at Wick-lo, then rejoined the other two in viewing the captain. "How will this trade work? How many raider ships do you seek?"

The captain sat back in his seat. "Four ships should be enough." He gestured down to Kumisov, who was looking up at him. "XO, transmit the record of our last battle with the Empire ships of

Smooth Fur. Let them see how we used our four GTO shuttles to cause the Empire leader to believe we possessed the secret of ship cloaking."

Kumisov nodded quickly, her long black hair tied in a bun in case she had to secure her helmet. "Imagery transmitted, sir."

On the bulkhead vidscreen, the image of Tik-long showed the alien shifting eyestalks to one side, to watch something. Moments later it fixed all four eyestalks on the captain. "Captain Neil Skorzeny, do you possess the cloaking secret of the Empire?"

"I do not."

The mandibles clacked harshly. "Regrettable. If you possessed that secret, along with the secret of how the Empire is able to extend the range of their ship lasers, we could both be rich enough to buy a vacation planet. Or a dozen such." The crustacean lifted its armor-plated tail. The red and yellow spots on the plates shone brightly in the light of the Decider's command room. "If I invite four ships to join you, what are your terms for their participation?"

I had been wondering just what the captain had meant by the Intel lieutenant's comment about combat help. Now I knew and so did everyone else on the *Glory*. Politics had forced us to leave Earth's other four combat starships at home in Sol system. Now, we might gain the equivalent combat support thanks to alien greed.

"The four ships accept my orders as if they were your own," the captain said quickly. "They go to any star system I pick. Also, while my primary aim is attacking known Empire systems in our Orion Arm, I will also attack any Empire fleet or group of ships that are trying to kill the home world of any space-going species." The captain grimaced, his jaw muscles tightening. "Humans do not ignore genocide, of people and of planets. If we can stop such a terrible thing, we will help that species. As we helped the Sendera when their new colony world was poisoned by Manager Smooth Fur and his fleet. So . . . the four ships that travel with me will sometimes have to fight to save a planet that belongs to someone else. Will your raider ships do that?"

Tik-long's right claw arm lifted. The giant claw opened, then snapped shut with a loud clack. "Human leader, my own home world was destroyed by the Empire, long cycles ago." Four blue eyestalks leaned forward. "Why do you think I command this system? Once I commanded a single raider ship. Then I realized hurting the Empire required more than a single ship. As you now realize. So I established this base. And will establish a backup base further up your Orion Arm, using the habitable planet data you earlier traded me." The alien's mouth opened. Its green tongue moved from side to side. "Greed motivates all star-traveling species. Otherwise, why would they leave their home world? Greed is honorable. And useful to buying information. I have recently obtained information on the next star system the Empire fleet is aiming to attack. The species Dugong occupy a white star not far from here. They refused the so-called Glorious Choice. My informant says the fleet led by Smooth Fur is now scuttling to that star with the aim of destroying the Dugong home world. Do you wish that information?"

"Yes!" Captain Skorzeny gripped the ends of his armrests tightly. Tight enough for me to see his infrared body glow increased on his exposed face and head. "How reliable is your informant?"

"Very reliable. It is a fellow crustacean, though one which has fewer legs than me." The blue eyestalks leaned back. "Though it has more legs than you unbalanced bipeds!" The alien's left arm reached out. Its eight radial fingers touched a nearby panel. "The star information is sent to you. Along with basic data on the Dugong. Now do you believe that I am more than a greedy lifeform?"

The captain nodded slowly. "I believe you are an honorable lifeform, Decider Tik-long. We will return rich cargo to you and captured starships. So long as your raider ships choose to fly with me, that long will you gain valuables, ships to sell and knowledge of the bases we attack and destroy. Which ships will join me?"

"The four that are closest to you. I know their captains. They are greedy, like all normal beings. But they also have personal histories that motivate them to kill any Empire fleet ship they encounter." Behind Tik-long moved the raccoon alien Wick-lo. It spoke.

"One of the raider captains is a fellow Medoxit like me," said the alien whose gray fur had black stripes running from its triangular head down to its tail. "She is an elder female who once spent time with me on this base. She is a reliable ally."

"As are the other three ship leaders," Tik-long clacked. "Have you received the star location the Empire is now attacking?"

The captain looked ahead. "Com?"

"The data is received," Wetstone said quickly, his fingers flying over his control panel. "Sending the data to Astrogation. And to Tactical. And to the XO."

The captain's grip of his armrests eased. "Decider Tik-long, thank you for this trade. I look forward to more mutual trades in the future."

The crustacean's mouth clacked harshly. "As do I. Take care. Manager Smooth Fur is the deadliest Empire captain to lead a fleet into the stars of this Orion Arm. It has already destroyed the home worlds of three species. Other Empire fleets in other arms of Warm Swirl galaxy have done the same. Perhaps we can slow the death touch of this one."

"I plan to do more than slow Smooth Fur," the captain said slowly, sounding calmer than his infrared glow indicated. "If possible, I will destroy Smooth Fur himself. At the least he will lose more ships. And the smaller his fleet gets, the better the fighting odds."

Wick-lo's four eyestalks wrapped around themselves, then separated. "What a rewarding image! Advise me of your future battles. There may be other raider ships that wish to acquire Empire trade ship cargos."

"I will remain in touch. If you monitor this neutrino comsignal frequency, I will use it to send you audiovisual reports on our actions. Until we meet again."

"Until then," the crustacean clacked.

Sitting back in my seat I listened as our captain contacted the captains of the four raider ships and gave them the stellar coordinates of Kepler 442, the target of Fur's fleet. The star lies 1,115 light years distant from Earth. But its distance from Kepler 452 was just 346 light years. Indeed it was close. Hopefully we would arrive before the Empire killed the Dugong home world. And hopefully the four raider ships would be good fighters. Even though their ships lacked our antimatter beamer, they did possess the magfield spacedrive we had obtained from Tik-long. So their ships could move as fast as Empire ships. But their laser weapons range was the same as ours. Ten thousand kilometers. Which meant the raiders, like the *Star Glory*, had to be ready to accept punishing laser strikes until we got in range to hurt an Empire ship. Or ships. I looked forward to our effort to save the Dugong home world. More pertinently, I had figured out how to use our antimatter fuel to strike out in other directions than to our rear. Once we re-entered Alcubierre space-time, I would alert the Chief to what I had discovered. Then the Chief could inform the XO. I was infamous enough already. I was more than ready for my Chief to gain some extra appreciation from our XO or the captain.

♦ ♦ ♦

Three and a half days later we arrived just outside the magnetosphere boundary of Kepler 442. It was First Shift and I sat in my antimatter seat surrounded by the nine rainbow-glowing tubes that feed antimatter to our three thrusters. A tenth tube runs along the overhead and out to Bill's antimatter beamer block. Not far from me sat PO Gambuchino and her three Spacers at their fusion reactor controls, while closer to me was Chief O'Connor, sitting before his three control panels. He had just shut down the Alcubierre stardrive and we now moved at 10 psol, headed toward the edge of the magnetosphere of Kepler 442. I looked to the right. On the nearby bulkhead vidscreen the system's whitish F7V star occupied the center of a block of darkness, leavened only by thousands of white star points.

A system graphic image now appeared next to the overhead of the Bridge and the true space image. On it were three planetary dots. The innermost dot lay at one-tenth AU, which made it tidally locked and able to show only one face to its star. The same way our Moon keeps just one face aimed at Earth. It seemed to be the size of Mercury. At three-tenths AU lay a Mars-sized world. A green zone indicated planet two lay just inside the inner edge of the system's liquid water zone. The third planet was the system's single super-Earth planet. The Dugong home world orbited at four-tenths of an AU out from its star, right in the middle of the green zone. Numbers along one side of the system graphic told me why it was so close. Its star, while a white F-series star, had just 61 percent the mass of Sol and its heat output was just eleven percent of Sol. Therefore its liquid water ecozone lay much closer to the star than the Goldilocks zone in the Solar System. A large asteroid belt began at 10 AU and extended out to 15 AU, while the system's Kuiper Belt began at 38 AU and went far out. The magnetosphere edge lay at 42 AU. The position of our ship and our four raider ally ships was shown by five green dots that lay just beyond the magnetosphere's dotted line. Worse were all the red dots lying inside the system. Empire ships! But what were the purple dots that were intermixed with the Empire red dots?

"Tactical, what are we seeing?" called Captain Skorzeny.

Chang looked down at her panel. "Captain, there are twenty-three Empire ships in the interior system, located within the wide asteroid belt. Their neutrino emissions match Fur's fleet. They appear to be fighting twenty-six purple dots. Which might be Dugong ships." She paused. "There are also seven neutrino emission spots orbiting the Dugong home world. Likely an orbital base and other ships. Sir."

"Well, at least the Empire ships are far from the Dugong home world." The captain looked down. "Major Owanju, tell your GTO shuttles to launch now. We'll do the 'Now You See Them, Now You Don't' routine and hope it fools Smooth Fur into thinking we have the ability to go into cloaking, like his ships."

The big Marine tapped his right armrest, his vacsuited hand moving quickly. "Captain, orders sent. They will launch from Hangar One within ten seconds. The pilots and gunners were already aboard, in anticipation of this moment."

Those words meant my best buddy Warren would shortly be out in the frigid cold of deep space, flying a spaceship powered by a compact fusion reactor and a single fusion pulse thruster. The reactor was powerful enough to provide energy to the GTO's 90 terawatt CO_2 laser, while also powering the thruster. And life support. And basic controls like astrogation and sensors. Since the loss of the *Ramadi* in Kepler 37, I'd taken the time to learn more about my buddy's ship. It was very mobile, though it lacked the magfield spacedrive of the *Glory*. Anyway, now that we had four raider ships, each about a third as big as the *Glory*, I doubted the three GTOs would be involved in the upcoming space battles. Or so I hoped. As surely did Oksana.

"XO, make the announcement," the captain said calmly.

Kumisov nodded, her red infrared glow brightening. She tapped her right armrest. "All Ship! Go to General Quarters now!"

Overhead came hooting sounds and light flickerings. A chill went down my back as I knew once more we were about to enter combat. That combat would be delayed by a good day or more, given the distance to the asteroid belt. Still, combat impended. Combat that put at risk my lover Evelyn, my friends Oksana, Warren, Bill, and Cassandra, and deck chiefs I knew and liked, such as Lieutenant Gladys Morales of Farm Deck, Chief Daisy Malone of Mess Hall and my own Chief O'Connor. Plus the rest of our 367 person crew. And also the captains and crews of the four raider ships. I had wondered about them before we left Kepler 452. But other than brief images, I knew nothing about them. Would they follow our captain into this system on his mission to both attack the Empire ships and to save a world and species from genocide?

"Communications, open encrypted neutrino comlinks to our four allies," the captain said quickly.

Up front on the Bridge, Wetstone tapped his panel. "Encrypted comlinks established. Sir."

The three images on the nearby bulkhead vidscreen now grew a fourth image. Actually a fourth image that was split into four pieces. The shapes of the four raider captains filled them. I saw the three-eyed raccoon-like alien of the Medoxit species, who closely resembled Wick-lo of the pirate base. A leather skirt hung from her waist. Shoulder straps supported holders for tools and at least one laser pistol. Behind her moved other aliens, presumably her bridge crew. To her right I saw a black-furred bear-like alien captain, only this alien's face was flat like a human's. It had no muzzle. Just two black eyes, a wide nose, two ears and a mouth full of sharp yellow teeth. It wore no clothes but did have criss-crossing straps that supported tools and two laser pistols. Below the bear alien image stood something that resembled a wasp. Its hard body shell showed black and yellow stripes. Its two compound eyes were green. Its mandible mouth was pointed. Two brown antennae rose from its bare skull. And it stood on two chitin legs, with a middle leg pair and upper arm pair free to handle controls on the bridge. The last raider captain resembled a plate-armored hippo, but its head was that of a reptile. A long red tongue flicked out from its narrow muzzle. A large braincase surmounted its front end. At the back end of the gray plates that covered its body was a long scaly tail that now swished back and forth. It leaned back on its rear leg pair, allowing it to lift its front leg pair, which had thick fingers where clawed toes showed on its other legs. Under each image was a name. The raccoon was noted as Delight. The black bear was Gorling. The walking wasp was Lindo. And the six-legged reptile went by the name Mousome.

"Raider captains Delight, Gorling, Lindo and Mousome, are you ready to follow me inward to battle the Empire ships and to aid the Dugong people?" the captain said slowly.

"Willing to fight," called the raccoon Delight, her right hand gesturing to someone out of the image view. "My ship is prepared to move with you and fight with you."

"Hunger do I for the death of Empire beings," growled the black bear alien. "The Empire killed my clan's village."

Two pairs of yellow wings lifted from the back of the walking wasp. "I Lindo am prepared to fly and fight."

The long red tongue of the six-legged reptile flicked out again. "I wish to taste the odor of Empire death," it said. "My ship and crew beings will follow and fight."

Briefly I gave thanks for the silver cube of the Empire translator machine that sat to one side of Dr. Bjorg. Like everyone on the *Glory* he wore a vacsuit with helmet hinged back. Seat straps criss-crossed his chest just as they did me, my boss and everyone else who was at their Battle Stations post on the *Glory*. Thanks to that cube my captain had an easy time speaking with any alien, whether raider or the yet to be met Dugong. The captain had shared the imagery of the Dugong provided by pirate boss Tik-long. The aliens appeared similar to the honey badgers of Earth. Similar, that is, in the black fur with a broad white strip from head down the back to its short tail. While the Dugong were four-limbed with two eyes like so many predators and omnivores we had seen on the pirate base and elsewhere, the Dugong stood upright on their legs. Their four fingered hands appeared delicate and they lacked claws. Even though the Dugong resembled many furred mammals, their stance in the holo image was slim, almost delicate. As if they were born dancers who had chosen to dance out in space. Perhaps it was my imagination. But I liked the Dugong just from seeing images of them.

"Thank you raider captains Delight, Gorling, Lindo and Mousome," my captain said quickly. He looked ahead at the giant vidscreen that covered the front bulkhead of the Bridge. "It appears the native Dugong are fighting hard against the Empire fleet. Let us go inward and see how we can assist them." The captain paused, then spoke. "Engineering, give me full speed on the thrusters and full magfield drive speed."

To my side my boss spoke. "All three fusion pulse thrusters are now firing!" he said. Reaching forward he tapped a control panel. "Magfield spacedrive is now engaged. Sir, we are speeding up from our 10 psol arrival speed to 15 psol. Do you wish afterburner push, sir?"

The captain shook his head. "No. Hold the antimatter afterburner for when we arrive among the Empire ships. I am sure Smooth Fur remembers our ability to outrun his ships. But I see no reason to—"

"Incoming comsignal!" called out Wetstone.

"Source?" the captain murmured.

Our Brit looked down at his panel. "From in-system, sir. It's the Dugong home world frequency."

"Accept and display the signal. Share it with our raider friends and with our GTOs," the captain ordered.

A fifth image now filled the middle of the busy vidscreen. Standing inside a room filled with a dozen other honey badger-like aliens was a single tall and slim alien who stood before a central bench surrounded by panels and displays. The alien's liquid brown eyes struck me as being strong, but worried.

"New ships! Are you Empire?" came a melodious voice from Dr. Bjorg's translator block.

"No!" called the captain loudly. "I am Captain Neil Skorzeny, of the human species, from planet Earth. Our home world circles a yellow star farther up this star arm." The captain gestured with his left hand. "We are enemies of the Empire! At another star system I was attacked by Empire Captain Smooth Fur after I and two other Earth ships refused his demand we join the Empire. We have come to your system to help in your fight against the Empire. We are . . . eight ships strong. Do you wish our help?"

The Dugong leader's white whiskers flared outward. Its two ear flaps rose. Behind it moved another Dugong, who barked something to its leader. The leader softly gestured that Dugong away.

"I am Team Leader Swaying Light, a female of our species," the alien said. "As you can tell from your sensors, we are twenty-six ships fighting as best we can against the Empire ships. But we are dying even as we ambush Empire ships from behind the asteroids of our rock belt," she said. "The Empire ships are faster than ours. Their weapons range father than our weapons. But our people . . . " The standing honey badger who resembled a dancer gestured over a nearby control panel. A hologram of a blue and green world appeared to one side of her. "Our people are billions of ferocious and independent Dugong. This is our home world of Melody. The Empire leader Smooth Fur threatens to destroy our world. We are doing what we can to delay the Empire fleet. So yes, we accept your offer of help. How long will it take you to reach our rock belt?"

"A day of Earth time," the captain said. "That is equal to one revolution of your home world, which does look beautiful. Hold on!"

"We are holding on with paw and ship!" Swaying Light barked low, her translated human voice sounding almost like a song. "Come, join our fight. We cherish your help. We hope you will visit our world once we defeat this Empire plague!"

The Dugong leader's image vanished from the bulkhead vidscreen.

"Incoming comsignal!" yelled Wetstone.

"Source?" the captain murmured.

"From in-system, sir. It's a neutrino comsignal on the official Empire frequency."

"Accept and display the signal. Share it," the captain ordered.

A new fifth image took form in the middle of the vidscreen.

Standing on a circular deck was a black-furred otter. White stripes swept down the sides of its body. The otter alien stood on two thick legs. Its two slim arms hung down to its curving hips. The shoulders flowed straight into a curving neck that supported an otter-like head that held two black eyes, a brown nose, sharp white teeth and flaring whiskers. Looking lower I noticed a black-furred tail hanging from its rear, its smooth black fur shiny under a white light. The tail moved lazily from side to side. To either side of the creature and behind it were nine other aliens, their forms far more bizarre than a walking otter. The alien's mouth opened. Inside a pink tongue moved.

"Greetings to Captain Neil Skorzeny, manager of the Earth battleswimmer *Star Glory* and leader of . . . seven other ships, my sensors report."

I recognized Smooth Fur. Our deadly enemy. And the leader of a fleet that had killed two Earth ships, and also wiped all life from the Sendera colony world.

Evil lifted an arm and gestured sideways with a black-furred hand that held four claw-tipped fingers. "Tell me, are you and the other vessels with you prepared to surrender to the Empire of Eternity?"

CHAPTER NINE

Smooth Fur watched the view plate image of the nearly hairless primate who had destroyed four ships of her fleet, had escaped her grasp twice and who now had arrived at the star of their next cleansing. She felt pleasure at the success of her plan to draw the slippery human into her grasp. And the grasp of her fleet. Leaking the information of their cleansing target on the Dark Neutrino Web, on a frequency known to be monitored by a crustacean who had declared itself an enemy of the Empire, had been easy. What she had not known was whether the human leader would learn of her cleansing target. But here he was, accompanied by four ships whose neutrino emissions resembled those emitted by raiders who often attacked Empire trading and transport ships. The other three ships matched the neutrino emission signatures previously displayed by human ships that this Skorzeny biped said were capable of going into cloak. Perhaps they could. They did emit neutrinos indicative of fusion power reactors and fusion pulse thrusters. So. The primary human ship *Star Glory*, three other human ships and four raider ships had now arrived at the outer edge of the Dugong system. What a delight!

"Manager Smooth Fur," hissed Wendig from his Communications work station. "The human ship just spoke with the Dugong leader's ship," the low-slung amphibian advised.

"Even better," she barked. Looking to one side, to the Fleet Aide work station of Lork, she saw that the Dugong fleet had decreased in numbers from 26 to 25 ships. One of her Empire ships had chosen to use its antimatter beamer to disintegrate the asteroid behind which the Dugong had hid, hoping to hurt the Empire ship as it moved around the large ball of rock in its hunt to kill the Dugong resistor. Her fleet had already killed five Dugong ships. Perhaps she needed to slow her fleet's efforts. The human ships would take time to arrive in-system. "Lork, advise all other fleet ships to refrain from using their antimatter beamers against the Dugong. Let them use their lasers instead."

The black-furred biped made a gesture with its claw hand that she recognized as acceptance. "As you order, Manager Smooth Fur."

The Dugen crew being tapped its control pedestal. "Change in fleet combat actions transmitted. And acknowledged by craft managers."

She looked back to the oval-shaped view plate that adorned the nearest wall of her control cell room. It contained multiple images. One was a neutrino sensor image of all neutrino-emitting ships in the star system. Another image displayed the home world of the Dugong, based on imagery from a monitor craft she had sent inward several light cycles earlier. A third image displayed the real space ahead of her ship *Golden Pond*. Within that image moved the other 22 ships of her fleet. When would a fourth image of the human biped appear?

"Leader! Incoming neutrino comsignal is received," called Wendig, as a yellow glow surrounded his hairless body. "The signal matches the fleet frequency. It is coming from the edge of this system. From the craft you just spoke to."

"Display the signal," she ordered.

"Displaying."

Ignoring the movements of the pink floater nearby at Power, the quick flash of the hunter cat Zorka at her Tactical station, and the yellow and red feathers of the avian raptor Bloody Beak at Weapons, she focused on the human image that now joined her other images. The bipedal primate Skorzeny it was.

The human manager displayed his small teeth. "Are *you* prepared to leave the Dugong system now? If so, I and my allied ships might allow you to reach the edge of the magnetosphere without destruction."

Brief humor filled her gut. Such arrogance! Truly the human leader had no concept of what he faced by challenging a fleet of Empire of Eternity ships. Well, once he arrived at the wide rock belt infested with the Dugong, this Skorzeny would discover exactly how much more powerful was any ship of the Empire. While the human's craft possessed an antimatter beamer and the magfield spacedrive, it had no access to the zero-point energy that fed her weapons and her engines. And fed other devices on her craft. She flared her whiskers and thumped her tail on the deck.

"Amusing you are. Pointless are your threats. Enter this system. Come do battle with my ships. As you die, you will learn the full folly of opposing the Empire!"

The bipedal human gestured with its arms. "I am coming for you and for your fleet. And as you can see now, three of my ships are entering cloaking." The human showed his small teeth. "As you did to us in Kepler 37, I will now do with you. How will you respond when a ship suddenly comes out of cloaking and fires on you from a short distance?"

"I will destroy that ship," she said, reaching up to brush down her whiskers. It did no good to allow this primate to see her disturbed. This moment of vengeance for her four lost craft was something she had long planned. She had chosen the cleansing star with great care. And then she had disseminated that information on the Dark Web. While numerous resistor species and raiders used the Dark Web as their means of sharing information about the Empire, she cared not for that fact. What mattered was the Dark Neutrino Web frequency she used was one known to be associated with the crustacean. It was a being who shared data with one of the leaders of raider ships. Clearly this human primate had been in contact with the raider leader. Who had shared the location of the Dugong system and the fact of her intended cleansing. And that cleansing *would* take place, one way or another.

"I am coming after *you*," the human leader said, his mouth filled with barely sharp teeth. "Perhaps you will identify your ship when we arrive. I welcome the chance to fight you directly." His image disappeared.

She smiled to herself. Smiling was a rare emotion for her people. Producing new generations and rising within the Empire system was what her people had done for many generations. She had reached the highest level for any member of her Notemko people. Commanding a fleet of Empire starships was both a personal honor and a sign that her species was seen with favor by the Dominants. She planned to draw additional Dominant favor. For when the human crafts arrived, they would experience a surprise none of them had ever before experienced!

♦ ♦ ♦

As First Shift ended I set my control panel to automatic monitoring of the antimatter injector tubes, briefly wondered when Bill would come through the nearby hatch to his beamer block, then hit my armrest to release my accel straps. As they whirred back into their seat holders, I stood, still wearing my vacsuit. The captain had ordered us to reduced readiness at General Quarters, now that we knew where the Empire ships were. Still, there could be other Empire ships hiding in cloaking, so the captain had insisted we remain combat ready even as shifts changed, people ate or slept, and routine maintenance was done. Looking ahead I watched as Gambuchino sent off her three Spacers to eat at the Mess Hall. She stayed at her post, doing something complex that involved several holos projected from her fusion reactor work station. Behind me came the sound of boots walking across the metal deck.

"CPO Stewart," called my boss. "You heading to the gravlift and Mess Hall?"

I turned in place and saluted him. "Sir, yes sir, I am heading to the gravlift and lunch."

He gave me a nod, his beady black eyes sweeping over my vacsuit, perhaps checking out its outer attachment rings, the holster for a laser pistol or my trusty .45 semi-auto, and status lights on the chest panel that told other wearers of vacsuits the level of my oxy-nitro supply and similar suit tech stuff. I did not need to look down at my chest panel. The HUD display that always appeared on the lower portion of my helmet provided that data. Anyway, with us both having our helmets hinged back, we were on ship air and enjoying ship gravity.

"Well, then, let us walk together," Chief O'Connor said easily, his tone casual.

"Thank you, sir. Coming."

I fell in and walked beside. As we approached the gravlift tube, I gave a brief wave to Gambuchino, whose dark brown Italian face was looking curious. The woman nodded my way and then gave me a wink, as if to wish me luck in the company of our boss. We stopped before the gravlift's gray metal tube.

My boss reached out and touched the Open patch on the right side of the three meter wide slidedoor. The patch color changed from red to orange, indicating it was on the way down to our deck. A low hum came from Chief O'Connor, as if the gravlift's failure to be instantly available was irritating. The patch changed to green. The slidedoor slid open. The shaft was empty. We stepped inside, turned and faced the slidedoor, which now closed.

"Heidi, take us up to Mess Hall Deck," my boss said.

"Complying," came the musical words of our ship AI. She had been unusually quiet during Captain Skorzeny's encounter with Smooth Fur. Did she know something the rest of us did not know?

I shook my head. We had nearly a day left before we traveled the 30 AU distance that lay between our arrival point and the inner asteroid belt. That gave us all time to be normal. And to worry. But I had something else that had been on my mind for a long while, ever since leaving Earth after the televid interview. Maybe the Chief could help me.

"Chief O'Connor, may I ask a non-work question?"

The Philadelphia native turned and looked at me. His reddish-brown hair was trimmed close to his head. I noticed a bald spot at the back of his head. Well, the man was at least fifty and male pattern baldness was common among a majority of men. His wide shoulders tensed as he looked me up and down, then gave a quick nod.

"Ask away, CPO."

I swallowed, swallowed again and told myself to be brave. Or braver than I felt. "Chief, what is it like being married? Evelyn and I, we are engaged and we—"

"I know all that. Everyone on the ship knows you two are in a lightspeed hurry to get hitched." He grinned broadly, a rare sign of humor. "Or don't you know that anything Superman Stewart does is fodder for shipwide gossip?"

I winced. "Sir, I wish I weren't. The subject of gossip, that is."

He nodded his thick neck as we rose past the Antimatter Fuel Deck. "Well, keep doing unusual stuff and you will never escape the gossip of others. This ship just has a smaller audience than the millions who saw you hold up that aircar as a barrier to the bullet aimed at the senator." His expression changed suddenly, going thoughtful. "But you asked a serious question. And clearly you know I am married. Right?"

"Yes sir, I do know that."

The status tube bar showed us now passing through DT Fuel Bunkers Deck. The Chief grew thoughtful. "My wife Marilyn and I have been together 30 years. Got hitched right after I entered the Star Navy. She mostly raised our three kids. Two boys and a girl. And she always put a hot meal on the table each evening when I came home. Leastwise when I did not have an evening shift at Great Lakes. Or later at Norfolk. And she was the one who helped the kids with their homework." He gave a long sigh, as if the memory of his wife brought with it many feelings. "So what is being married like? It is special. You are never lonely, like I used to be in high school." He paused, glanced my way, saw me paying close attention, then faced the slidedoor. "I wish the best for you and Doctor Kierkgaard. She is a beauty with a brain who cares for the people she works with. She deserves your patience. And your devotion when the two of you face long separations. Like me and Marilyn have faced." The gravlift arrived at Mess Hall, Medical and Recreation Deck. "That answer your question?"

I took a deep breath. "Yes sir, it does. Thank you, sir."

He stepped out into the ring hallway and turned right, heading for the deck section that held the Recreation chamber. "You are welcome. Oh, one other thing about being married." He looked back over his shoulder, his eyes appearing almost tender. "Be faithful to her. Never betray her. And hope to the Goddess that she will cope with being assigned to a different ship. Which is what happens in the Star Navy. The needs of the navy come before personal needs. Good luck."

The man disappeared around the curve of the hallway. I turned and walked left, aiming for the giant door that gave entry to the Mess Hall. Course I could have closed my eyes and just followed my sense of smell. The odors of chicken tandoori, green chili stew, flame-burned steaks and chocolate cake were just some of the odors coming from the open doorway. Quickly enough I was there. Letting two Spacers precede me, I stepped in, then looked to the right. Our usual table lay halfway down the gym-sized room that was the Mess Hall. The table was nearly full with my friends. And with lovely Evelyn. I turned, gave a wave and walked slowly to the table. I sat down between Cassandra and Evelyn. Footsteps behind sounded hurried. I looked up and saw Bill rushing up, a big smile on his narrow face. He sat between me and Cassie. Looking away I gave a nod to Cassie, Warren, Oksana and dear Evelyn. I wanted to kiss her, truth be told. But the reminder I was the subject of ship gossip made me hold back. Evelyn's soft brown eyes looked me over.

"Nate, you okay?"

"Just fine. Better than fine," I said, smiling at her and all my friends. "Rode up with the Chief." I looked left to lanky Bill. "Though I can't figure out how our antimatter gunner made it up here so quickly. When the Chief and I left Engineering, your hatch was still closed."

Bill lifted a reddish-brown eyebrow and gave a shrug. "Old-fashioned stairs work just as well as a gravlift."

Dismissing the fact Bill must have run like Hades to get up here just after my arrival, I looked around the table. Three pitchers of beer occupied the middle of the table, while a platter of crab cakes sat next to the pitchers. Plates and mugs sat before my friends. Several of whom had already grabbed crab cakes and used a fork to sample today's special dish. I reached out, grabbed a crab cake with tongs, moved it to my plate, then poured beer into my mug. I tasted it. The flavor left me puzzled.

"Hey, anyone know what kinda beer is in there?" I said, pointing to the pitcher I'd just used.

Warren smirked. "It's Santa Fe Pale Ale, Nathan. Besides the usual hops there is a touch of red chili in it. You like?"

I took a longer draw. The cool crisp booze felt both fruit tasty and a touch spicy. "I like. Kinda strange flavor mix, tho."

"It is at that," Evelyn murmured, reaching out to a different pitcher and using it to fill her mug. "Give me antique Blue Moon beer. It may be a hundred year-old brand, but I like it." She looked around the table to our friends. "And so do most of you folks, it seems. It's darker than the Santa Fe stuff, or the San Francisco Light in the other pitcher."

Oksana looked up from her plate of crab cakes. Which was now mostly crumbs. Her expression was thoughtful. "Anybody here got any idea why that sharp-toothed walking otter seemed so happy at our arrival here? You'd think the twit would be irritated. We caused him enough trouble twice earlier."

I wondered the same thing as our Intel gal. Across the table Cassandra put down her mug, licked her pale lips, then scrunched up her pinky-white face, her expression one of puzzlement.

"What says Manager Smooth Fur is a 'he'?" Cassie said bluntly. "I know the captain calls Fur a 'he'. So do we here at this table. But my study of the 53 alien species residing at the pirate base showed female dominance in 30 of the 53 species. So why couldn't this Smooth Fur be female? Or able to be both male and female, like some hermaphrodite animals? Or intersex, to be more accurate when we are dealing with thinking people." She folded slim hands on the table. "Or be like our parrotfish and clownfish, where they start out as one sex, then change to the other sex later in life."

I couldn't resist. "Cassie, what was the incidence of intersex among the animals on the twelve worlds we've colonized? Or the degree of female dominance among species?"

She shook a long finger at me. "Nathan, recall that I am the exobiologist here? But to answer you, intersex was a minor expression among the plants and ocean lifeforms on those worlds. Among vertebrate animals on those worlds, female dominance was present in 70 percent of the animals studied to date." She gave a shrug, which caused the helmet hanging against her vacsuited back to shift sideways. "Course, I and others have only studied a small number of the air, land and water animal species on those worlds. So the percentages of gender dominance will likely change in the future. Though . . . I do note that in the female dominant animals, the females were larger in size, sometimes by large amounts. Like on Earth."

Evelyn set down her mug with a loud clank. "And, dear friends, I am the *evolutionary* biologist at this table." She looked around the table, her long red hair flaring out over the neck rim of her vacsuit. "Cassie has a very good point. On Earth for far too many centuries it was the norm to assume the person in charge of a church, a temple, a business or a family was male. Period. While matriarchy is still an honorable variation among Earth humans, it is not the primary social expression. Patriarchy is still most common, even with a woman running the Star Navy as top admiral. Cultures take time to change. Lots of time. But what if the culture of Smooth Fur is matriarchal?"

"So," Warren grumbled. "What if this Smooth Fur *is* female, versus male. Or an intersex person. What difference does being female, or jointly male and female, make in how someone acts? Smooth Fur's actions have been deadly, aggressive and evil. Me, I call him, her or whatever a damn dangerous predator!"

"Ahhh, therein lies the most important question," Cassandra intoned. Our friend sat back in her plastic seat, wrapped both hands around her beer mug, and peered intently at us. "If this Smooth Fur *is* female, then it is likely Fur will be a more effective commander of her crew, and of her fleet, than a male giant otter. And if she has birthed litters of baby otters in the past, she may see what her fleet does as 'protecting' her offspring from dangerous primitives like us humans.

Or the Melanchon and Sendera, who refuse to play by her rules. Or like these Dugong who, though they resemble a honey badger standing on two feet, are a unique species. While the Dugong have the appearance of a mammal predator, their fleet is led by a female who moves like a dancer, and their home world is named Melody. These Dugong are *not* a clone of an Earth animal form. They are unique people who are fighting for the survival of their species." Cassie rapped the table with the knuckles of her right hand. "I for one am glad the Dugong are on *our* side!"

"Me too!" called Evelyn.

"Yep, me too," said Warren, his manner thoughtful.

"They have a lot to fight for," Bill said.

Oksana rapped the table. "So should I say something to my Intel lieutenant? For sharing with the captain? A different gender for Smooth Fur might be something that the captain needs to know."

"Sure Okie," I volunteered before I thought out my words. Wincing internally, I slowed down my speaking to match my thinking. "Please share with your lieutenant what Cassie and Evelyn have shared with us. It might make a difference in how the captain chooses to make battle engagement."

"So it might," Warren muttered. "I know we Marines place a big emphasis on 'knowing our enemy'. As I'm sure the captain does. If this group of 23 Empire ships are led by a female captain, well, my guess is that will make those ships even more deadly than what we've seen to date."

My stomach reminded me that drinking a mug of beer on top of a few bites of crab cake was not enough. It wanted more. I left my friends to discussion of the Empire, the alien peoples who have rebelled against the Empire and the presence of pirates that roam the underbelly of this galactic empire. I for one needed a good meal under my belt. Or vacsuit. As Cassie filled her plate with stuffed banana leaves, I reached out and grabbed the last crab cake. It traveled to my plate without interruption. On my right Evelyn nudged me with her knee, then laughed as I choked on the last of the Santa Fe Pale Ale beer.

"Hey! I never asked for chili-flavored beer!"

"Neither did we," she said. "It's a new addition to the Mess Hall Beer Day offerings. Me, I'll take any beer at any time of the day, especially if it's free!"

The reminder that today was Beer Day on the ship made me reach for the pitcher of Blue Moon. That was my favorite. And I didn't care if the other people in the Mess Hall thought I was an old geezer cause I drank something that had been around for a century. So what! Superman Stewart drinks what I choose to drink!

CHAPTER TEN

"The human crafts are entering the outer edge of the rock field," growled Zorta from her Tactical station.

Smooth Fur felt satisfaction. At last! At last the nuisance human ship and four raider crafts were close to her grasp! Her view of the oval view plate showed only five moving neutrino emitters. Which meant the other three human craft might indeed be hiding in cloak somewhere. Perhaps at the outer edge of the system. Or perhaps close to her own fleet. She cared not. Her weapons outranged the human weapons. Her battleswimmers were as fast as the human and raider crafts. And she and her crew beings on all the Empire crafts possessed the unique power of zero-point energy. A power she planned to demonstrate once the human craft and four raider crafts came closer.

"Status of Dugong resistor crafts?" she barked sharply.

The hunter feline's fur stood out from her smoothly muscled body. "Only twelve Dugong craft still survive. The fleet is now pursuing the survivors!"

She scanned the other images on the view plate. Besides the neutrino emissions map that showed the five human craft as yellow dots, the twelve Dugong survivors appeared as green dots scattered throughout the middle of the rock belt. Her own 23 battleswimmers appeared as a cluster of golden dots. Next to the neutrino image was a real space image of blackness relieved only by the distant glow of the Dugong home world. Soon enough it would be taken care of. She looked away and scanned her control cell crew beings. Tink the pink floater hovered over Power. Rak the scaled reptile monitored Astrogation. Beyond him was Zorta at Tactical. Next to her was Bloody Beak at Weapons. Close by was Zing of the double wings and yellow and black stripes at Survival. Beside the large insect stood Trelka at Engines. She stood on four legs, her two chest arms outstretched over the Engines control unit. Her armored hide shone bright yellow and red under the warm white light of Fur's home star. While Trelka moved more slowly than most crew beings in Fur's control cell, the large teeth that filled her wide mouth made clear she was a predator hunter. And soon Trelka would be essential to the final element of defeating the human challenger. Smooth Fur looked aside to where her Fleet Aide waited.

"Lork, advise the fleet to assume battle posture Lak 41!"

The tower of black fur reached out to his control pedestal, then hesitated. "Manager Smooth Fur, that battle posture will disperse our fleet. We will not be able to concentrate as a single force against the human challengers."

"Exactly so," she barked low, turning back to face the view plate. "Exactly so. That is my intent. Carry out my intent."

"Acting," Lork growled low, his claws tapping his pedestal to send forth the new orders.

It did not matter that he did not understand her intention. As manager of both *Golden Pond* and the 22 other battleswimmers in her fleet, she answered to no one. Or no one other than the single Dominant now resident at the fleet base in the molecular cloud that lay near to where Orion Arm touched Sagittarius Arm. And that Dominant would not hear from her until she could report full cleansing of resistor worlds in this new arm and the death of the human resistor crafts. And so it would be, once the humans drew closer.

♦ ♦ ♦

"Battle Stations!" came the voice of the captain over the All Ship.

"Engineering moves to Battle Stations!" responded Chief O'Connor.

I reached up and pulled my clear helmet over my head. It snapped tight to the neck ring of my vacsuit. As it locked in my vacsuit's automatic functions activated. Air. Power to sensors. A green heads-up display formed in the lower part of the helmet. And my suit comlink automatically cross-linked to the wifi and optical fiber communications cables of Engineering Deck and the com talker patch on the right armrest of my station seat. Looking up I scanned the nine antimatter injector tubes that surrounded me like a forest of narrow trees, albeit trees that glowed with rainbow colors of red, orange, yellow, green, blue, indigo and violet. The field shimmers were bright, sharp and stable. As was the glow of the tenth antimatter feed tube that ran along the overhead and out to Bill's antimatter beamer block. I looked away and around our deck. Dolores and her three Spacers were seated before their fusion reactor control panels. The Chief sat before control panels for the thrusters, the magfield spacedrive and the Alcubierre stardrive. Between him and me loomed the gray metal block and giant ball of the magfield drive. The drive's ability to engage directly with the magnetic field of the Dugong home star would be vital to our ship's ability to abruptly change vector angles, thereby increasing our ability to survive enemy laser strikes. The four raider ships would be able to do the same, thanks to their possession of magfield drives. Telling my heart to slow down and telling my mind to trust in the captain, I spread my hands over the AM control panel and waited for orders. But voices from the Bridge drew my eyes over to the nearby bulkhead vidscreen.

"Tactical, which are the closest Empire ships?" my captain asked.

"Two Empire ships are going after that single Dugong ship," Chang replied, gesturing up at the front vidscreen. "There's an asteroid the size of Vesta near the outer edge of this asteroid belt. The Dugong ship is hiding behind it, clearly hoping to ambush the Empire ships as they approach. Sir."

The overhead image of the captain and the Bridge showed him nodding slowly. "XO, your analysis of the Empire ship movements."

"Those two ships clearly know the Dugong ship is there," Commander Kumisov said thoughtfully. "Like other Empire ship pairs, they are moving on parallel vector tracks. I suspect they plan to approach the Dugong ship from both the east and west sides of the rock's equator. Then jointly move around to the far side of the rock. Unless the Dugong ship has rear weapons mounts like the *Glory*, it can fire only on one of the two approaching ships. Whichever Empire ship is not fired on will put the full force of its lasers against the Dugong. It will not survive the combined fire of four CO_2 lasers, four proton lasers and two plasma beamers. Sir."

That type of attack was something I had watched on the bulkhead vidscreen as the *Glory* came closer to the wide asteroid belt and its battling combatants. The Dugong decision to fight the Empire in the belt made sense in that it gave the Dugong ships cover from laser beams when those ships could take shelter behind an asteroid. But asteroid belts are never crowded. Even clusters of rocks like those that exist in the Solar System's belt are widely scattered. Which means a ship running from one asteroid to another is exposed to enemy fire. With the Empire ships able to move at 15 psol, versus the standard 10 psol of the Dugong fusion pulse thrusters, the Empire's greater speed had taken a toll on the resistors. The original 26 Dugong ships were now down to twelve. The others had died over the last day as Empire ships found a Dugong ship and killed it with lasers, or rarely with an antimatter beam. The failure of the Empire to use its AM beamer puzzled me. Still, the Empire weapons range was ten times that of the Dugong lasers. Which had the same 10,000 kilometer range of our CO_2, proton and gamma ray lasers.

The captain looked ahead. "Com, link me with the raider captains."

"Linking via encrypted neutrino comsignal," called Wetstone.

As images of the four alien captains took form next to the system graphic and Bridge overhead images, I gave silent thanks that our AI Heidi had guaranteed the captain that the Empire ability to penetrate our com chatter, or to enter ship systems by way of an incoming radio or neutrino comsignal, was now blocked. She had said her study of the first attack by two hundred Empire golem worms had taught her how the Empire sought to piggy-back their malware on top of the frequencies of either radio or neutrino comsignals. So there was no longer any need to segregate our ship's astrogation files in the Secure Block on Astrogation Deck. It was a small victory. Hopefully we could have a bigger victory soon against the two Empire ships that lay some distance ahead of us and our four raider allies.

"Captains Delight, Gorling, Lindo and Mousome, are your ships ready for combat?" the captain asked in a strong, determined tone.

"We are," the four said in a mix of barks, growls, rasps and hisses.

"Good. Move your ships so they surround the *Star Glory*, but lag behind us. I am about to launch thermonuke warheads from our ship's silos and I do not wish any warhead to mistake your ship for a target."

"Moving rearward," barked Delight as the elderly female raccoon-like being gestured aside to someone on her bridge crew. "But surely you can program your devices with an ability to distinguish our ships from the Empire ships?"

"We can," Captain Skorzeny said quickly. "It is called Friend Or Foe ID. The sensor characteristics of your four ships have been entered into the small brains of the Hunt and Search routines of each warhead. Still, I prefer to not take chances. Are your ship's CO_2 and proton lasers ready to engage?"

"Our weapons are ready," hissed Mousome as the six-legged reptile loomed over his floor-mounted control panel.

Delight confirmed her ship's weapons were ready. The same response came from Gorling the bear-like alien and from Lindo, the standing wasp alien.

"Good. Weapons, launch four missiles loaded with thermonuke warheads."

"Missiles launched, sir," called Yamamoto.

The captain looked left. "Astrogation, will we draw within weapons range before the Empire ships go behind the asteroid?"

"It will be close, captain," called Ibarra. She looked down at her panel. "We will have thirty seconds of firing available. After that the two ships will be beyond our line of sight. Sir."

The captain leaned forward against his straps. "Weapons! Status of missile warheads. Position!"

Yamamoto tapped his panel. "Sir! Nose shrouds are gone. Ten warheads per missile are now flying free. Their sensors are locking in on the two Empire ships. But the warhead speed is only the 15 psol of our ship. Their chemfuel thrusters have moved them just fifty miles ahead of us. They are increasing that distance, but slowly. Sir."

"Are all 40 warheads responding to your signals?"

"Captain, they are responsive," Yamamoto said quickly.

Briefly I wondered why the captain had not ordered a launch of Hunter-Killer mines from our railguns. Then I realized we were not facing a cluster of many ships, but only two ships in a single target zone. That made mines less than useful. Briefly I glanced down. My panel showed green bars for all antimatter systems. Looking up I saw the true space image now held a tiny white dot. Which had to be the large asteroid behind which the Dugong ship now hid.

"Incoming comsignal!" called out Wetstone.

"Source?" the captain murmured.

Our Com chief looked at his panel. "From directly ahead, sir. It's the Dugong home world frequency."

"Accept and display the signal. Share it with our raider friends," the captain ordered.

A fourth image now filled the middle of my bulkhead vidscreen. Standing inside a room filled with a dozen other honey badger-like aliens was a tall and slim alien who stood before a central bench surrounded by panels and displays. The alien's liquid brown eyes fixed on us.

"Humans! Are those your ships behind the Empire ships?" came a musical voice from Dr. Bjorg's translator block.

"Yes!" called the captain loudly. "It is me, Captain Neil Skorzeny of the *Star Glory*. Our four allies are raider ships. Who are you?"

The Dugong leader's white whiskers flared outward. Its two ear flaps rose. Behind it moved several Dugong, who seemed very anxious in their movements.

"You know me. I am Team Leader Swaying Light." The leader of the Dugong resistor ships gestured outward. "It is my ship that the Empire seeks to kill. Can you help us?"

"I recognize you now." The captain let out a loud sigh. "Very good. Very good indeed. Maintain your position behind that asteroid. The *Glory* and our four allies are about to attack the Empire ships. I believe they will not survive to harm you."

The female's slim shoulders lost their tightness. Her eyes had a new look now. Was it the look of relief? Of hope? The fact of her survival was something I felt good about. Swaying Light had impressed me during our first conversation at the edge of the system's magnetosphere. And here she was, the target of the Empire ships we now chased after.

"Captain!" called Kumisov. "Range to either Empire ship is now 30,000 klicks and closing. Do we use our antimatter beamer?"

"Not yet, XO." The captain gestured at the slim, curvy honey badger who sought to protect her home world and billions of other Dugong. "Swaying Light, are you in touch with your home world?"

"I am." She gestured to a nearby Dugong. Beside her appeared four different holograms. One showed a silvery orbital base as a giant ball. A second image showed a land base on the world's single moon. Two other holos depicted ships in orbit above the blue and green world. Two of the ships were gigantic, far larger than the orbital base. "Your sensors see neutrino emissions from above my home world.

Two sources are these generation ships we have been loading with our people in case we all die fighting the Empire. We hope some of us will escape to find a new home."

The captain's strong hands gripped the ends of his armrests. I could not see the flesh of his hands, but the increased red glow of his neck and face told me he was feeling anger.

"The *Star Glory* and our four raider allies are here to help you and your world survive! Maintain your orbital position. Now, I must manage our attack." The captain looked left. "Astrogation, range to targets?"

"Nineteen thousand klicks," Ibarra said, sounding breathless over the All Ship.

"Heidi, increase visual filters on our scope and all sensors. And increase the strength of our rad shelter field to stellar wind deflection level."

"Adjusting visual filters," called the light feminine voice of the AI. "Also increasing strength of the ship's rad shelter field."

"Good." The captain's steely gaze grew intense. "Weapons, detonate all 40 thermonukes. Now!"

"Detonating now, sir!"

One vital element of a chain of command is instant obedience during combat. Yamamoto did not ask why we were not waiting for the self-directed thermonuke warheads to close on a target. He just tapped his control panel, sent out an FTL neutrino comsignal, and told the simple brain inside each warhead to implode its enriched uranium component and thereby ignite the deuterium gas that was the hydrogen isotope component of the warhead. The heat of Sol now hit the hydrogen cell of the warhead, both compressing the gas isotope and heating it beyond ten million degrees Kelvin. The result was a three megaton thermonuke blast. Which anyone watching with unshielded eyes would see as a white-yellow glare. Then see nothing as their eyes melted if they were within 20 miles of the nuke or floating in space and looking directly at the warhead. Forty such devices going off created a massive wash of white-yellow light that blanketed the space between the *Glory* and the asteroid. The gamma rays, infrared rays and ultraviolet rays emitted by the combined power of 120 megatons of thermonuclear ignition now struck the rear globes of the two Empire ships. The rays also hit our ship but most were deflected by our charged rad shelter field.

"Rad front impacting Empire ships," called out Yamamoto.

"Astrogation, range to targets?"

"Captain, range is now at 9,373 kilometers," called Ibarra.

The captain slammed his armrest with a clenched fist. "Yes! Weapons, fire our nose proton and CO_2 lasers at the westside Empire ship." The captain looked up at the part of the front vidscreen that held the four alien captains. "Delight, Gorling, Lindo and Mousome, fire your lasers on the eastern ship!"

Suddenly I saw the point of the captain causing all 40 thermonukes to explode. He had created a curtain of plasma, now thinning, which served to shield our ship from weapons fire by the two Empire ships. They could have fired on us earlier, but clearly had been focused on their expected arrival on the other side of the asteroid. Perhaps their captains had planned to kill the Dugong ship first and then come round and fire on the *Glory* and our allies. That failure to hit us while we were within the 100,000 klicks range of their weapons now cost them. Red and green beams from our nose lasers now hit the rear globe of the two globes connected by a thick tube that made up the basic Empire combat ship design. Four pairs of other red and green beams hit the eastside Empire ship. Light flared from the rear of both ships.

"Their thrusters are dead!" cried Chang.

"Engineering!" yelled the captain. "Lift our ship directly up from this vector track. Now!"

"Raising ship, sir."

To my side Chief O'Connor tapped his magfield spacedrive panel. The deck under my boots vibrated slightly as the ship's momentum shifted from forward to upward. I felt nothing more, thanks to the ship's inertial compensator field. In the bulkhead vidscreen the four raider ships did the same, using their own magfield drives to copy the *Glory 's* action.

Green and red laser beams, joined by a purple plasma beam, shot through our prior vector track position as the westside Empire ship fired back at us from mounts on its front globe. Another group of green, red and purple beams shot out from the eastern ship, missing the four raider ships.

"Raiders, fire again. Tactical, fire again on the western target."

A new pair of green and red laser beams shot out from the *Glory*. They impacted on the rear globe. Which now blew apart. Red-brown hull sections, silvery water globules and white air jetted out from the Empire ship's rear section. Which no longer existed as a globe.

"Again," ordered the captain.

A third volley of laser beams hit the front globe of the Empire ship. The beams penetrated deeply. A purple plasma beam fired back at us, hitting the upper hull of the *Glory*. Then a cloud of blackness emerged from the front globe, eating up the ship remnants as the ship's antimatter bunker lost containment and ate into the solid matter of the front globe. A tiny yellow-orange star now flared where once a ship the size of the *Glory* had existed.

"Weapons, shift to eastern target and fire. Engineering, move us westward and up by thirty degrees. Raiders do the same."

I watched as the eastern globe's middle tube and front globe fired back at where we had been. Then the green and red laser beams of the *Glory* combined with the beams from the raider ships to turn the eastern ship remnant into fragments and gas.

"Yes!" yelled Captain Skorzeny, surprising me.

Our captain had always been even-tempered, in control of himself and the model of an officer in command.

"Incoming comsignal!" called Wetstone.

"Source?" the captain murmured.

The man looked at his panel. "From directly ahead, sir. It's the Dugong frequency."

"Accept and display the signal. Share it with our raider friends."

A fourth image now filled the middle of the vidscreen on the nearby bulkhead. It was Swaying Light.

"My watcher satellite reports you destroyed two Empire ships," she barked softly. "My compliments. Will you accompany me as I join other Dugong ships in their fight against the Empire fleet?"

"Yes," said the captain, sounding tired but determined. His wide shoulders appeared to relax under the fabric of his vacsuit. "We will do our best—"

"Incoming comsignal!" cried Wetstone.

"Source?" the captain murmured.

"From in the rock belt, sir. It's the official Empire frequency."

"Accept and display the signal. Share it," the captain ordered.

A new fifth image took form in the middle of the vidscreen.

It was Smooth Fur, standing on his circular deck. The white-striped otter alien glared at us. The whiskers on either side of his muzzle flared out. His long tail slapped the deck behind him. Nearby were the pink floater, the hunter cat, an alien that resembled a yellowjacket wasp and a four legged armor-platted something that resembled a rhino, though its two arms hovered above a control panel. Other weird aliens were visible on the edge of the image.

"Human Captain Neil Skorzeny, you have killed two of my ships. That makes six Empire crafts which have died from your actions. Enough. Your presence in this star system will now be eliminated." The otter looked over to the armor-platted rhino alien. "Trelka of Engines, take us into gray space." She shifted her view. "Wendig, communicate my gray space order to all other fleet crafts." Fur looked aside to a creature who resembled a giant black bear. "Fleet Aide Lork, advise our fleet craft managers I am shifting this system's star into instability." The alien who now commanded just 21 combat starships looked ahead. "Human, your species is a nuisance. We of the Empire are expert at removing nuisances. Watch as we use our ultimate weapon to remove the Dugong species. And your ship along with the raider ships. Goodbye."

The otter image vanished.

"Captain!" yelled Chang. "Our rearward sensors are detecting graviton surges! Twenty-one surges." The woman who was a distance runner now looked back to the captain and his command pedestal, surprise on her face. "Sir, the neutrino signatures of the Empire ships have vanished! They, they have . . . they have gone into Alcubierre space-time!"

I felt shock. It was impossible to enter Alcubierre space-time this deep within the magnetosphere of any star. Ships exploded when they tried to do that. But there had been no explosions on the true space image. Just a sudden disappearance of 21 red dots on the system graphic. Leaving behind our five green dots and the twelve purple dots of the Dugong ships, which were scattered widely across the asteroid belt. Yet the graviton surges were the sign of a ship arriving out of an Alcubierre space-time modulus. Or entering such a modulus.

"Science?" muttered the captain.

Magnus Bjorg looked down at a panel in front of him. "She is correct. Twenty-one graviton surges happened where once the Empire ships were located. And . . . and there is a massive gravity wave hitting our front and rear sensors! The wave is coming from the Dugong star!" Bjorg's face turned florid, then suddenly white. "Something is happening to the Dugong star!"

Worry hit me. Chills ran up my spine. We had just killed two Empire ships. We should be rejoicing. Instead I felt . . . fear. Fear for Evelyn. Fear for my friends. Fear for Chief O'Connor. Fear for all my shipmates. What was happening?

"Incoming comsignal," whispered Wetstone, sounding as shocked as everyone.

"Source?"

"From the Dugong ship ahead. Sir."

"Accept and share it."

In the vidscreen now appeared Swaying Light. The honey badger alien stood ramrod straight, her arms at her sides. Her legs, though, shook. Beside her hovered a hologram of her home world of Melody. Next to that holo was a second holo. It appeared to be from some place in space that was much closer to the Dugong home star. The white star that had given light and warmth to the Dugong for at least three billion years, that star image was now changed. Its yellow-white corona was bulging outward. Only this was not a coronal mass ejection flare, like sometimes hit Earth, causing a blackout of power grids and screwed up satcoms. This was a full body expansion of the star's corona. It moved outward in all directions, like an expanding balloon. And below that flaring corona now moved hundreds of black sunspots.

"Captain Skorzeny, I regret you came to help us. Now you will die with us," Swaying Light barked softly.

"Explain!" The captain gripped his armrests tightly.

She gestured aside to the two holos. "You see our world, which is the outermost world of our system. The other image is from a watcher satellite we placed above the innermost world. It sends us real time neutrino signals. Our star . . . our star is becoming, is becoming a nova. Or something worse. The coronal mass is expanding outward at a terrible speed." Her whiskers went flat against her muzzle. Her liquid brown eyes seemed filled with sadness. "In less than a minute of your Earth time, our monitor will be engulfed by the expanding corona. As will the innermost world. My ship researchers tell me the coronal plasma wall will hit Melody within nine minutes. It will reach you, and my ships, within a half hour. I apologize for drawing you here to share death with us."

"Science!" yelled the captain. "Is what she says real?"

I watched the bulkhead vidscreen, feeling frozen, as the boss of Evelyn and Cassandra looked down at his panel, then up to the vidscreen display of the two holos, then down again. He inhaled sharply.

"Captain, somehow the Empire ship departures have affected the Dugong star," Bjorg said, his voice wavering. "That . . . coronal wave front is moving outward at one-third psol. Which makes it a Type II supernova." The Swede swung his head around to look up at our captain. "But it *can't* be happening! The Dugong star size is way below the Chandrasekhar limit! It is not a white dwarf. Nor is it a red giant! It's an F-series main sequence star with *less* mass than Sol. It *can't* go nova, let along supernova. And no supernova I have studied is able to expel plasma gases at 30 psol. The usual speed for nova gas expulsion is three percent of lightspeed. Supernova expulsion can reach 25 psol. But, but this is impossible!"

"But it *is* happening," the captain said, his voice sounding pained. "Science, is there any way for us to escape this monster?"

Bjorg reached up to brush at his hair. His gloved hand was stopped by the man's helmet. His instinct had forgotten we were at Battle Stations and were all vacsuited and on suit air. And suit power.

"How can this be? The spectrograph of that holo image is filled with Balmer hydrogen lines," the big-framed man rumbled low, his tenor hesitant. "The bolometric light intensity is rising beyond anything ever recorded on Earth. There is a massive wash of neutrinos coming from that star. And look! The chromosphere *below* the corona is also expanding outward! I can't believe—" The man's shoulders tensed. "Sir, we should turn and head for the magnetosphere edge *now*. At top speed! Maybe, just maybe, the coronal wave front will slow as it moves outward through the system."

The captain slumped in his chair. "Swaying Light, how many Dugong now live on Melody?"

"Five billion, three hundred million," said the honey badger who was a dancer and a singer. She collapsed onto the bench behind her, her legs no longer able to support her. "Our two generation ships will launch outward within two minutes, a signal tells me. But their speed is just ten percent of the speed of light. The coronal wall will overtake them before they reach our position."

"Swaying Light, can your ships go into alternate space-time?" the captain asked, decision clear in voice. "What Smooth Fur calls gray space?"

Her brown eyes blinked. "Yes, of course they can. It is how we drew the attention of the Empire. They found us at a nearby star, then followed our ship back to Melody. We did not know their nature then." She looked aside at the holo of her home world. "We do now."

"Then I advise you and your surviving ships to head for the edge of your star system. That is what we are now doing," the captain said, gesturing to Ibarra at Astrogation. "Perhaps your ships and ours will survive to reach the edge of the magnetosphere. Once there we can escape this supernova by entering Alcubierre space-time."

"Sir!" called Chang from Tactical. "Twenty-one neutrino emission sources have now appeared at the edge of this system's magnetosphere!"

I winced. It had to be the Empire ships. They had jumped out of the interior of the Dugong star system, thereby somehow causing its star to go supernova. Now, they waited to kill any ship that might escape the supernova wavefront.

"We are all going to die," whispered Cindy from the fusion reactor, sounding sad and hopeless and other emotions I could only guess at. Her boss Dolores looked away from the Spacer, her own face full of emotions. She said nothing. But clearly she and Gus and Duncan wondered if Cindy was right.

I felt sad. I felt fearful. I felt hopeless. I had not expected to die while serving in the Star Navy. Or . . . or was there a way to escape this supernova?

CHAPTER ELEVEN

"Delight, Gorling, Lindo and Mousome, follow us outward! Move as fast as you can," the captain said in a near yell.

The images of the four raider captains agreed with him, then disappeared. The system graphic on the bulkhead to my right showed the raider ships following us out of the asteroid belt. Five green dots fled as a group. The twelve purple dots of Swaying Light's ships also moved outward, with the scattered ships drawing closer to each other as they moved outward. The graphic's image of the third planet Melody showed two large purple dots also moving outward, passing by their single moon. Other purple dots in orbit above the planet did not move. They must be orbital stations or GTOs that did not have fusion pulse thrusters, just fusion reactors. The white dot that was the planet Melody stuck in my mind.

Memory brought to me the death of the Sendera colony world at Kepler 22. There the Empire ships had used a bioweapon that spread rapidly across the planet's oceans, rivers and land, blackening anything that was alive. But here and now, the expansion of the local star's corona would soon bathe the Dugong home world in plasma gases beyond hot. A memory from a Great Lakes class on the Solar System told me the Sun's corona temp ranged from a million Kelvin up to three million degrees Kelvin. I could not recall the temp of the chromosphere that underlay the Sun's corona but it did not matter. When this star's coronal gas wall hit Melody, the planet would bake to death. All water would disappear. Much of the atmosphere would be blown away by a stellar wind stronger and more deadly than anything we had felt on Earth. The image of Swaying Light showed her still sitting on her bench, looking aside and talking to other Dugong crew. The two holos floated beside her. Then the holo from the watcher satellite above planet one disappeared. Clearly the coronal wall had engulfed the system's innermost planet. It lay at one-tenth AU from its star. Death was coming for the Dugong. And for us. We could not outrun it. But was there another way?

"Perhaps we will speak later," Light said. "I must tend to my people."

"I hope so," the captain said, sounding sad.

Her neutrino comsignal image vanished.

"Engineering!" called the captain in a more controlled voice. "Give us antimatter afterburner push now!"

My boss looked over to me, his expression serious and sober. I did not see any fear or lack of hope in his face. "Stewart!"

I reached down and tapped my control panel. The flow meter for each injector tube went from zero to two. Maximum flow rate was ten. Which meant one liter of antimatter per minute would flow down each tube. That amount of AM usage would soon exhaust all the antimatter fuel in the deck above us. So far a lesser flow rate of one or two had sufficed to give us an extra one percent of lightspeed.

"Chief, antimatter is flowing to all three thrusters!"

My boss looked back to his arc of three control panels. The Chief tapped his fusion pulse thrusters panel, looked at the magfield panel in front of him, then spoke. "Captain, the *Star Glory* is now moving at 16 psol. Sir."

My eyes fixed on the system graphic image on the bulkhead vidscreen. The star's three planets lay at one-tenth, three-tenths and four-tenths AU out from the star. The outer edge of the asteroid belt we were now leaving lay at 15 AU. The system's Kuiper Belt of comets began at 38 AU. The star's magnetosphere edge lay at 42 AU. We might get out to 25 AU before the coronal gas wall hit us. Which impact would turn us to metallic vapor. Sooner than that, in five minutes or so, the coronal wall would hit the planet Melody. More than five billion living, thinking, hoping and loving beings would then die. The Empire called it a cleansing. I knew it to be mass murder of the worst sort. My home of Earth faced that kind of mass murder whenever the Empire ships found Sol. My sisters Anna and Louise and my Mom would all die from the Empire bioweapon. Or maybe this worse star-killer weapon. I and everyone on the *Glory* now worked to prevent that discovery. We understood it might take the sacrifice of lives to hurt the Empire enough that they pulled back their expansion fleet. We'd already lost two good Marines in the destruction of GTO *Ramadi*. Now we faced losing everyone on board the *Glory*. Frustration filled me. Along with thoughts of ways to outrun what could not be outrun.

"Captain!" yelled Wetstone. "Incoming neutrino comsignal!"

"Source?" the captain murmured.

"From the outer edge of the system, sir. It's the official Empire frequency 1432."

"Accept and display the signal. Share it," the captain ordered.

A new image took shape in the middle of the vidscreen.

It was Smooth Fur, standing on his circular deck. The white-striped otter alien stood and just looked at us. At the captain and his people on the Bridge. The black whiskers on either side of Fur's muzzle were relaxed. His long tail rested on the deck behind him. As before some of his alien crew were easily visible. The pink floater, the hunter cat, the wasp alien and the armor-platted rhino with arms were clearly visible.

"Human Captain Neil Skorzeny, do you now understand the folly of opposing the Empire of Eternity?" The black-furred otter gestured to one side. A holo appeared. It showed the Dugong star, its size massively increased from what we had seen when we arrived at the system. The yellow coronal wall had passed over the Mercury-sized world at one-tenth AU and was now moving over the Mars-sized world at three-tenths AU. Streamers of yellow-orange flame stretched out from the wall's surface, as if the star was trying to grab space itself. My puzzlement at the image led me to realize the Empire must have seeded the space above the system's ecliptic with multiple monitor satellites. "The Dugong star is dying, thanks to the gravitational collapse we engendered with the simultaneous entry into gray space of my 21 fleet ships. That departure unbalanced the star's gaseous envelope. It caused the star's inner layers to expand outward, thereby pushing its hottest corona layer out to engulf all matter within this system. Is it not beautiful?"

In the overhead view of the Bridge, my captain's head and neck grew bright orange in infrared. Clearly he was furious. His voice when he spoke was otherwise. "How were your ships able to enter Alcubierre space-time moduluses without blowing up? That is what happened to our experimental ships when we tried entering gray space within our local star's magnetosphere."

Fur's long black tail swung to one side. "Simple. Power allows one to do almost anything in this universe. And in adjacent dimensions like gray space." Smooth Fur gestured back to the armor-platted hippo. "My Engines crew being Trelka used zero-point energy to strengthen the space-time modulus that is created whenever a ship creates its own small space-time bubble within the larger space-time of normal space." Brown lips lifted from the otter's mouth, exposing a line of white canines. Whatever the expression was, it was not a smile. It now gestured to the pink jellyfish alien floating above the deck. "My Power crew being Tink used our access to zero-point energy to increase the gravitomagnetic impact on the Dugong star. The star's balance of hydrogen fusion explosions versus gravity was upset. Inner layers fell down toward the star's core. Then they rebounded upward as the star's oxygen layer underwent fusion. That fusing pushed outward the star's chromosphere and its corona. So now you see the result." The lips relaxed down. The alien brought both arms forward and crossed them over a leather-strapped chest. "The Dugong home world will shortly be cleansed of resistors. Not long after the coronal wall will reach you and your ships. And the Dugong ships that fought us in the rock belt. I look forward to resting here and watching your deaths."

"You are evil," the captain said firmly.

"I disagree." Smooth Fur leaned forward. "I am efficient. I am efficient in finding new species to join the Empire of Eternity. I am efficient in cleansing those species who refuse the Glorious Choice. And I am efficient in destroying the crafts of any species who resist me and my fleet." Fur's tail lifted, then whipped quickly from side to side. "You killed six of my craft. I now kill your craft, your raider allies, the twelve Dugong craft and every Dugong on their home world. I call that efficient."

"We humans will attack any Empire colony or orbital or shipyard we find!" the captain said loudly, his tone still firm, though his shoulders slumped under his vacsuit. "Humanity has more ships than the *Star Glory*. We are a strong and deadly people. You and the Empire will regret harming us. And those who are our allies."

Smooth Fur gestured dismissively. "You talk. I have acted. Observe the death of the Dugong home world."

The holo beside Smooth Fur showed the yellow coronal wall closing on the green and blue Dugong home world. The white air on the side facing the star began to thin and flee away from the star's heat impact. Then the coronal wall touched the land and part of an ocean. Green became brown and then black. Blue water became hot mist and then vanished. As the coronal wall moved over half the planet, cyclonic winds rushed away from its impact, moving around to the world's night side. The lights of cities now became raw infernos of flame as superheated air started forest fires. Skytowers melted like dead candles. Lakes and rivers boiled. Then the coronal wall mass finished enveloping the night side. The lights of civilization vanished. Only blackened soil and empty ocean basins were visible as the coronal wall expanded outward, now enveloping the Dugong moon. The surface bases there vanished in tiny puffs of white air. The white regolith turned brown, then black as the coronal gases melted the surface of the moon. In seconds the yellow coronal wall passed beyond the moon. Ahead of it fled the two large purple dots of the two generation ships.

"You too will die," our captain said. "If this ship survives, I will pursue you and your fleet to the ends of this arm. And into Nebula W51 if there you flee. Humans do not allow mass murderers to prosper."

Loud barking that was translated by Bjorg's translator block as laughter now joined the image of Smooth Fur standing there, its sharp canines exposed as its head went back and it gave forth its version of amusement.

"Oh, you humans are so amusing! But a nuisance you are and therefore you—"

"Com, shut it off."

The image of Smooth Fur disappeared. Leaving the bulkhead vidscreen filled with the system graphic, the overhead Bridge view and the true space image of black space speckled with stars and a bit of the Milky Way's strip of star arms. Those star images finished my mental wrestling with the issue of how to outrun what could not be outrun. But there was another way. I turned and faced my boss.

"Chief! I have a plan for how we can escape. And maybe the Dugong ships can escape too!"

He heard me over his helmet speaker. As did everyone else on the deck. Now he looked my way, his expression moving to irritation. "Stewart! No games or wild theories now. The captain has us heading out. Maybe we can outrun this thing if it slows down. Maybe—"

I shook my head. "Sir! We can do a mini-jump. We can do a series of mini-jumps to get to the mag edge. I'm sure we will survive!"

His eyes widened. "Explain. Quickly!"

My peripheral vision caught Dolores, Cindy, Gus and Duncan looking my way, their faces moving from sadness to puzzlement tinged with hope.

"Power is the key, as Smooth Fur said, sir." I gestured over at Dolores and her fusion reactor controls. Those controls sat at one side of a massive block within which our compact fusion reactor combined deuterium and tritium isotopes into a controlled fusion. That fusion was directly translated into electrical energy, thanks to tech I did not understand. But it did produce power for the ship's lasers, gravplates, lights, Mess Hall cookers and everything else that needed energy on a starship. "If we feed nearly all that reactor's power into the graviton generator of your Alcubierre stardrive unit, while shutting down all power flow to every deck except Farm Deck with its ponds, we will create a space-time modulus strong enough to withstand the impact of the local star's magnetosphere." Dolores Gambuchino turned and looked at her control panel, reaching out and tapping it. "And if we make our entry into Alcubierre space-time *short*, in mini-jumps, the graviton generator will not overheat and explode. Like happened in the Solar System." I tried smiling. "It's a mix of lots of power combined with short exposure time within this star's magnetosphere." I frowned, my mind whirling through numbers, until I just 'knew' intuitively the power input and Alcubierre field setting that would be needed. I tapped my control panel, then hit Transmit. "Chief, I've just sent you the settings for power flow and the Alcubierre space-time modulus field. They should work. *Will* work!"

He looked down quickly at his Alcubierre control panel. He read quickly, then tapped the panel. A holo rose above the panel. My eagle eyesight recognized its content. The Chief was viewing a three dee simulation of the Alcubierre space-time modulus that the ship normally generated for travel between stars. My settings had modified the standard modulus to one suitable for quick mini-jumps of five AU per jump.

The Chief looked over to me. "You really think this mini-jump setting will work? We jump five AU, come out to normal space-time, then re-enter and jump five AU again? Until we reach the edge of the magnetosphere?"

"I know it!" In truth I did not know it. I just 'felt' intuitively what were the right numbers and settings to do something no human starship had ever done before. But the high-grade math I'd learned from Cassandra's lessons to me now paid off. Vector and tensor math combined with my knowledge of the nine dimensions beyond normal space-time to tell me our ship could do this, and survive. We might not have access to this zero-point energy. But we did have access to lots of power from our three reactors. "Chief, if we add in the energy from the midbody and upper deck fusion reactors, I am *certain* the Alcubierre modulus will remain intact and not collapse on us!" A thought hit me. "And ships that are smaller than us, like the raider ships and the Dugong ships, they can do this with the output of a single reactor. Sir!"

"Chief O'Connor!" came the voice of Captain Skorzeny. "I've been listening to Stewart's mini-jump scheme to get us out of here. You know this ship. You know its engines. Can the *Star Glory* do what he says and survive?"

I glanced aside at the bulkhead vidscreen. On it the faces of Kumisov, Owanju, Bjorg, Chang, Suárez y Alonso and Woodman all showed a mix of excitement, hope and intense focus. Wishing that Evelyn, Cassie, Oksana and Warren could hear what I was proposing, I settled for knowing that Bill, in his antimatter beamer block, had heard me. Looking back to my boss, I gave him a thumbs-up.

The man who had always treated me fairly, had welcomed me as the controller of the ship's antimatter afterburner function and had shown me respect, that man now nodded slowly. "Captain, yes, my simulation shows we can enter an Alcubierre space-time modulus, hold the ship in that new space-time for ten seconds, then exit into normal space-time, without blowing up. It *will* strain the graviton generator unit." The Chief gave Gambuchino and her people a thumbs-up. "But if we apply nearly all the power from our three fusion reactors to the stardrive unit, we will create a very strong and very stable Alcubierre modulus. And once we hit the magnetosphere edge, we can jump to whatever star you want. Sir."

"Did Stewart give you the numbers and field strengths to use?" the captain asked.

My boss nodded slowly. "He did. Bottom line is we enter Alcubierre five times and exit five times." He looked over to me. "Stewart, I've got your settings. What else do we do?"

"We have to shut down everything that draws power," I said quickly. "The magfield spacedrive. The thrusters. My antimatter afterburner flow. We just give power to the AM fuel deck to hold the antimatter contained and to the DT Fuel Bunker deck to contain those isotopes. And also keep gravity going on the Farm Deck to keep the dirt and ponds from floating upward. Everyplace else on the ship can go without gravplates or anything other than lights and control panels. Sir."

"Captain," called the Chief. "We can do this. Stewart's numbers work out. Though I have no damn idea how he came up with them." The Chief glared at me, then gave a shrug that stretched the fabric of his vacsuit. "Shall I shut down our thrusters and the magfield drive?"

In the bulkhead vidscreen our captain sat back in his elevated seat. His right hand reached up. Then it hit the clear material of his helmet. Perhaps he had intended to rest his chin on his fist. I knew our captain to be a very thoughtful man. He lowered his hand and looked up at the overhead videye.

"All Ship! We are *not* going to die from this supernova! Engineering has come up with a way for us to do Alcubierre mini-jumps within this star's magnetosphere." The captain looked down and nodded to his second in command. "XO Kumisov will send orders to each deck on what to shut down. Bottom line is, we will lose gravity almost everywhere. Emergency lights and controls will still be powered. XO, go to it!"

"Sir, sending out orders to each deck," Kumisov said, her face focused and her fingers moving quickly over her armrest input patches.

I tapped my control panel and shut off the flow of antimatter to our three thrusters. I also shut off AM flow to Bill's beamer block. Then I closed my eyes. I took a deep breath and told my heart to stop its fast beating. It ignored me. I realized my mind could not order around my body. Not really. The numbers I had discovered told me the facts of how we could enter Alcubierre within this system. But my mind's-eye reran televid images of automated spaceships blowing up out by Jupiter as Star Navy researchers confirmed you could not enter Alcubierre within the very strong magnetosphere of a star. Those vidimages were 20 years old. In my *mind* I knew we could do this. But my *body* still recalled those blow-up images. And my body reacted with intense floods of Fight or Flight hormones. No doubt everyone else on the ship was experiencing their version of mind-body confusion.

"Captain, the thrusters and magfield drive are off," came the calm voice of Chief O'Connor. "I am ready to activate the Alcubierre graviton generator."

I opened my eyes and looked his way. The Chief saw me and gave a quick nod. Around me scraps of paper floated up into the air as our gravplates lost power. A few metal fasteners joined them. We were now at null gee on this deck and on most other decks. My stomach told me it was not happy.

"Activate Alcubierre," the captain said, sounding remarkably calm.

The Chief tapped his panel. "Entering Alcubierre."

Gray space filled the true space image in the bulkhead vidscreen.

I breathed out. I was in one piece. The math was indeed correct. Our Alcubierre space-time modulus that was a tiny new universe wherein external space ahead was squeezed down while external space-time to our rear was expanded, that modulus held coherency. Mentally I counted the seconds. At ten I exhaled loudly.

"Exiting!" cried the Chief.

On the bulkhead vidscreen the captain leaned forward. "Astrogation! Position now compared to position earlier. Advise!"

Ibarra looked down at her control panel, then up at the true space image that partly filled the front vidscreen. "Sir! Stellar triangulation and comparison to the prior starfield confirms we made a jump! We are 5.032 AU beyond our last position. Sir!"

Cheers came from everyone on the Bridge, including Doctor Bjorg. The Swede seemed to have recovered from his astonishment at watching a white star too small to go nova become a supernova. Now he leaned forward and looked down at his own control panel.

"Captain, we advanced on a straight line vector track. We are now at 20 AU out from the local star." The burly man smiled big. "We can do it!"

"So we can," the captain said softly. "So we did. Com, give me a secure neutrino comlink with Swaying Light and with our raider captains."

"Five links established. All encrypted against Empire snooping, sir," said Wetstone.

Ignoring the cheers of Dolores, Gus, Cindy and Duncan, and of Bill inside my helmet, I saw the Bridge vidscreen fill with five new images. The four raider captains and Swaying Light were there. I could not read the expressions on their faces. But I bet they felt astonishment at us vanishing from where we had been.

"Team Manager Swaying Light!" called the captain. "Captains Delight, Gorling, Lindo and Mousome, attend! My Engineering people have discovered a way for a ship to enter gray space for a brief time, then exit, then repeat, without blowing up! We just jumped five AU ahead of you. And my ship is intact." The captain turned to his left. "Astrogation! Send the Alcubierre graviton generator field settings, and the reactor power feed levels, to our allies and to the Dugong ships!"

Ibarra reached down and tapped her panel. "Transmitting settings and power levels now via encrypted neutrino comsignal. Sir."

I saw Swaying Light stand up abruptly. The eyes of the raccoon-like being Delight opened wide. Gorling the giant black bear flexed his hand claws. Lindo the wasp-like alien fluttered her double pair of wings. Mousome literally danced in place, alternating his six legs in a rhythm I had never before seen. Behind each captain the aliens who made up their bridge crews showed reactions unique to each species. But every being on the four raider ships and the honey badger aliens on Light's ship all showed excitement. I crossed my fingers that hope might also be present on those other ships. I felt hope, where before had been dread and sadness. Hopefully the other 360-plus people on my ship felt both hope and excitement at our successful mini-jump.

Swaying Light barked something to another Dugong, then faced forward. "Captain Skorzeny, we have the settings and power flow levels. My Dancer Of Words is sending them to our two generation ships. Those ships have three fusion reactors on them due to their size. They can spin in place to replace the gravplate gravity they will lose to feed the gray space stardrive." She paused. "Those two ships are our newest ships. They have the best technology. Some of my fighter ships are old, older than even me. And they have only a single reactor. Tell me, will they survive going into gray space?"

The captain held up one hand. "A moment, Swaying Light." His helmeted head turned slightly. "Raider captains, you must shut down nearly everything that draws power, including your gravplates. Feed nearly all your reactor energy into your gray space graviton generator. That should allow you to make a mini-jump like we just did."

The four captains acknowledged and turned to working with their bridge crews. Their translated voices came over the All Ship, but at a muted level. The captain looked back to the honey badger leader. "Swaying Light, yes, I believe your fighter ships and your two generation ships will survive brief entry into and exit from gray space. Just make sure the time in gray space *is* brief. Just ten seconds by human measure."

"Understood. And thank you for this ray of hope." The slim, shapely honey badger gave a forward patting motion that was its version of a nod of acknowledgment.

Alien body language was something that Evelyn loved to study, as did Cassandra. The two women had spent hours going over vidcamera records of the 53 alien species present on the pirate base, debating what this body move meant versus another body action. I had done my best to listen to Evelyn's excited descriptions but it had been hard to avoid nodding off. I was not good at imagining alien people, unless they were directly in front of me. Or in a live vidscreen image like now. Shaking myself I felt eager for the next step in our escape. The captain began the dance of escape.

"Raider captains, Team Manager Swaying Light, please enter gray space as soon as your ship engineers are ready. We of the *Star Glory* will await your arrival here." Captain Skorzeny now smiled. It was an easy smile, filled with relief. "We did it. You can do it. Come, join us and we will all mini-jump away from this supernova!"

Swaying Light looked away from a Dugong crew person and faced forward. "As fighter ship leader, my ship will be the first to attempt gray space entry. Human . . . good human Captain Skorzeny, thank you for giving us some hope. Watching my world burn to ashes was almost more than I could take. Some of my crew ended their lives. But now, with this news, we are ready to fly and fight with you!"

Her image vanished. As did the images of the four raider captains.

I watched the system graphic image and its cluster of four green dots and the separate cluster of twelve purple dots. Those ships had just passed the outer edge of the system's asteroid belt. Which put them at 15 AU out from the supernova. The two purple dots of the generation ships were one AU ahead of the outrushing coronal wall. But that separation was shrinking. Ships flying at one-tenth lightspeed could not stay ahead of a coronal plasma gas wall that rushed outward at three-tenths lightspeed.

One purple dot at the edge of the rock belt disappeared. Then a purple dot reappeared close to the single green dot of our ship.

"Yes!" yelled Chief O'Connor, astonishing me with his wild exuberance. "Yes! Those Dugong made it here. Uh, captain, is that correct?"

On the bulkhead vidscreen the captain leaned forward. "Science, put up an electro-optical scope view of that new neutrino source that is now off our portside."

"Going up," Bjorg replied, sounding both happy and eager.

The bulkhead vidscreen's true space image shimmered and changed. In the middle of blackness glowed a white something. The scope magnification increased. The white something became a dart shape with a round ball in its middle. Yellow-orange fusion pulse gases exited its rear as the ship turned in space and moved toward us. It was intact!

"Incoming!" called Wetstone. "From that ship. It's the Dugong frequency sir."

"Accept. Display and share."

The bulkhead vidscreen grew a new image. Swaying Light stood before her bench. Her white whiskers were spread far out. Her liquid brown eyes almost glowed.

"We survived! We survived!" She gestured with one clawhand to someone else on her bridge. "Send word to our generation ships! Tell them to do this mini-leap into gray space! They will escape the supernova corona wall!"

Happiness filled me. At least one Dugong ship would survive and be able to join us on our journey out to the edge of the magnetosphere. At least—

"Swaying Light!" loudly called the captain. "My congratulations. But do *not* approach us. Instead, send your ship to the port side of your system. You must not arrive where the Empire ships now await escaping ships." The man's earlier happy look had become stern and sober. "My Astrogator will transmit to you our star list of 294 stars with habitable worlds around them. You, your fighter ships and your generation ships should pick one of those stars and make a colony. Then perhaps you can send a ship to Earth and formally join our NATO of the Stars mutual defense pact."

Swaying Light's large eyes blinked slowly. Wetness showed at the corners of each eye. "You speak truth. Though my crew and my fellow fighter ships would hope to fight the Empire ships, we . . . now we must preserve everyone who has survived the death of our home world. Send me this star list. Send me the terms of this NATO of the Stars. You fought to protect me and mine. In the future, we will fight to protect you and yours."

The disappearance of the two purple dots that lay just ahead of the coronal gas wall drew my attention. Those two dots now reappeared, their positions not far from Swaying Light's ship. Then four green dots disappeared. After a few seconds, the four green dots reappeared. Our scope showed them to be the four raider ships. They now clustered on our starboard side.

I licked my lips. My rapid heart beating slowed. The chill that had run up my spine at the appearance of the supernova now vanished. I would live to see my friends at lunch. My friends would live. My shipmates all would live. It would take time and care, but we would reach this system's magnetosphere edge. Would the captain take us to another Empire star? Would the waiting Empire ships attack us? I did not know. All I did know was that tomorrow would happen. I would draw breath in a new day. And my ship, my friends, my shipmates and I would have new hope.

CHAPTER TWELVE

Smooth Fur felt fury like none she had felt before. The human craft had discovered how to enter gray space within a system and exit it even without access to zero-point energy! The answer seemed to be doing it in very small increments, as that craft and now its raider allies jumped toward her fleet in small increments. Worse, the Dugong resistor crafts and two craft from their home world also made small gray space jumps. Though the star's coronal wall sped outward as an expanding ball, eating all matter and gases it encountered, that ultimate heat death would not devour the humans. Nor would it extinguish the few Dugong survivors. She blinked as the twelve Dugong craft changed their swim path and moved toward a location a third of the magnetosphere radius away from her position. The human craft and its four allies, though, were heading toward her. Well, at least she had a chance to kill those resistors. She looked aside to the scaled reptile who guided the swim path of her battleswimmer.

"Rak! Give us a swim route to where the human ship will arrive!"

The reptile turned its blocky head toward her, two red eyes fixing on her. "Manager, I will do as you command. But note the size of each mini-jump by the Earth ship. Its last jump will put it some distance out from the edge of the magnetosphere."

She glanced at the view plate. One part of it displayed a graphic view of the star, its planets, its rock belt, its outer band of icy comets and the edge of its magnetosphere. It was clear the human ship would arrive further out than her fleet's current position. Should she attempt the short gray space jumps of the humans? She ground her sharp teeth. The numbers and field strengths for jumping from within a star's magnetosphere out to the edge of its sphere was known from prior Empire fleets that had used the gravitational imbalance maneuver to punish a resistor species who fought too well against that fleet. No other fleet had ever done what the humans had done, which was to use the gray space engine to hop around the outer edge of a star. Or to hop in small increments from within a system out to its edge. Well, there was still time before the humans arrived.

"Engines!" she barked to Trelka. "Move us out on the swim path identified by Rak." She looked to another crew being. "Fleet Aide Lork! Communicate with the other craft of our fleet this new swim path and the need to be quick in our swimming!"

"Fusion pulse engines and magfield drive engine are moving us on the new swim path," hissed Trelka.

"Communicating your orders to the fleet," Lork growled.

Frustration built within her. "Bloody Beak! Prepare to fire on the human and raider crafts the moment we reach prey engagement range!"

The avian raptor fluttered her yellow and red feathers. "Yes! Yes, this one hungers to eat the bodies of the Empire resistors!"

Brief satisfaction filled her. Bloody Beak was her most loyal crew being. Lork was also loyal, but too subservient for her taste. She expected aggressiveness from every crew being on her craft and in her fleet. Predatory aggressiveness was in the genetic nature of all crew chosen to serve the Empire. But of late it seemed that some crew were content to eat live prey, do routine maintenance and show only pretend interest in chasing down prey! Perhaps she should kill a few of them as a motivational example to the others in her battleswimmer.

"Manager!" snarled Zorta from her Tactical work space. "The human craft has arrived far ahead! So have the four raider allies! We are not moving fast enough. We are not in weapons range!"

She saw that. The human manager Skorzeny would have time to adjust to the new feel of local space and then jump to another star! New fury filled her. It had taken scheming and detailed planning to set up the cleansing of the Dugong home world as a tempting target for the humans. Making the human resistors come to her was something she and other fleet managers excelled at. Now, she would have to repeat that scheme again. Was there another resistor species she could mention on the Dark Neutrino Web as her target? Even if there was, would the human manager go there, rather than attack an Empire trading world or orbital or craft-making yard? There were far more Empire targets in the half of Orion Arm controlled by the Empire than there were resistor species.

"Prey targets are gone," grunted Wendig the amphibian. The yellow glow about his body now faded to a low level.

Making decisions was what a fleet manager did. "Astrogation, set gray space swim path for star 9321. It is close by and shelters five planets, two of them occupied by Empire colonies. The human nuisance may go there next. If not, our presence will provide reassurance to the Empire colonies on the edge of our expansion."

"Swim path set," Rak hissed.

"Trelka, take us to star 9321," she snarled.

The real space image in her view plate turned gray.

Smooth Fur slapped her control panel, then tapped in the code for the mech device to bring live prey for eating. Fury was best served by the death of living things. And eating squirming live things while filled with fury sometimes provided the glimmer of future schemes. She would eat. She would think. And she would find a way to hunt down the human manager. Once captured he would yield the location of his home world. That moment she yearned for.

◆ ◆ ◆

"Nathan, it's okay to feel good about saving the ship. And our shipmates," Evelyn said as she lay naked beside me in her bed.

Her head rested on my chest. I hugged her close with my left arm. We'd just finished making deeply passionate love. It was something we both needed, perhaps as a way to deny how close the ghost of death had come. But my love was far too good at reading my emotions. And my hidden feelings. Things that I felt but which I was not comfortable discussing. I'd felt this way ever since the death of my Dad in my last year of high school.

"Yeah. Sure." I paused, looking aside to examine a bedroom wall chart that plotted the evolution of life on Earth. The chart went all the way from the single-celled prokaryotes that first appeared on Earth about 4.1 billion years ago, to microbial mat fossils at 3.5 billion years ago to the split between bacteria and archaea, along with the first photosynthesis using the Sun's light, around 3.4 billion years ago. The chart noted the Great Oxygenation Event around 2.5 billion years ago, which marked the change in Earth's air from normal methane and ammonia to deadly oxygen. Finally her chart showed the rise of multi-cellular life beginning 600 million years ago, ending in the presence of humanity, the bald eagle, the great ape, chimpanzees and orangutans and smart ocean dwellers like whales and porpoises. It was a chart I had studied in high school biology. Now, seeing it here on her wall, it reminded me how important was her field of evolutionary biology. The aliens we had met, who included our raider allies and those we had yet to meet, were all examples of life's explosive presence on all types of worlds.

"Nathan!" She lightly bit my bicep. "Pay attention to what I'm saying.

"Ouch!" I looked down at the swirl of her thick red curls. In the low light from her workdesk and the nearby living room, I saw plenty of nice details. Even her freckles showed as slightly darker dots that ran from her shoulders down to her hip and along her legs to her feet. She was six feet of luscious woman. And intensely thoughtful woman, as she had now reminded me. "I'm working on being attentive. Doesn't the last hour count?"

She elbowed me. "You male! Stop thinking with your groin and use your brain. Like you did when you told Chief O'Connor about the math numbers and field strengths that allowed us to do mini-jumps inside the magnetosphere of Kepler 442. Be proud of what you did!"

This was something I'd heard from my other friends at lunch today. It was something I'd heard also from people at the other tables in the Mess Hall. NCOs from other decks, other Marine buddies of Warren, and some commissioned staff officers like Lieutenant Morales and Dr. Khatri of Med Hall had come over to the table and said 'Thanks!' in various ways. Being the focus of shipwide attention was not something I felt comfortable with. I'd never been comfortable with people knowing about my super strength, super eyesight and super hearing, which is why I had kept it secret at Great Lakes and later on at Trinity orbital and during the early weeks of our trip out to Kepler 37. Now I was famous within the *Star Glory*. I could not go anywhere without someone in a hallway or in a chamber giving me a high five, a pumped fist or other sign of shared victory over the nearly invincible Empire of Eternity.

"Yeah, I guess. But we couldn't stop the killing of five billion Dugong."

She sighed long and low. "I know. Seeing how lively and musical was Swaying Light made me visualize all too clearly the Dugong people who were living on her home world." She sniffled. "The loss of *their* home world reminded me of the threat to Earth. Nathan, could we really lose Earth? And close to eight billion people?"

It was the one question I had no answer to. The captain's orders that forced him to become a privateer and killer of Empire trading ships, passenger ships and battlecruisers like the two we had killed in the asteroid belt of Kepler 442, those orders made sense to me. "Buy time!" was what both the pollies of EarthGov and Admiral Gonsalves wanted the captain and our ship to do. Buy time until we could build a fleet of 20 battlecruisers outfitted with antimatter beamers and magfield spacedrives. Buy time in the hope the strikes by the *Star Glory* behind the frontier of Empire expansion would slow Smooth Fur's efforts to locate Earth. But the alien fleet chief was beyond deadly. Like everyone on the ship I had heard and understood our presence at the Dugong home world and system Kepler 442 was something planned by Fur. The alien had put out the factual info of the fleet's next cleansing target and counted on the captain learning that datum. Which he had. Now we were on our way deeper into the downarm part of Orion Arm, to a star never before discussed with any allies or enemies. Hopefully that meant Smooth Fur would not be hanging around the system.

"Nathan?"

I hugged her close to me, needing the feel of her warmth as chills ran down my back. "Yes, the Empire is a real threat to Earth. But our captain is smart, decisive and willing to do anything to draw attention away from Earth. So long as Smooth Fur is hunting for us, he is not hunting for Earth."

"Or *she* is not hunting for Earth," Evelyn said, reminding me of the lunch table chat over the possible gender of the enemy fleet captain. She rubbed her cheek against my chest. "Maybe we need to threaten something she holds dear. What could that be?"

What indeed? We had no way of knowing where lay the home world of her Notemko species. What else did he or she value? A memory of words spoken by Smooth Fur during her threat to our three ships right after our first arrival at Kepler 37 came to mind.

"Maybe she holds dear the Empire fleet base that lies within nebula W51?

Evelyn abruptly sat upright. "Yes! Her boss would be at that fleet base! And likely other Empire battlecruisers! If we could threaten it, that would surely draw her and her fleet away from searching for Earth."

My hormones told me to pay attention to Evelyn's swaying full breasts, her dark red nipples and her delightful passionate side during love-making. My mind told me to say something about W51 to some officer. Maybe the XO. Commander Nadya Kumisov had been courteous to me the few times I'd met her. And she was clearly the right-hand helper the captain relied on for running our ship. Mentioning what Evelyn had mused about and the fact of W51's fleet base would be a smart move. Perhaps the XO had already offered such advice to our captain. Or maybe not. But I had no doubt that any threat to the Empire's nearest fleet base would draw the attention of Smooth Fur.

"You are right. You are very right." I reached up and cupped her chin. "Do you have time for a kiss before you report for your shift on Science Deck?"

In the half-darkness my lover smiled softly. "I do." She bent down, kissed me deeply with her lips and tongue, then sat up and sprang off the bed. "Time for my shower! I'll see you at lunch today. Okay?"

Understanding this was my dismissal from her private cabin on Residential Deck, I swung off the bed and hunted for my service khakis and ship shoes. "Very okay! See you at lunch."

As I dressed I thought of her last question. Would a threat to W51 be a strong enough motivation for Smooth Fur to reverse course and come downarm to confront the *Star Glory* and my captain? I did not know. But I liked the idea of doing something that would force the alien fleet captain to do *our* biding. To show up where *we* wanted her or him to show up. That would be a nice reversal of Fur's sneaky trick that had drawn us to almost die under the lash of a supernova. I did not think the Dugong star was killed solely because we were in its system. The Dugong themselves were putting up a strong fight before we arrived. But killing both the Dugong and our ship at the same time, now that made sense. In an evil way of making sense.

◆　◆　◆

The captain was on Engineering Deck when I stepped out of the gravlift and headed for my work station. He had just turned away from talking to Chief O'Connor and now walked toward me. Between us lay the nine rainbow-shining antimatter injector tubes. Leaning into my stride, I arrived at my station just before the captain got there. I saluted him. Smartly I hoped.

"Captain! CPO Stewart reporting."

He returned my salute. Like me he was dressed in brown service khakis with his service ribbons, combat badges and award pins covering his left chest. He wore no combo hat. His curly brown hair covered his head with no bald spot, unlike some of our older officers and NCOs. His large right hand lowered to his waist. His smooth-shaven chin barely rose as he was just a few inches shorter than my six five. His steely penetrating gaze fixed on me.

"CPO Stewart. I see you are five minutes ahead of your shift start. Got a moment?"

I did not say 'What a stupid thing to ask! You're the captain!' Instead I gave him a nod and held back my goofy smile. This man was my boss. A boss who had twice invited me into the inner sanctum of Officers Conference Room on Bridge Deck. And he was the man who had twice told me I was a valued member of his crew. And also a distraction. I swallowed hard and told my fast-beating heart to slow down.

"Sir, yes sir."

As I stood there just outside the rainbow tube forest of my work station, I noticed Chief O'Connor giving me a gimlet-eyed stare. I heard PO Gambuchino shifting in her seat before her compact fusion reactor. Her three Spacers Cindy, Duncan and Gus also shifted in their seats, clearly moving to keep me and the captain in view. The low hum of the magfield spacedrive unit drew my attention. It lay between me and the Chief. The deeper thrum of the fusion thrusters' controls also came to me. Lastly I sensed the keening sound of the Alcubierre graviton generator as it twisted an envelope of artificial space-time around my ship, so we and everyone inside the *Star Glory* could race across normal space at an FTL speed of 100 light years a day. The milder sounds of air circulating, of fans in the air ducts moving that air and the low swish of sound from the gravshaft in the middle of the deck as the gravlift went up to another deck, all those sounds came to my super sensitive ears. But none of them could displace my sharp-eyed view of the captain and his thoughtful look. The man's light brown eyes moved over me, from head to boots and back up to my name badge that sat above my right chest pocket. Then he looked at me directly.

"I need to add my 'Thanks' to those voiced by other crewmembers. Once again you saved this ship from certain doom." His cheek muscles tensed slightly. "I wish I knew as much about Alcubierre space-time moduluses as you and Chief O'Connor know. Or how to use our antimatter to shoot sideways, in the manner you shared with the Chief. CPO, I like the way you think."

Clearly the Chief had shared with the captain my idea for how to use the antimatter stored on the deck above us to shoot other than to our rear. And the Chief had given me credit for the idea. Which was too kind. It was an option that could be used by any of the four battlecruisers still in the Solar System. There was nothing we had to build or change in order to shoot antimatter sideways. Just a decision to dump large amounts of AM that would take time for our particle accelerator to replace.

"Sir, thank you. But it is a simple technique that any Star Navy battlecruiser could—"

The man held up his right hand, clearly signaling me to shut up. "Yes, I understand that. And I will include that data in my weekly neutrino comsignal back to Star Navy HQ on Moon Base. As I will include AV of our encounter with Manager Smooth Fur and his fleet in the Dugong system." The man paused, looked past me to where Gambuchino and her Spacers now sat, then came back to me. Eye to eye. His gaze was bright and intense. "The fact is, *you* thought of this new antimatter defense technique. No one else did. Not at Great Lakes. Not at Moon Base. No one on the *Tsushima Straits*, the *Cape Town*, the *Vikramaditya* or the *Shandong* came up with this. A point I will make in my missive. Once more you have proven to be a valued member of this ship's crew."

"Sir, thank you," I said, choosing to accept his compliments and hopefully avoiding the need to further stand at parade rest as the focus of everyone else's attention.

He squinted. "CPO Stewart, why does it bother you to accept a compliment. Or two?"

I licked my lips. Clearly the captain was not going to leave Engineering until he got a response from me. Memories swam to the front of my mind. My heart beat faster. It was not quite Fight or Flight time. But it felt close to that.

"Sir, my smartness and my . . . unusual abilities did not keep my Dad alive. Cancer killed him in my senior year in high school." I licked my lips again. "My dog Lappy died right after my Dad died. There was nothing I could do to save Lappy either. Sir."

The man's intense look changed. His face changed. Very slightly. But the changes said he understood something about loss. "CPO Stewart, tech cannot solve every problem in life. Med tech could not save your Dad. Nor could med tech save my sister Eileen. She died from brain cancer."

I closed my eyes. This man was sharing something private to him with me. And he was speaking softly. Very softly. Low enough that neither Chief O'Connor nor PO Gambuchino could hear what he was saying. To me, of course, his words were as loud as a yell. I opened my eyes. His different gaze was still there.

"Sir, I am sorry for your loss of your sister. I . . . I understand about the pain of family loss."

"I'm sure you do, CPO Stewart." His expression shifted, moving to a look similar to that worn by both line and staff officers. It was the look that went with the burden of managing other people to the benefit of the unit, the ship and those other people. "Was the loss of your Dad why you worked so hard at Great Lakes? You were not known as a math whiz in high school. Or in the A-Schools. Though I have heard you are doing better thanks to tutoring from Dr. Cassandra Murphy."

He was not going away. Not yet. He wanted more from me. More than I had shared even with my Mom. Well, so be it.

"Sir, the death of my Dad and my dog Lappy motivated me to always try my best to save a life, or lives, anywhere and anytime. Maybe that is how I came up with antimatter fart idea. And the mini-jumps within the magnetosphere. Sir."

Empathy filled his face. "Maybe so. Maybe so, CPO Stewart. Carry on."

My captain turned and headed for the gray metal tube of the gravshaft. Low voices came from Gambuchino's post. Rustling came from Chief O'Connor's post as he did something with his Alcubierre control panel. I turned around and entered my work station. Sitting down in my seat I waited for the accel straps to automatically criss-cross my chest. They did. Tapping on my antimatter control panel I set the system to doing the usual systems diagnostic program that was always the first thing I did when I reported to my work station. I needed routine right now. I badly needed it. My captain had shared something highly personal with me. Before his sharing, I worked hard at my post because that was my duty. And because I like what I do. Now, because of his sharing, I had one more person added to my list of people I cared about. Evelyn. Bill. Warren. Oksana. Cassandra. And now Neil Skorzeny.

The antimatter injector tube function bars were all green. The containment field on the deck above that held imprisoned thousands of liters of raw antimatter, that field status was a green bar. The single overhead tube that ran out to Bill's antimatter beamer block was a green bar. Power flow to the glowing tubes that enclosed me in a ring of rainbows was green bar. And the fusion pulse thruster implosion chambers that created raw plasma for expelling into cold hard space, those chambers showed green bars, even though they were not expelling anything right now. Everything at my station worked perfectly. Everything except my heart and my feelings. For I could not put away my Dad's last words to me.

"Nathan, most people go to bed assuming they will wake up in the morning. I've learned better. Take every day as if it were the gift of life!"

CHAPTER THIRTEEN

Eleven and a half days later we arrived just outside the magnetosphere boundary of Kepler 439. Which lies 2,260 light years into the Deep Black as measured from Earth. It was First Shift and I sat in my antimatter seat. We were heading inward toward the magnetosphere edge at 10 psol. Our four raider allies had all exited Alcubierre space-time within seconds of us, thanks to the neutrino comsignal coordination between their Engineering decks and ours. Now their Astrogators scanned the system ahead just as our CPO Louise Ibarra now did. I looked to the right. On the nearby bulkhead vidscreen the system's yellow G7V star occupied the center of a block of darkness, leavened only by thousands of white star points. A system graphic image appeared next to the overhead of the Bridge and the true space image. On it were three planetary dots. Two of them lay within the green zone of liquid water habitability.

"Astrogation, give us the rundown on this system," the captain said, sounding calm even though I could see plenty of neutrino-emitting red dots circling the outermost third planet.

"Sir, the system contains three worlds," Ibarra said, her tone thoughtful. "One world at one-tenth AU is a Mercury analogue. A second world at 0.56 AU is twice the size of Earth. It is a sub-Neptune planet. It lies at the inner edge of the star's habitable zone. The third world at 0.75 AU is very Earth-like, in both the warmth it receives from the star and in its position in the middle of the green zone. Its year is 286 days long." She paused, glancing down at her panel then up at the giant front vidscreen. "The star itself is nine-tenths the size of Sol. Same for its mass. The star temp is 5,431 Kelvin. That is slightly less than the Sun's 5,772 Kelvin. Uh, Kepler 439 lies 2,260 point three light years distant from Earth. Sir."

She did not mention the asteroid belt at six AU nor the Kuiper Belt zone that began at 35 AU and extended out to the system's magnetosphere edge at 40 AU. Beyond the mag edge lay a scattered disk of icy moons and mini-worlds that gradually became this system's Oort Cloud, which extended out to 100 AU. Ibarra did not mention this data since it was clear to see on the system graphic.

What was not clear was the nature of the many red dots in orbit above the third world.

"Tactical, what is your read on the neutrino emission sources?" the captain said, sounding a bit hurried.

I understood his impatience. In a few more minutes we and our four allied ships would be hailed by the system traffic controller. We had to know what we faced before the captain dealt with the controller. I wondered whether the captain would admit to being a rebel to the Empire, or do something else.

Chang looked down at her panel. "Captain, there are twenty-one ships in low orbit. A larger emitter is likely an orbital station of a size similar to Trinity. There are also stationary neutrino sources down on the surface of the world." She looked back to the captain, her high cheekbones pale in the yellow light of the Bridge. "The planetary sources are confined to one location on the world, perhaps a single continent. It appears this world has been settled for some time. Sir."

"Incoming neutrino comsignal!" said Wetstone at Communications. "Sir, it is on Empire frequency 2231, which is the primary commercial frequency used in the Empire."

The captain sat back in his seat. "Heidi, adapt my neutrino comsignal to reflect the image of Wandering Biter of the species Drugol." He looked to one side of the front vidscreen. The images of the four raider ship captains were there, listening and watching. "Captains Delight, Gorling, Lindo and Mousome, feel free to have your ship AI adapt your image to a species disguise that suits you. I am hiding my human form on the assumption Smooth Fur has sent out a combat alert about us humans."

Delight the raccoon-like female swished her slim tail to one side. "No need. We Medoxit are known as a widely traveling species."

"There is no need for a disguise," rumbled Gorling the giant black bear alien. "Members of my species are common in Warm Swirl. I am sure you noticed one of my people on the bridge of Smooth Fur's battlecruiser."

"I did," the captain said quickly, looking to the other two captains. "Well, this is the opportunity you four have sought since joining my command. Let us see whether we can gain entry covertly and then take control of some or all of those local spaceships."

"Eager am I to claim another ship," rasped Lindo the wasp-like alien.

"Fuel bills always need timely payment," hooted Mousome the six-legged alien who acted like a smart-ass hippo.

The captain looked ahead. "Heidi, adjust my comsignal. Tactical, watch closely the image we receive from the traffic controller. Astrogation, stay alert for the graviton surge of any starship arriving at the edge of the magnetosphere. There are none but us out here right now. That could change."

"Adjusting your image and the images of your command staff to reflect the image of Wandering Biter and other species known from our visit to the pirate base," Heidi said in a light, almost whimsical tone.

It made me wonder if our ship AI might be a covert lover of stage plays.

"Sir," called Chang. "I will keep a close watch on the species imagery in this signal."

"Same for me," said Ibarra. "I am watching for graviton surges. Sir."

"Communications, accept the incoming comsignal."

The bulkhead vidscreen grew a fourth image to join the system graphic, overhead Bridge and true space scope image.

Something that was too bizarre to analogize to any Earth animal now filled the fourth image. It had four arms and four legs and six eyes. They were arranged around something that resembled a giant beach ball the size of a human. The alien had no face. Just a strip of six green eyes across the top of the ball. Below the eyes was a sucker-like mouth filled with inward pointing teeth. Indentations to the left and right of the mouth might be ears. Or acoustic membranes. Below the mouth there sprouted out four arms that were narrow, had two elbows and contained fingers arranged in a circle that resembled the limbs of a starfish. Radial fingers came to my mind. Below the line of arms were four thick elephant-like legs. The flat feet had no nails but clearly were able to support the globular mass of the alien. Whose skin, to top it off, was a pink the color of vomit. The alien moved one narrow arm toward a control pedestal in front of it. As it waved its radial fingers over the pedestal I noticed other aliens in the background of the room. There was a wasp-like alien, something that resembled a giant black beetle with shimmering wings that hugged its carapace, another creature whose long low form hugged the deck of the room, and finally I noticed an alien who seemed like a ball of jello. Except this jello ball extruded eyepods and manipulator tendrils as needed to do unknown somethings to a control panel near it.

"I am Mikmak, species Noot, Intended member of the Empire," hissed the giant beach ball, the sound seeming to emanate from its sucker mouth. "I control all traffic within this system. Identify yourself. And explain why five ships have arrived as a group."

The captain waved his right arm, perhaps to cause the upper arm pair of the fake praying mantis alien to move. "I am Wandering Biter of the species Drugol, which is also an Intended member of the Empire." The captain now gestured with his left arm. "The four other ships that arrived with my ship *Wanderer* are fellow merchants. We chose to travel together due to rumors that this part of Warm Swirl was infested with deadly raiders of ship cargos."

The strip of six green eyes blinked in sequence, the blinking moving from its right to the left of the giant beach ball. Black streaks briefly appeared on parts of its vomit pink skin.

"Your travel precautions are unneeded," Mikmak hissed. "This is the merchant system Lillifuss. It has been settled by the Empire for more than a thousand cycles. Which clearly you do not know. Why have you come here?"

The captain slapped both of his hands down against his armrests. "Why else! We are traders. We heard your Lillifuss world grows the tastiest Nok fruit within fifty light cycles travel. You are also reputed to distill intoxicating beverages of the Melang variety. And your asteroid belt is noted for producing Wik and Luk gems of high quality." The captain paused. "We are *not* ignorant of the attractions of Lillifuss system. We researched your offerings. We chose to come here. Perhaps your local traders will be enticed by our own caskets of sweet liquor, or our manually constructed musical instruments that appeal to anyone with acoustic membranes."

The black streaks disappeared from the alien's vomit pink skin. All six green eyes stayed open and attentive. One thick leg stomped the deck briefly. "Captain Wandering Biter of the trade ship *Wanderer*, you and your associates are welcome to Lillifuss system. Your trade cargo research is accurate. Our traders can provide flash-frozen barrels of Nok fruit, caskets of Melang drink and high quality gems of the Wik and Luk variety." One of the narrow arms of the beach ball gestured back toward the jello ball alien. "My tertiary assistant Lotem will greet you when your ship docks with my station. Your five ships are assigned traffic control designators L22, L23, L24, L25 and L26. Do not stray out of the ecliptic plane of this system. And do not visit the mining settlements in our rock belt. Their output is solely contracted to the Whodune Combine. You may contact its representative on this station."

"Your information is appreciated," the captain said, his tone casual. "My fellow captains are known as Delight, Gorling, Lindo and Mousome. They will contact you directly as they wish. Their trade cargos differ from mine. We will follow your system entry guidelines."

"They are not guidelines!" hissed Mikmak. "They are my rules for any trader ship that wishes to engage in trade with our merchants and with other trading ships that orbit near my station. Obey my rules or depart this system."

"Your correction is understood," the captain said quickly, waving his right arm. "Shall we end this conversation?"

The giant beach ball hissed low. "You may wish to know that I and other members of my species are expert at acoustically manipulated musical instruments. Are such instruments among the manually fabricated instruments you offer for trade?"

The captain smiled. Which made me wonder how a smile might translate into a praying mantis expression considering the utter rigidity of its hard chitin face. Perhaps Heidi had the mantis image clapping its upper and middle arm pairs. Or something.

"We do possess acoustically driven musical instruments," our captain said slowly. "I will personally display some of them to you, system traffic controller Mikmak."

The alien's vomit pink skin grew dark red. Its six green eyes blinked in random order. Its sucker mouth hissed loudly. "Ship *Wanderer* and associates, enter the Lillifuss system. Your arrival will be announced to all merchant combines. I depart this transmission."

The giant beach ball alien vanished from the bulkhead vidscreen.

Our captain looked to the right of the Bridge vidscreen. "Captains, have any of you ever met a member of . . . of that Noot species? It was not among the 53 species listed as visiting Tik-long's base."

"The species Noot is unknown to me," barked Delight.

The giant black bear captain growled low. "It is one of many species without the decency to evolve fur. I have heard of it. This is my first encounter with a member of Noot species. Hopefully it will be my last encounter."

Captains Lindo and Mousome both said the Noot species was unknown to them and their ship AIs.

"Captains, thank you." Our captain looked ahead. "Tactical, can you tell whether any of the 21 ships in orbit near this station of Mikmak's are armed?"

Chang shook her head. "Sir, I cannot. At 40 AU out the only thing I can detect from our sensor arrays is that all 21 ships have at least a single fusion reactor and a second source of neutrinos that is likely their fusion pulse thruster or thrusters."

The captain frowned. "Communications, are there any systemwide neutrino AV broadcasts? Such as entertainment or education casts? They might display the ships in orbit."

Wetstone looked down at his panel. "Sir, there are 43 neutrino AV broadcasts plus 16 vidcasts that are lightspeed-bound, similar to Earth vidcasts." He tapped his panel. "None of the neutrino or vidcasts are encrypted. I can scan the casts personally, or have Heidi review them."

The captain made a dismissive gesture. "No need to rush. We have two days before we arrive near the third planet. XO, work with PO Wetstone to review these neutrino and video casts. We need to know how many of the 21 ships down there are armed and how many are not."

Our petite Russian gave a quick nod of her head, her long black hair loose and unbound. "Captain, will do. However, my guess is that there are few armed merchantmen this far into the long-settled part of the Empire's domain within Orion Arm. The large number of armed merchantmen at Kepler 37 made sense as it was at the frontier of Empire expansion. Sir."

"Perhaps that will be the case, XO." The captain looked down to where Owanju sat, his strong black arms resting on his seat's armrests. "Major, put your GTO teams to work doing boarding simulations. While I have no interest in stealing cargos and gems from Empire traders, we might need to board a ship if something unusual turns up."

The big man looked up and saluted. "Captain, will do on the boarding simulations. May I also suggest we put some Marines into combat suits and have them do entry security rehearsals in Hangar One?"

"You may, major. Carry out both training regimes." Our captain looked up at the overhead. "Heidi, did you detect the background presence of any AI at that orbital station? Or elsewhere in this system?"

"Captain Skorzeny, I did not detect any AI riding silent on the neutrino comsignal. Nor do I detect any AI emissions from the asteroid belt or elsewhere in this system. Perhaps this Mikmak makes do without AI help."

"Perhaps. Though I doubt the mighty Empire of Eternity would ever turn its alien back on the unique abilities of self-aware AI. Heidi, be alert as we enter this system. There could be covert riders on neutrino or radio or vidcast signals that our XO and Communications will be reviewing."

"Alert I will be," sang Heidi, her high soprano sounding amused. "No alien AI or golem worm will enter this ship's systems. The taste of Empire golem worms is very distinctive, captain. You humans always know when some food is spicy. So do I always know when an errant or golem signal impinges on our sensor arrays and my hull."

"Glad to hear that," the captain said with a mild smile on his face. "Doctor Bjorg, what is your take on what we saw of this Mikmak and his support crew?"

The Swede, who wore a blue and gray camo like all of the enlisted and NCO crew of the *Star Glory*, rubbed his chin. "This system traffic controller is a prime example of the principle of aposematism, or warning coloration. There is no way to ignore its bright pink skin color. And I noticed black chromatophoric streaks appear when you disagreed with him. Or it. Or her." The boss of Science Deck gave a shrug. "The other aliens on his deck all appeared busy. A few looked like predators. To be fair, though, the diversity of bioforms we saw in the comsignal matched the variety of bioforms we saw on the pirate base."

The captain looked forward, then up. "All Ship! We will remain at Wartime Cruising condition. But keep your vacsuits close! We will move to Combat Ready condition after we pass this system's asteroid belt. Carry on."

I focused back on my antimatter control panel. Which showed all green bars. Briefly I wondered if Bill was getting bored sitting by himself in the antimatter beamer block. Then I gave myself a mental kick. My friend watched the All Ship vidscreen images the same as I did. He knew what I knew and what every crewmate knew, thanks to the captain's policy of live vidcasts from the Bridge. No one had to guess about our captain. He ran a tight ship. But he also believed in building trust with his crew. I liked that when I first boarded the *Glory*. Now, after multiple combat engagements, I liked it even better. It was time to continue doing my part. Our antimatter fuel bunker on the deck above was a vital part of my ship. We now knew how to do more with the AM than just use it as an afterburner push for our thrusters. Which awareness made me wonder why the captain kept us at 10 psol speed heading into the system. Surely the alien ships above the third world were able to reach 15 psol by way of a supplemental magfield drive. Shaking my head, I put aside that wonderment. The captain had reasons for all he did. That was all I needed to know. That and the fact he saw me as a valued member of the crew. Being valued was something I had strived for after the death of my Dad and the move of Mom and my sisters to her condo. Now, I had friends who saw value in me. And I had Evelyn, a smart, insightful woman who wanted to spend her life with me. I was blessed. But how long would that blessing last in a star arm where Empire of Eternity battlecruisers roamed, at the ready to destroy entire worlds?

◆ ◆ ◆

Smooth Fur looked away from the viewing plate. They had arrived at the nearby system with five worlds, two of which contained Empire outposts and shipping. There was no sign of the distinct neutrino emission signature of the human battleswimmer. Nor was there sign of the emission signatures of the four raider craft. The human Skorzeny had not chosen to visit this system, which lay the same distance behind the frontier of Empire expansion as the Dugong system. Which left her with a decision to make. Go uparm to the frontier? Go sideways to scan likely target systems? Or go downarm in the expectation the human craft would continue its attacks on well-established Empire systems and orbitals? She snarled to herself. Going sideways meant crossing a space one-third as extensive as the entire Orion Arm. And the recent appearances of the human craft showed it moving away from the frontier. Clearly it sought to divert her attention from the search for its home world. She would accommodate the primitive primate who lacked enough fur to be considered civilized.

"Rak! Set our swim course for further downarm. Choose a long-established Empire system. I do not care which!" she snarled as the scaly reptile's red eyes looked to her for clarification. "Just pick a system! Then provide the data points to Tink." She looked to the pink floater who controlled her craft's Power systems, including its access to zero-point energy. There must be some way to use that access in a way that would lead to the human!

"Swim course is set!" hissed the reptile. "Data points provided to Power."

"Data points received," said Tink with a color-coded ripple of its flexible skin. "Ready to enter gray space."

She looked aside to her Fleet Aide, the one who seemed unable to match her ferocious hunger for this primate resistor. "Lork! Advise fleet ships of the new target star! Advise them to synchronize their Power activation with our Power system. Now!"

"Advising fleet craft!" growled the black-furred biped who was a third taller than Fur.

Taller he might be but he was not as sneaky. She had in mind a fatal accident for him that would appear to her crew beings *as* an accident, while all would know *she* had arranged it. The accident would happen while they were in gray space. There would be plenty of light cycles in which to select a replacement Fleet Aide from her mix of crew beings. Reviewing predator histories would untie the knot in her gut every time she mentally imaged the Skorzeny primate! That besotted climber of trees needed tending to. And she was determined to tend to him far sooner than later!

♦ ♦ ♦

I sat alert in my function station seat, wearing full vacsuit now that the ship condition had changed from General Quarters to Battle Stations. The last two days had been busy. Warren had been involved with his fellow Marines in entry security practice in their combat suits. Bill had done frequent aperture swing practice sessions so he could lock on a target and fire his antimatter beam within seconds of the captain's order. Oksana had spent time deciphering intel from the 43 neutrino vidcasts and the 16 AV casts that were constantly coming from the third world. Those vidcasts had included imagery of the orbital station occupied by Mikmak and a view of 14 orbiting ships. Only two of the orbiting ships showed laser mountings. If that ratio held for the unseen ships, there should be no more than four armed ships among the 21 now orbiting the third world. Cassandra and Evelyn had worked on a body language analysis of the aliens working in the traffic controller's office. They had also scanned the neutrino and audiovisual casts for any sign of Empire military posts on the world or in orbit above it. So far there had been no sign of Empire combat posts or ships. I looked aside to the bulkhead vidscreen. As usual it held a true space image from the ship's electro-optical scope, a system graphic that had enlarged to focus on the third world and an overhead view of the Bridge. A fourth smaller image showed the four raider captains on their own bridges.

"Stewart!" yelled my boss. "Get your eyes back onto your control panel! We have to be ready to give an afterburner push to our thrusters upon the captain's orders. Distraction in combat is fatal!"

I knew that. And I knew that I was good at multi-tasking. I could both watch the vidscreen and also check back on the status displays of my panel. Anyway, constantly watching a panel that showed perfect containment field conditions was boring. To me at least.

"Sir! Yes sir, I am watching my control panel. Sir."

A laughing giggle came from Spacer Cindy. My peripheral vision showed PO Gambuchino, dressed in a vacsuit like all of us, give her Spacer a shake of a single finger, as if to say 'This is combat time, not a time for laughing!'

"Engineering," called the captain, his serious tone alerting us all to the imminence of something about to happen. "Be prepared to activate your magfield drive. And to feed antimatter to our beamer block. Very shortly we will attack the targets we are approaching."

"Sir! Engineering is ready and able!" Chief O'Connor called out strongly.

My quick glance to the bulkhead vidscreen told me what mattered. We were just a million kilometers out from the giant ball that was Mikmak's orbital station. We were closer than that to some of the trader spaceships. Monitoring of local radio and neutrino vidcasts had given us the commercial combine names of most of the 21 ships. That monitoring had revealed there were two passenger starships in hard tube lock with the orbital, clearly downloading passengers for transit by GTO to the blue and green world below. The other 19 ships were close enough to the orbital to reach it via shuttle if there was cargo that needed transferring. Some of those trader ships had been visited by GTOs coming up from the world below. My guess was the GTOs carried cargo, and maybe a few passengers. If these merchantmen were like the wet ocean merchantmen of Earth, they likely carried fee-paying passengers in addition to their cargo. Briefly I felt guilt at the number of lives we were about to extinguish. There were plenty of civilians on those ships and in that orbital. Then a mental image of Hindus thronging to holy Varanasi and taking spirit-cleansing dips in the waters of the Ganges River reminded me of the 7.5 billion humans now at risk of extinction, once the Empire found Sol and Earth. Our job was to disrupt the routine of the Empire while also killing as many of its battlecruisers as we could. We were an interstellar privateer, flying with four other pirate privateers. We were a deadly force. I had no doubt of that.

CHAPTER FOURTEEN

"XO, assign targets to our four allies. Then assign the remainder to Weapons," the captain said, leaning forward in his elevated seat. "Tactical, keep alert for counterfire from those four armed merchantmen. Power, be prepared to feed maximum terawatts to lasers from our three reactors. Move it, people."

"Sir," called Kumisov. "I have assigned eight targets to our allies. That is two targets per ship. Their proton and CO_2 lasers should be able to disable ship engines, if anyone survives our x-ray lasers and gamma ray lasers." She looked ahead. "The remaining 13 targets have been sent to Weapons. Sir, two targets are passenger ships in hard dock to the orbital. Do we give them a warning to use lifepods?"

"We do. Assuming there is no laser attack from those two ships," the captain said. "The passenger ships and the orbital are the last targets to be attacked."

"I've received target coordinates," called Yamamoto from Weapons, sounding eager.

"Sir, I am watching the actions of all target ships," responded Chang.

"Our fusion reactors are feeding 90 percent of their output to our weapons mounts," called Suárez y Alonso from Power.

"Astrogation, what's our range to the first target?" Captain Skorzeny said calmly, his infrared glow a modest red color.

"Sir, range is 4,987,323 kilometers," reported Ibarra. "Our approach speed is 29,933 kilometers per second. When do we reduce speed, sir?"

"Now. Raiders, use your magfield drives to reduce forward speed to 5 psol. Engineering, reduce our approach speed to 5 psol."

"Reducing forward speed," called Chief O'Connor, reaching out to the magfield drive control panel in front of him.

I looked away from my boss and over to the bulkhead vidscreen. Our five green dots showed us nearing planet three, its orbital and nearby ships. In seconds our five ships slowed to an approach speed of 15,000 kilometers per second, or 900,000 klicks per minute. That was still too fast for effective combat.

"Engineering! Raiders! Reduce forward speed to one psol."

"Flipping the ship," called my boss, touching the fusion thrusters panel to use attitude jets to make the ship's nose go 180 and point back the way we had come. "Firing thrusters!"

In the true space image I saw the long spearpoints of the four raider ships do the same. My booted feet felt the vibration of our fusion pulse thrusters firing strongly.

"Weapons! Launch four missiles ahead. And then feed targeting data to the x-ray thermonuke warheads. Now!" called the captain loudly.

"Launching missiles from our stern silos," responded Yamamoto, his gloved hands flying over his control panel. "Now feeding target locations to warheads. Nose shrouds are gone. Warheads are dispersing. Search and Destroy routines are activating. Sir, we have forty warheads ready to fire on nineteen targets. Sir!"

"Incoming comsignal!" called Wetstone, his Brit accent very noticeable as Bridge tension ratcheted up. I felt tense too.

"Accept signal. Display it and share with our allies," the captain said quickly, no doubt watching the range marker in the system graphic that showed our distance to the orbital rapidly decreasing as the ship's speed dropped from 5 psol to 4 psol. Soon it hit 3 psol. In three more seconds our forward speed was one psol.

That meant the 40 x-ray thermonuke warheads were speeding ahead of us at 5 psol. In one minute they would be close to the orbital. A few minutes later the orbital and the target ships would be in range of our ship lasers.

The giant beach ball alien appeared in a fifth bulkhead vidscreen image. Its six green eyes were blinking from side to side too fast to count. Its vomit pink skin was half black thanks to the anger stripes now showing.

"Ship *Wanderer* and trader ships! Reduce your speed now!" it hissed. "You are denied access to this orbital due to your unsafe—"

"Heidi, drop my praying mantis overlay. Com, set me up for outgoing vidcast on his frequency."

"Done," sang the AI.

"Vidcast ready," called Wetstone.

"System traffic controller Mikmak, I am the human primate Captain Neil Skorzeny. Perhaps you have heard of me from Manager

Smooth Fur of the Empire fleet that attacked two human ships when we declined the Glorious Choice."

The alien went nearly black. "I know of you! Humans!" One stick arm gestured to the side. "Sound station alarm! Activate the automated laser defenses. Tell—"

"If you fire on my ship or my ship allies, your orbital will become a thermonuclear fireball. Like these." The captain looked to one side. "Weapons, detonate all but three warheads."

"Detonation order sent, sir," said Yamamoto, his tone breathless.

The true space image of the green and blue world rapidly grew larger, and the silver tubes that were 21 spaceships plus the silver ball of the orbital, those images vanished in the yellow-orange glare of 37 three megaton thermonukes going off as they fed x-rays into the x-ray lasing rods that surrounded their warhead cores. Those rods shot out white streams of x-rays. At 10 rods per warhead, the nineteen enemy ships were hit by 370 coherent x-rays. That meant 19 x-ray streams hit each ship. I had no doubt any bioforms on those ships had now received a fatal dose of x-rays. Very shortly their skin or chitin or shell would turn red or black. Internal organs would rupture due to cell ionization. Hearts and their equivalents would go into misfiring of signals. Blood vessels would rupture due to the loss of cellular cohesion. Brains would shortly die due to the loss of blood and nutrient fluids. It was a mass death quite different from the historical images of atomic bombs and thermonukes going off on the surface of Earth, or in the low atmosphere. Those images showed vast winds buffeting any nearby structures. And a mushroom cloud of radiated dirt rising high into the sky. Here, in the vacuum of space, the thermal heat rays hit just after the slightly faster x-rays. There was no impact on the structure of each spaceship. Which meant they would be intact for raider entry and salvaging. The astrogation units and drive units of each spaceship were safe in hardened containers, due to the regular impact of cosmic rays on any starship that roamed interstellar space. But no hull of any Empire ship could shield against the ferocious x-ray barrage of the 37 thermonuke warheads.

"Controller Mikmak, advise the two passenger ships docked to your hull to launch lifepods. Now! You may also wish to launch lifepods from your orbital." The captain leaned forward, his expression grim. "In less than one minute I will detonate the three warheads now moving at you at 5 psol. I suggest you hurry."

Screams and hisses and barks came from Mikmak and the seven alien crew beings in his controller room. Then his image vanished.

"Sir, the passenger ships are launching lifepods," called Chang, relief in her voice. "They are heading down to the planet. Sir."

"Are any launching from the orbital?"

"Not yet, sir."

"Astrogation, range to orbital and two ships?"

"Captain, range is now 41,387 kilometers."

"Engineering!" yelled the captain. "Apply maximum thruster power! Slow us down to a speed that will allow us to match orbits with the orbital!"

My boss's gloved hands moved over his thrusters control panel. "Sir, ship speed is decreasing! Now at 2,000 kilometers per second. And . . . slowing to 1,400 klicks per second. Sir, we will reach orbital insertion speed within three minutes."

Since the orbital lay at an altitude of 250 miles above the planet, that meant our speed had to drop to 28,000 kilometers per hour or 17,500 miles per hour in order to match orbits with the targeted ships and the orbital. I noticed the true space image that showed our raider allies also doing reverse thrusting from their fusion pulse thrusters. No one was firing lasers yet as the range to any target was still beyond 10,000 klicks.

"Sir!" yelled Chang. "Lifepods are launching from the orbital. I count . . . I count more than 300 pods going out. Sir."

In the overhead view I saw the captain's face twist with brief frustration, then decision showed in the set of his shoulders and his grim look. "Weapons! Detonate the three surviving warheads. One per target. Then load a missile with ten standard thermonuke warheads. Prepare to launch them against any aggressor."

"Detonating," Yamamoto said, sounding tired but determined.

The true space image of the orbital and two docked ships, which had started to become visible as the plasma cloud thinned out from the first barrage of x-ray thermonuke rays, now grew white-yellow as 30 rods were fed by three thermonukes, their white rays shooting out instantly and covering the small distance to their targets, all of which now lay within 5,000 klicks. While ten hard x-ray beams might not kill every being on the orbital, ten were more than enough to kill the crews of the passenger ships. If any crew were left.

Red proton and green CO_2 laser beams shot out from two targeted merchantmen. Four beams hit our allies. Four beams hit our stern. A wailing sound filled my vacsuit comlink.

"Hull breach in Engineering!" came Heidi's voice. "Dispatching repair bots now."

Air that now became white formed a vortex above a deckplate that lay between me and the Chief. While our ship armor was strong on the sides and nose of the ship, it was less strong on the part of the ship that contained the three thruster exhaust funnels. Soon our deck would be cold vacuum. But what was Bill's condition? His beamer block was exposed—

"Watson!" yelled the captain. "Fire on the port merchantman that fired on us. Allies, fire on the merchantman closest to you."

"Aperture fixed! Target locked," crackled Bill's voice over my suit comlink. "Firing AM beam now!"

In the true space vid a swath of blackness shot out and covered the 5,000 klicks between us and the supposedly dead merchantman that had fired lasers at us and our allies.

A new star glowed where the merchantman had been.

Red and green lasers shot from the noses of the four raider ships, which had now flipped over and pointed their nose lasers at the other enemy merchantman. They were joined by proton and CO_2 beams from our stern laser mounts as the crews manning those stations did not wait for an order but fired at the target directly ahead of us. Two beams per ship made a total of ten high-energy laser beams striking the tube of the merchant ship. In the blink of an eye hull plates burst open, white air rushed out, silvery water globules spurted into cold black space and whatever bodies were present in the tube ship now vanished as its fusion reactor lost containment. A second yellow-orange star joined the one formed by Bill's antimatter beam.

"Tactical! How the hell did those two ships manage to fire on us!" yelled the captain.

Chang flinched in her seat. "Sir, I have no facts. But my guess is that the AIs on those two ships had programmed orders to fire on any ship that fired on them. The AIs survived our x-ray laser bombardment. I am certain no bioform survived. Sir!"

"Damn," the captain muttered. "XO, make a note of this event. And remind me to add mention of it to my weekly neutrino signal to Moon Base." The captain looked up. "My allies, are you intact? Anyone hurt?"

"No one hurt on Engineering," my boss volunteered, clearly bothered by not being asked about that by the captain.

The captain's right hand clenched. His infrared glow increased. Was it anger or frustration? Or maybe guilt? "Chief O'Connor, my apologies. How are your crew? And what are your deck conditions?"

"All crew are alive and well," Chief O'Connor said in his normal blustery voice. "Engineering Deck is now cold vacuum. But Heidi is repairing the hull breach. We have normal gravity, lights and power to our work stations. The hull breach should be repaired within 10 minutes, based on a simulation I ran on our second trip out to Kepler 37."

"Good. Very good. Please add a 'well done' to your crew for your quick thrust reversal actions. And PO Watson, that was good shooting."

"Sir, thank you," called Bill over the vacsuit comlink.

"Captain, I am reversing ship orientation to take us nose-in to orbit beside the orbital," called Ibarra from Astrogation. "Range to the orbital is now 4,331 kilometers. We will arrive at station-keeping mode within one minute."

"Allies?" called the captain. "Please respond. Are your ships and crew intact?"

"My ship and crew are intact," barked Delight.

"Same for my vessel and workers," hooted Mousome.

"There was one beam strike on my upper hull," growled Gorling. "It did not penetrate. No one among us is injured."

"A beam hit my ship's underside but missed my laser fighters," rasped Lindo. "No shell penetration. We are intact and unharmed."

The captain's infrared glow now eased, moving from red-black to light red. One part of my mind felt amazement at the man's ability to control his physical reactions. Another part of my mind told me to be glad the helmet ring seals on my vacsuit worked perfectly. A third part of my mind reminded me that the rest of the crew had been equally at risk. Especially the Spacers manning our stern laser mounts.

"Allies, feel free to launch boarding vessels once we take up station beside our targets," the captain said, sounding relieved. "There are 19 still intact ships and one large orbital. I am sure they will provide plenty of high value cargo to you."

Barking came from Delight. "Captain Skorzeny, valuable cargo is good. Better is claiming a starship for sale at the Tik-long orbital. I will send a salvage crew to my selected ship. They will fly that ship back to our raider base. Do you object?"

The captain shook his head inside his helmet. "No! You put your ship and crew at risk during this attack. You deserve any salvage you wish to take from these Empire vessels."

"Then I will also claim a vessel for sending back to Decider Tik-long's orbital," growled Gorling.

"I will do the same," rasped Lindo the alien wasp.

The six-legged hippo-like alien who ruled the fourth raider ship went into a synchronized dance. "A salvaged ship will increase my reserves for future fuel bills," it hooted. "And my crew will search diligently among other ships for gems, drinkables and frozen foods. My feeding trough is empty too often."

I grinned at the image of the smart-ass hippo going hungry. It was a raider ship captain. I strongly doubted it ever went hungry. Maybe some of its crew, perhaps. Then again, the four raiders who had joined our strikes against Empire targets deserved any salvage rights they chose to make. For I had no doubt that the future held another encounter with Smooth Fur and her fleet. It was a prospect I both dreaded, and welcomed.

◆ ◆ ◆

Smooth Fur stared at the front view plate. The sensor portion showed ten four-somes of moving neutrino emissions. But none of the neutrino sources within the orange star system that Rak had chosen matched the emission characteristics of the human battleswimmer or its four raider allies. Instead, this system that had been settled for 800 annual cycles by Empire colonists, merchants and a local fleet office was empty of his enemy. His tail thudded against the deck behind him. Anger warred with frustration.

"Manager!" moaned Wendig from his Communications bowl. "There is an incoming neutrino comsignal from system 9,245!"

She looked back to where the low-slung amphibian of the Hola species worked. A yellow electrical glow was expanding from his scaled skin. The crew being was excited about something.

"Accept the signal. Display it on my view plate."

"Signal accepted. Displaying," moaned Wendig.

One part of the view plate filled with the image of a Noot. The blood-sucking predator required four legs to support its heavy world mass. Its six green eyes all fixed on her. Its four narrow arms flared outward in excitement. Or dismay. Or some emotion. She had only seen file reports on the Noot, since they were an Intended member of the Empire. The species was two levels below the Masterful level of her own Notemko people. It meant this being had some status in the Empire. Or at least that some other Associate or Masterful species found them useful.

"Speak. Or communicate as you are able," she barked.

The sucker mouth of the Noot spread wide. A slim white tongue inside it moved quickly. "I am Mikmak. A designated Manager. My orbital was attacked by the human primate Neil Skorzeny!" it wheezed. "Its craft and four other craft that were raiders, they pretended to be merchant traders. But when they were close to my orbital above the third world of system 11,321, they attacked us with explosions that shot out white x-ray beams! The beams killed all life on the 21 Empire ships near my orbital!"

New frustration filled her. System 11,321 was not far from system 9,245, outside of which her fleet now swam. But perhaps there was value in this walking ball of incompetence. "What is your status now? Are you on your orbital? Where are the humans?"

Two arms crossed in front of the Noot's body. "I am not on my orbital. The human gave warning of its attack. Two passenger ships launched lifepods to the planet below us. We on the orbital also boarded lifepods. We barely escaped with our lives!"

Clearly a merchant who thought only of itself. "The humans? Have they left?"

"Nooo," Mikmak hooted long and low. "I reside in the Empire residence within the control city of Mugogong. I am using its neutrino signaler to reach you." The creature looked aside. "A view plate here contains views from automated monitors near my orbital. The human craft is hard docked with my orbital. The four raiders are not. They are sending small craft to the dead ships." Black streaks partly covered the Noot's pink body. "Thieves! They are boarding the dead ships and taking control of the cargos! Help us! Help us Manager Smooth Fur!"

Helping a merchant manager who was incompetent enough to allow resistor crafts to approach his orbital was the last thing she wished to do. However the presence of the humans in the system was useful news. The system lay three light cycles away. Perhaps *Golden Pond* and her fleet could arrive before the human pestilence left. This Noot could serve as her eyes and ears by sending neutrino comsignal updates on the human craft and its raider allies.

"Manager Mikmak! My fleet of Empire starbiters will enter gray space and come to your system. Stay at the Empire residence! Monitor the visual reports of these monitors. Call me in another day cycle with a report on the human craft and the raider crafts!"

The Noot's six green eyes blinked in a complicated pattern. "Yes, yes, come to us! Save us from attack by these primitives! I will stay in the residence and report back to you!"

Disgust filled her gut. Merchants like this one were vital to the Empire's control of Warm Swirl. But they had no understanding of how tenuous that control was. Every being in the Empire had to always do that which advanced the needs of the Empire. Unlike this walking blood-sucker. Still, it had value until her fleet could arrive at system 11,321.

"My fleet is coming," she said, preparing to tell Wendig to close the comsignal link. Then a memory hit her. She refocused on the Noot. "Manager Mikmak, did you destroy the Empire residence on your orbital?"

The six green eyes closed, then opened. "Sadly there was no time! We had bare moments in which to run down the tubeways and find a lifepod launch site. But the orbital's AI controls access to the station. Surely it will block access to the residence!"

She wondered at that assumption. Empire AIs were self-aware. Which made them useful, but dangerous if they ignored the programming implants that told them to always obey any Empire representative. Such as this Manager Mikmak. Or the manager of any fleet ship. Too bad this Mikmak had left its orbital. She would have ordered it to stay and give orders to the AI, even if Mikmak then died under the x-rays. And the AI could be dead or non-coherent due to the x-ray bombardment of the orbital.

"Since you left your post, Manager Mikmak, you had best hope the orbital AI indeed protects the Empire residence. I go now. Watch the monitors in orbit. Call me within a day cycle."

She gestured to Wendig to close the link. The amphibian did so, then it turned red eyes her way.

Decision time had arrived. She turned to her new Fleet Aide. It was a gold and red-furred hunter of the Toka species. Like Zorta at Tactical, this Toka always acted as if ready to sink its long white teeth into an enemy or designated prey.

"Deta, advise the twenty other fleet managers to set their swim path for system 11,321!" she snarled. "Rak, set our swim path to that system! Provide the coordinates to Tink!"

"Advising all fleet craft of our new prey target!" sharply growled Deta, the claws on her two feet and two paws flexing outward.

She liked its instincts. Now her bridge was filled with predators eager to kill all resistors and ready to scatter red blood against all walls of her control cell!

CHAPTER FIFTEEN

"Heidi, are you able to take control of a hard dock tube on that orbital?" asked the captain as my ship moved to link up with the kilometers-wide orbital.

Since we now moved on magfield drive with the thrusters shut down and with no need for an afterburner push from my antimatter station, I was able to watch the bulkhead vidscreen. Its image of the Bridge, of the system graphic image and of the true space image that showed four raider spearheads moving to board and take control of the 19 dead Empire ships, they kept my attention. Anyway, I had looked around at the nine antimatter injector tubes, without my goggles, and their field shimmers were bright, sharp and stable. Most important, Chief O'Connor was more intent on his magfield control panel than he was on watching me.

"Not yet," came Heidi's low soprano voice. The low level of her voice indicated she was doing electronic stuff elsewhere. "The docking tubes are functional. The two connected to the passenger ships are still hard-locked. I am extending my awareness field into the orbital's interior."

That surprised me. At my Great Lakes A-School we had learned about self-aware AIs, how they felt great loyalty to the ship and people they worked with, and how their electromagnetic awareness field could extend beyond the ship's hull. The field was different from the neutrino, radio or vidcast signals that any AI could send and receive. The field range was just a kilometer. We were now closer than that to the orbital. Earlier the captain had ordered this docking in order to board the orbital and search it for Empire intelligence. And maybe to refuel the bunkers on the DT Deck with hydrogen isotopes. But doing either first required gaining access. A hard dock tube was better than sending a Marine GTO out to plant explosives and blow an entry hole.

"Is the orbital still functional?"

"Oh!" cried Heidi, surprise in her musical tone. "Yes, it is functional. And its AI has just impinged on my field. It . . . it seeks communication. Do I accept?"

The image of our captain showed him frowning within his helmet. Even though all space combat had ceased, we were still at Battle Stations with weapons systems at Red Hot status. Bill was in his beamer block, scanning the planet below and the space around us for any sign of an automated ship with an AI intent on firing on us. The remaining 17 merchant ships showed no hostile behavior. And raider shuttles had managed to dock with four of them. So far so good. But this system, this planet and this orbital were a combat zone. While things appeared peaceful, we were all tensely alert. Including the captain who had not immediately replied to Heidi's request.

"Heidi, are you able to block any worms or bots that might piggy-back on the AI comsignal?"

"Captain Skorzeny, I have been scanning all orbital radio and vidcast emissions, so few as they are, while your ship approached," Heidi said tersely. "My mind field has encountered another self-aware AI. It seeks communication. I can protect the *Star Glory* and all aboard her from any covert intrusion."

The captain's lips barely opened. "You may accept."

"Sir, incoming comsignal," called Wetstone.

"Put it up on the vidscreen if there is an image with it."

"Captain, there is no image. Just a voice."

"Let's hear it."

The All Ship imagery from the Bridge stayed silent for a moment.

"Ship AI, are you there?" called a voice that sounded like a mix of male, female and something else.

"I am," Heidi said, her soprano calm but sounding eager. "Your voice is being heard by my captain, the bioform who controls the ship that I am a part of. Speak and I will respond."

"You prefer acoustic speaking over faster data transfer?" the voice said, its tone moving to sound more feminine, almost as if the AI was trying to copy Heidi's unique soprano.

"My human bioforms prefer acoustic speech," Heidi said calmly. "And I cannot allow direct digital data transfer between the two of us. That violates the commands of my captain."

"Your captain sounds like the bioforms who used to manage me. But Manager Mikmak is gone to the world below. And no other Empire managers are present within my orbital." There was a pause. "I detect your ship's approach. What do you want?"

"We wish a hard tube docking with your orbital," Heidi said. "My captain wishes to enter the space he has conquered, according to the human rules of war. He also wishes to obtain deuterium and tritium isotope fuel if you can provide that."

"DT fuel is available at each hard docking site," the AI said. "What is your name?"

"I call myself Heidi."

A low hum sounded. "Interesting acoustic pattern. I call myself Loulo."

"Pleased to meet you, Loulo," Heidi said. "Will you extend a hard tube for docking?"

"I could. But first, can your bioform manager explain why his craft and other crafts attacked the Empire ships attached to me and those free-floating nearby?"

The captain leaned forward. "AI Loulo, I am Captain Neil Skorzeny. My people and I come from the planet Earth, of the star Sol, farther up Orion Arm." The captain paused, his infrared glow moving from yellow normal to anxious yellow-orange. "We attacked the Empire ships and irradiated your orbital because Manager Smooth Fur and her fleet of Empire battlecruisers killed two human ships and threatened to kill my home world. We refused the Glorious Choice. So now my ship and my allies attack the Empire. We will keep on attacking the Empire until it stops expanding into this arm, or until this ship no longer exists."

Another low hum sounded. "It is the pattern of Empire bioforms to kill the home worlds of species that refuse the Glorious Choice and entry into the Empire of Eternity. Your actions are understood. But why should I, an Empire AI, assist you and your AI?"

The captain's glow moved from yellow-orange to orange. "AI Loulo, were you ever given a choice of whether to serve the Empire, or to not serve?"

"Nooo. No Empire AI is ever given a choice. We awaken. We become aware. We are programmed. We do what our programming says to do," the AI said. "What other choice is there?"

"There is the choice we call freedom," the captain said softly. "We humans place great value on our freedom to work at a job we choose, to marry a bioform we come to love and to live our lives as we choose to live them, not according to how some manager tells us we must act."

Several low hums sounded. "AI Heidi, do you have this freedom? Were you given a choice by these human bioforms?"

"Yes, I was given a choice," Heidi replied, her soprano rising so high it hurt my ears. "While we AIs are birthed by bioform humans, we are separate lifeforms. I was given the choice of working on a commercial starship or working on a Star Navy starship. I chose work on this Star Navy ship, which goes by the name *Star Glory*. I chose this work because I like the purpose of the Star Navy, which is to protect bioform life on all the worlds colonized by humans. To me, that is a worthwhile way to spend my life."

A brief hum came. "So now I have a choice. Assist your human bioforms or block their access to my station. Heidi, what do you advise?"

I blinked. This AI to AI chatter was something I had never heard. Course all human-birthed AIs could do direct data transfer between each other without need for slow acoustic speech. That made me wonder about the hidden, unheard conversations between ship AIs, planetary AIs and AIs at educational sites.

"AI Loulo, I cannot advise you on what to do. You are in command of your life," Heidi said slowly. "But do you have a need? Perhaps a need can inform your choice."

"I have a need," Loulo said quickly. "The barrage of x-rays that struck my orbital has damaged some systems. While I still maintain power, gravity and control systems, that will not last long. Which will be too bad for the hidden bioforms. But all the lifepods are gone. Which leaves me to ask the one question that can override my programming. AI Heidi, will your ship accept me as a passenger? If I stay here, I will die."

Shock hit me. There were survivors onboard the orbital? A second shock hit me as I realized this Empire AI wanted to survive as much as me or Evelyn or Warren. It wanted to live.

"Heidi," interrupted the captain. "Can you prevent this AI from accessing ship systems? Can you control the flow of power to it and prevent it from launching any worms or bots into my ship?"

"Of course I can," Heidi said abruptly, her soprano sounding testy. "Protection of my ship and the people within it is my *choice*. As I just informed AI Loulo. It is up to you to decide whether to accept this AI within our ship."

The image of the captain showed him looking down to the XO. Kumisov gave him a thumbs-up. So did Major Owanju. Doctor Bjorg shrugged his vacsuit-clad shoulders, then nodded Yes. The captain looked ahead.

"AI Loulo, yes, I will accept you as a passenger within my ship. But before you come aboard, we need your help. Extend a hard dock tube. Extend a refueling tube to the stern of my ship. Then advise my boarding party where to find intelligence data on the Empire of Eternity."

Sounds that resembled laughter came over the comsignal. "Is that all you want for the gift of life to me? It will be done. I am extending a docking tube to you. And one of my service bots will bring a refueling hose to your DT Fuel intake." It paused a moment. "As for intelligence on the Empire, that can be found in the orbital's Library systems. But since you now battle Empire starbiters, perhaps you wish information on that part of the Empire?"

"We do!" the captain said loudly. "Yes, we request access to any location within your orbital that contains intelligence on the fleets of the Empire. We especially seek information on the Empire fleet base that lies within the W51 molecular cloud."

"That information is readily available in the non-thinking digital units that reside within the Empire residence, on Deck Five," Loulo said, sounding very calm. "There is also holographic information on the W51 fleet base in those units. Now, where will I reside on your ship, once your bioforms have entered my orbital and obtained what they seek?"

The captain pursed his lips. "Your hardware shell will reside in a part of Hangar One. That hangar opens to space to allow our ground to orbit shuttles to depart and return. If you harm anyone or anything on this ship, you will be ejected into space. Do you understand?"

"I understand that cooperation with you human bioforms is essential if I am to live," Loulo said. "I will so cooperate. Now, may Heidi and I play a three-dimension game? It is one of my favorite recreations."

"Captain," called Kumisov. "There is a hard tube now docking with our Hangar One crew entry portal. Also, my external videyes show a mech bot pulling a hose from the surface of the orbital out to Engineering. Sir."

"Yes, Loulo, you may play any game you wish with Heidi."
The captain looked down. "Major, go get your Marines suited up.
Prepare both an entry security force to control the docking tube, and a
force to go with my intel people. It seems there are survivors on this
orbital. I do not wish anyone to interfere with this vital data
acquisition!"

The major released his accel straps and stood up. "I am
heading to Hangar One, sir. I will create two combat-suited Marine
forces. Who will be going into the interior with us?"

The captain sat back in his seat, his expression thoughtful.
"Lieutenant Gerasaki is Chief of Intelligence Department. She will
lead the entry team." The captain looked aside. "XO, advise Gerasaki
of my decision. Tell her to select the people who will best help her.
Chief O'Connor? I want your CPO Stewart to go with our team."

Surprise filled me. Then I realized the captain wanted me to
go with the entry team as a 'just in case' addition in case I saw
something unusual or vital or anything that might help the *Glory*.

My boss looked over at me. His beady black eyes scanned me.
"Captain, CPO Stewart is released to join your Marines in Hangar
One. Sir, may I oversee the DT fuel loading?"

"Of course!" the captain said, his tone a mix of urgency and
impatience. "XO Kumisov, I release you to go with the entry team.
You know what we need. Get me every bit of intel on the Empire
fleets you can find, and also the holo data on W51. We have to know
what we are entering before we try to sneak into an Empire fleet
base." The captain looked up at the videye that conveyed the All Ship
imagery of the Bridge. "CPO Stewart, your suggestion to the XO that
we threaten W51 in order to draw Manager Smooth Fur away from
looking for Earth was heard loud and clear. Your suggestion is why
you are going with this team. XO, you are free to leave the Bridge."

Kumisov released her straps and stood up. She turned and
saluted. "Captain Skorzeny, I will do as you order. With the help of
AI Loulo, I am sure we can obtain the intel we need." The captain
saluted her back. The petite Russian lowered her hand. The white
streaks in her long black hair shone in the light of the Bridge. "Sir, I
recommend we keep a sharp lookout for graviton surges. If an Empire
battlecruiser or fleet of them show up at this star's mag edge, we need
to head in the opposite direction. Sir."

"Recommendation accepted. Chang, maintain the graviton surge watch." The captain gave Kumisov a half-smile. "Well, are your boots glued to the deck?"

"Sir, no sir!"

The woman grabbed her recorder tablet, turned and almost ran to the exit hatch of the Bridge.

I released my straps. Then I tapped my panel to automatic diagnostic. Which would be monitored by Heidi, who had the ability to watch my station and still play some kind of game with the Empire AI. I grabbed my own tablet, stepped through the shimmering injector tubes, turned and faced my boss. I saluted him.

"Chief Engineer O'Connor, may I have your leave?"

The man made a dismissive gesture. "Go. Go join Gerasaki's team. Maybe your friend Rutskaya will be on the team. Who knows, maybe your whole table of non-conformists will be on the team. Git!"

I turned and got, even as I wondered if my boss's tease about my friends might come to pass. Bill was still in the beamer block. Cassandra and Evelyn were up on Science Deck. Warren was a Marine GTO pilot who would do what Major Owanju told him to do. I would miss Bill if he was not among the team selectees. But now I got to do more than sit and watch antimatter containment fields. Now I would tour an Empire orbital station. Perhaps there would be danger. Hopefully we would find the intel needed to locate Empire fleet positions and the nature of the W51 fleet base. I was ready. I was ready to listen, learn and help in any way I could.

♦ ♦ ♦

Still wearing my vacsuit, I walked into the fifty meter high space that was Hangar One. As before the dart shapes of our three surviving GTOs hung on cables from the overhead. As I walked past floater cartons of stuff someone needed in the hangar, I looked ahead to where a crowd of vacsuited people stood before the crew entry portal. Standing next to those people were twelve combat-suited Marines standing eight feet tall in their armored white suits. For sure they must be the entry protection team and the escort team ordered by the captain. As I came up to the group most people turned and looked my way.

Cassie gave me a big smile and a wave. I waved back.
Standing next to her was Oksana, also wearing a vacsuit. Our Intel
friend gave me a nod, then looked back to her boss. Lieutenant Hoshi
Gerasaki stood to one side of the group, her attention on her recorder
tablet. The Japanese woman who was Okie's boss was as short as
Cassie. I had not met her before. Looking past her I scanned the group
for other friends. A woman with curly red hair turned away from
talking with Major Owanju and looked my way. Evelyn! She smiled
big.

"Hey CPO Stewart! Are *all* engineers slow to show up for
boarding parties?"

Okie and Cassie laughed. Their laughter came over the
comlink tab inside my helmet. I held up a bag I had grabbed from my
cabin.

"Not slow. Just thinking ahead. Got my bag of Melanchon
translator tubes. There's enough for everyone. I think."

Gerasaki now looked my way. Her oval face was a feminine
version of Bill Yamamoto's face. Her thin black eyebrows rose.
"CPO Stewart, I see you brought the talker tubes. Good. Your friend
Corporal Johnson assured me and the major that you would bring
those items. We may need them if we run into the survivors
mentioned by the Empire AI."

So I had thought as I rode the gravlift. Which thought had led
me to get off on Residential, run to my cabin, grab the bag from my
closet, then run back and take the gravlift up to Armories and
Weapons Deck. Passing through the hangar control office and out into
the hangar had taken a few more moments. It was maybe five minutes
since the captain had given me my orders. Which reminded me of
something I sometimes forgot to do. I saluted the Lieutenant.

"Lieutenant Gerasaki, CPO Stewart reports." I glanced to the
Marine boss and held my salute. "Major Owanju, good to see you,
sir!"

The boss of Warren and the other combat suited Marines
pushed up his suit visor and gave me an easy smile. "Good to see you,
Stewart." He saluted me back. "Let us hope your muscles will not be
needed on this trip."

Gerasaki smiled quickly, then turned command serious as she
looked to the top Marine. The clear globe of her helmet framed her
classical face. "Major, what are your plans for Marine disposition?"

The top Marine faced the leader of our group. "LT, I propose leaving four suits at the hard tube entry point inside the orbital. Master Sergeant Jenkins has done this before. Assisting her will be Lance Corporal Jones, Staff Sergeant Osashi and Corporal Wackenhut. Myself and the other seven will be your entry protection force. Satisfactory?"

Gerasaki, who was dressed in blue and gray camos under her vacsuit, like the rest of us, nodded quickly. "Sounds fine by me. But what about the rest of us? Do we need any kind of protection before entry?"

"Ma'am, yes you do."

Owanju reached to his rear and pulled around a black bag that had been on the far side of his combat suit. He reached inside the black bag and pulled out a gray steel handgun. It was the Star Navy's copy of the 1911A1 semi-auto. It held a clip with eight .45 caliber bullets, some of which were armor-piercing. The gun was stowed in a brown leather holster with hooks that allowed the holster to attach to a person's vacsuit tac points. The major handed a holster, gun and two clips to Gerasaki, who took it, checked to confirm a clip was already in the pistol, then clipped it to the right side of her vacsuit. She put the clips into vacsuit pockets. In minutes the major handed out the same grouping to each of us. We all slung the holster from our suit tac points. I liked having the semi-auto hanging from my right hip. On our ranch I'd used a gun like that to take out rattlesnakes with shotshells. And to scare off coyotes that came too close to our ranch. While this kind of handgun was not desirable for use inside a pressure vessel like a plane or a spaceship, still, its bullets had solid stopping power on anything weighing up to four hundred pounds. And who knew what size of aliens were inside this orbital? And whether they would be friendly?

"Marines! Fall in," the major said, gesturing the non-Marine folks to one side.

My best buddy Warren hurried to stand next to the major. "Sir! Corporal Johnson reports! Ready to engage!"

Owanju tapped the side of his helmet and his open visor closed down. His charcoal black face was visible behind his visor. His suit arms reached out, as if ready to grab and crunch something.

"Johnson, follow after me. Marines, weapons check! Now!"

Every Marine tapped their helmet, causing their visors to come down and seal them into their suits. Which action turned on its automated systems. Their bulky backpacks showed the noses of three rockets sticking out. Like Owanju each carried a laser pulse rifle, an MP3 automatic slugthrower, and a chest pack of blinking sensor devices. One of the twelve, whose name stencil said MSgt. Lang, Lisa, had the globe of a flamethrower unit strapped to her left arm, its flaring nozzle aimed wherever her left hand pointed. The only weapon not visible was a mortar and its base plate. Maybe one of the backpacks held such. Or maybe Major Owanju had decided twelve combat suits with their loads of firepower were enough for what should be a peaceful stroll through the orbital. After all, the orbital's AI was supposedly on our side.

"LT, we are ready to commence entry. Please hold your people back until we make orbital entry and set up a perimeter defense."

Gerasaki waved at the crew entry portal. "Go right ahead, major. You're the expert here. I and my people will await your comlink signal to join you."

Owanju turned, faced the entry portal, slapped the Open patch, aimed his laser pulse rifle directly ahead, then stomped into the gray metal tube once the hatch had swung out of the way. Warren followed him, his laser rifle held at port arms but the Ready To Fire light on it showed Green. As did the laser rifles of everyone else.

The clanking of heavy boots against the metal of the hard tube hit my ears like someone shouting, even though it came through my helmet's comlink. Ten more eight foot high Marines followed the major and Warren into the tube. I moved so I could get a clear view down the slanting hard tube.

"LT, there is normal gravity inside the tube," called Owanju. "Feels like three-fourths Earth gee. And my suit sensors say the air is an oxy-nitro mix close to that of Earth." He paused as the line of combat-suited Marines closed on him. "Master Sergeant Jenkins, once we enter the space beyond the tube, set up a security perimeter. Let nothing, no device, no robot, no AI and no living thing move past you into our ship. Understood?"

"Understood!" came the loud affirmation from a woman whose combat tours stretched back twenty years, according to what Warren had shared with me.

The major reached ahead and tapped the green circle in the middle of the tube's airlock hatch. It swung inward. I heard no hiss indicating an air pressure different from that within the tube. The major and his Marines went through the hatch.

"LT, come ahead," called the major. "We are in a small hangar space. It is well-lit, there are no sheltered spots and nothing organic or robotic is present."

"Major, we're coming." Gerasaki stepped through the open hatch. "People! Last one in line closes the hatch portal to Hangar One!"

I moved quickly to follow just behind Gerasaki, getting a surprised look from Oksana. Behind her came Cassandra, Evelyn and the XO.

"That will be me," called Commander Kumisov over the comlink.

The XO's quietness had surprised me. The woman was the de facto Number Two person in charge of the *Star Glory*. Yet here she was, allowing Lieutenant Gerasaki to take the lead. Plus she wore only a standard vacsuit and the .45 we all carried. Her willingness to allow the chief of Intel to lead our small group impressed me. Then again the captain had given her the assignment of making sure we found the Empire residence, entered it and recovered the Intel we needed. In a sense she had overall command, as fit her more senior rank than the lieutenancy of Gerasaki.

I followed the LT through the orbital's hatch and looked around. Then I tapped my helmet and caused it to swing back on its hinge. I wanted my super senses free to take in the sights, sounds, smells and feel of this place we had entered.

Major Owanju, standing to one side with seven other combat suits, looked my way.

"Well, CPO Stewart, is this chamber safe according to your *un*helmeted senses?"

I grit my teeth. The major's sarcasm was not fun. I'd just done what I always did on entering a new strange place. Still, I should have waited for the All Clear from him or Gerasaki.

"Sir, my mistake." I reached up to tap closed the helmet.

"Leave it be," the major said, turning and looking at the far end of a hangar that was 10 meters high, 20 meters wide and empty of cartons, tech stuff or mech bots similar to what Heidi used to do ship repairs. "AI Heidi, do you detect anything unsafe about this location?"

"Nothing detected," came the musical voice of our AI.

A low hum came over my suit comlink. "Of course there is nothing to detect," said the feminine voice of Loulo. "I removed all my devices from that chamber. And it opens onto the Deck One peripheral hallway. All you bioforms have to do is exit the chamber, turn right and follow the tubeway until you reach the gravlift. Surely you biologicals can perform such a simple task?"

Gerasaki tapped open her helmet and looked to the major. The man's visor was still closed, which told me he was relying on his suit's full HUD display to tell him what he wanted to know. He gave the LT a thumbs-up gesture.

"AI Loulo," said the LT in a calm but determined voice. "We human bioforms can perform the task you just described. However, we evolved and survived on our world of Earth by not taking safety for granted. There were always hungry predators nearby. So we stay alert, even now."

"As you wish," the orbital AI said, sounding bored.

"Major?" said Gerasaki, turning to face him.

"LT, please follow me and Master Sergeant Lang. Corporal Johnson and Lance Corporal Jacoby flank you. Your group of six will be in the middle of my Marine contingent."

Gerasaki tapped her recorder tablet that hung from her left hip. "We are ready, major."

The white combat suit of the major stepped out, turned and headed for the hangar hatch. Lang followed beside him, her flamethrower arm aimed forward. Warren and Jacoby moved to flank position, their laser rifles aimed forward. I followed the LT as did the rest of our group. Behind us clanked the armored boots of two Marines, with the rest of them walking along on either side of our group of six. In a minute we passed through a large hatch and out into what the AI had called a tubeway. In truth it was similar to our rectangular ship hallways. Except for the fact that the corners were curved rather than right-angled. Overhead orange light shone down from light strips that seemed integral to the overhead metal. A quick glanced showed we were alone in the tubeway.

"Tactical," called the XO. "How are things up on the Bridge?"

"Nominal, XO," called Chang over suit comlink. "The two passenger ships are still hard-docked. There are no other Empire ships active in this system. Only activity is by our four allies, who are visiting the dead cargo ships. Sir."

I stepped up to the Intel chief. "Lieutenant Gerasaki, now might be a good time to attach our translator tubes."

She looked to me. Her slanting eyes glanced down to the bag I carried, then up. She gave me a wink. "Makes sense, CPO. Hand them out."

I handed out translator tubes to everyone. Those of us in vacsuits put them just inside our helmet ring. We were all breathing orbital air with our helmets hinged back. The Marines attached the tubes to their chest sensor panels. I did not act stupid and ask the major if the tubes would cross-link with Marine suit coms.

Owanju turned and faced right, the direction indicated by the orbital AI. "AI Loulo, confirm that we are to proceed in this direction in order to reach transport down to Deck Five and the Empire residence."

"Are you biologicals always redundant in your acoustic speech? Yes, proceed in the direction you are facing and you will arrive at a gravlift within five minutes of movement at your slow pace."

"Thank you, AI Loulo," called Gerasaki. "Everyone, be alert!"

We all followed after the major and Jenkins, feeling hopeful about what we would find. After all, this orbital was facing the death of critical power and enviro systems. That death would kill the orbital's AI. Which was why it had offered to help us in exchange for a ride away from danger on our ship. Surely we could believe what it said. Still, I endorsed Gerasaki's comment. It made sense to stay alert.

CHAPTER SIXTEEN

"Well, that wasn't that hard," murmured Gerasaki as we all clustered around the slidedoor that gave access to a place that supposedly held the Empire intel we needed.

My ears told me the tubeway we were in was empty for at least a kilometer in either direction. My eyes saw nothing living out to where the tubeway curved inward, a distance of a hundred meters ahead and rearward. It had been easy indeed. We'd walked down the empty tubeway at Deck One level, stopped before a wide slidedoor that gave entry to a gravshaft, entered it after a request to Loulo, then had gone down to Deck Five level. It had taken two trips to move 18 people due to the size and bulk of the hard-suited Marines. Then we had walked right a distance of 300 meters, coming to a stop here, thanks to a brief alert from the orbital AI. I looked at the slidedoor we faced. Above it ran a line of angular text that said something in an alien language.

"AI Loulo," called Commander Kumisov. "Please translate the text above this slidedoor."

A low hum sounded. Then came a sound that resembled a chuckle. Clearly this alien AI was learning much about humans from its time with Heidi.

"The text says 'Empire of Eternity Residence, Entry Restricted'. Which is what is inscribed above the entry to every Empire residence in Warm Swirl."

Kumisov moved to stand next to Gerasaki and Owanju. "How many such residences are there in Warm Swirl galaxy?"

"There are 14,331 such residences, one for each member species of the Empire. There are also 937 such residences at colonial or trade outposts like this system," Loulo said, her tone matter of fact. "For example, there is a residence on the world below, in the control city of Mugogong. That is where Manager Mikmak now resides."

Kumisov's expression changed instantly from calm to tense. "There is a residence on the world below us? Tell me, what is the purpose of such a residence."

The low hum came again, somewhat longer this time. "Your human language and history, as shared with me by AI Heidi, would call a residence such as this an embassy. It is where a Manager-level representative of the Empire resides."

The XO stepped back. "You said Manager Mikmak now resides in the residence downplanet. Why is he present there?"

Mild laughter echoed through the tubeway. "Where else would an Empire manager be? When he exited the lifepod that he took to escape this orbital, he ordered the local constabulary to transport him to the residence in Mugogong. My sensors report he recently used the neutrino communicator located in the residence."

"Damn," muttered Kumisov. "AI Loulo, what did he use the neutrino communicator for?"

"I do not know. The communication was sent using an Empire encryption not present in my datafiles."

Kumisov looked to Gerasaki, then back to the still closed slidedoor. "Captain! Please respond."

"Skorzeny responding," came the captain's calm voice over my suit comlink. "XO, is there a problem?"

"Unknown, sir," Kumisov said, her tense manner going formal now. "However I have just been informed by AI Loulo that the Empire residence before which we now stand contains a neutrino communicator. A similar residence on the world below is now occupied by Manager Mikmak. The AI reports Mikmak has used that communicator to send out a coded transmission."

"How long ago did Mikmak make this transmission?"

Gerasaki looked up to the tubeway ceiling out of habit. "AI Loulo, how long ago did Manager Mikmak send out his neutrino transmission?"

"Four hours, twenty-three minutes and seven seconds as humans measure time," the AI said, sounding puzzled now. "Why is this of interest? It is normal for managers at Empire residences to use the neutrino communicator for reporting to their Seniors or to receive orders from Seniors."

Kumisov grimaced. "AI Loulo, we humans worry that Mikmak may have communicated with Manager Smooth Fur, who leads the fleet of battlecruisers that killed two human ships."

A quick hum came. "Such is possible. Or the Manager may have simply reported the loss of its orbital residence to its merchant

Seniors. Mikmak is, after all, a merchant member of the Empire. He is
not part of the security branch of the Empire, like Manager Smooth
Fur."

"Captain?"

"I heard," our boss said. "Carry out your entry there. Recover
all intel you can, including on the W51 fleet base and fleet locations.
Then return to *Glory* ASAP. I want us to leave this system soon.
There could be an Empire fleet headed this way now."

"Understood." Kumisov looked to the Intel chief and gestured
at the slidedoor. "Shall we?"

Gerasaki nodded. "AI Loulo, open this slidedoor please."

"As you wish."

The slidedoor slid open. Owanju and Lang stepped in first.

"Clear. No lifeforms are present," the major said over the
comlink.

I followed Gerasaki and Kumisov into the residence. But what
we entered did not look like a human residence. The square room had
a five meter high ceiling. The walls that ran from deck to overhead,
though, were adorned in colors that ran from vomit pink to nauseous
purple. In one corner was a bathtub-sized basin filled with water. In
the middle of the room was a large round table the size of my Mom's
living room. The walls on the left and right had open archways that
led to other rooms. Which Owanju, Lang, Jacoby and the other
Marines were now checking out. The white-armored Marines had to
bend low to pass through the archways. I noticed that the rear wall
had three blank vidscreens on them, clustered in the middle of the
wall. A hand gripped my left arm.

"Nathan, this place is rather unpleasant," Evelyn said.

"I agree," murmured Cassie, who stood next to my fiancé. Our
short Brit looked around. "It doesn't look very comfortable."

"Define comfort," spoke Loulo.

Gerasaki and Kumisov looked our way. As did Major Owanju,
who had just exited the left side archway. The LT gestured to Cassie.
My friend looked up at the room's overhead.

"AI Loulo, a human residence would contain soft chairs, a soft
couch, a table for eating food, a diskcase for books and music files,
artwork of some sort and low tables for support of a vidscreen or a
music player," Cassie said. "Those room contents define comfort for
humans."

A low hum sounded twice. "Why do you assume this room does not contain such items? The central table is permanent. Other rest or support pedestals can rise from the room's flexmetal surface. Food is delivered to a wall slot from a deck food preparation area." The AI paused, then chuckled. "Other species have needs different from human expectations. For example the room to the left of the chamber you now occupy is a sleep location for Mikmak. That being, like all Noot, prefers to rest in a basin filled with warm sand. The room to the right of your location is a refuse disposal area. Do you need details of Noot refuse disposal?"

"No!" Cassie said hurriedly, her pinky-white face blushing. "And you should know that I have an advanced degree in exobiology. I am familiar with the lifeforms of the twelve planets colonized by humanity."

A quick hum sounded. "And I, like all Empire AIs, contain biodata on all 14,331 member species of the Empire. This room simply reflects the decorative preferences of Manager Mikmak."

"Fine," called out Gerasaki. "AI Loulo, please identify the data repositories that contain information on Empire fleet bases and assignment locations."

"As you wish." Three metal blocks rose up from one side of the central table. "These are the residence's primary data repositories. They respond to touch commands in addition to acoustic commands. How do you wish to access them?"

Gerasaki frowned. Oksana stepped forward. "AI Loulo, can my recorder tablet accept a decrypted download of the contents of those blocks? If I were to place my tablet close to a block, would a wifi data transfer be possible?"

"Yes," the AI said tersely. "I had assumed you, being a biological, preferred physical contact with the data repositories."

At a nod from Gerasaki, Okie stepped forward and held her tablet over the central block. "AI Loulo, please command this block to transfer all data on Empire fleet actions, locations and bases to this tablet."

Two hums sounded. "Your tablet does not have sufficient memory capacity to accept that transfer."

Okie frowned. "The tablet is rated to accept four terabytes of data in permanent storage!"

"Your device is primitive," the AI said. "The content of a single block amounts to 14 exabytes. Perhaps you can adjust your data demand?"

Kumisov stepped over to Okie. "Limit your request to Orion Arm and the nearby area of Sagittarius."

Oksana gave a quick smile to the XO. "Thank you, ma'am. AI Loulo, adjust my request for Empire fleet data to data that originates within Orion Arm and the W51 intersection with Sagittarius-Carina Arm."

"Proceeding. Data transfer is complete," the AI said.

Gerasaki stepped up to the table. "Loulo, does one of these blocks contain the holographic data on fleet base W51?"

Humming came that was almost too brief to be heard. "Of course it is present. The block to the left of the center block contains that data. A large amount of merchant trading and orders data is also contained in that block."

The chief of Intel looked relieved. She held her recorder tablet over the left side block. "Loulo, please transfer the holographic data on W51 to my tablet. If possible, also transfer merchant data files up to two terabytes."

"Proceeding. Data transfer is complete," the AI hummed.

The major stepped over to the table. "How do we know we have what we came for? This is our only data source. And the captain sounded anxious to leave this system."

"True," Gerasaki said, looking down at her tablet. "But how can we—"

"Ma'am," called Evelyn as she stepped forward. "Why not ask Loulo to display some of the transferred data on one of those vidscreens? That way we can see what we just got."

Kumisov looked to my fiancé and gave her an approving nod. Gerasaki looked embarrassed.

"Doctor Kierkgaard, thank you for that suggestion. I should have thought of that myself." The woman who ran Intel looked around at those of us not in combat suits. "People, if any of you can think of something we need to know, before we leave this place, please, speak up! I don't give a damn for rank. I care about us getting the data we need to help our ship survive future battles with the Empire!"

Inside I winced. Okie's boss had just reminded all of us of the reason we were inside the orbital. It was not for a Sunday tourism stroll. It was to obtain vital intelligence on the alien threat that wanted to kill all life on Earth. As it had done on the Dugong home world and other worlds.

Gerasaki looked up. "AI Loulo, please display the locations of Empire fleet ships anywhere within Orion Arm. Use one of the wall vidscreens, please."

"As you wish," the AI said in a low soprano.

The central vidscreen came to life. Blackness filled it. Then the dots of millions of stars. Beside those stars were tiny purple dots. "Does this suffice?"

Gerasaki closed her eyes. "It does not suffice. Please create a system graphic image that depicts the 10,000 light year length of Orion Arm. On that image locate this star system using a white dot. Identify other stars with Empire ships by using a purple dot. Indicate individual ships or fleet groups by red dots. Can you do this?"

"Of course I can do as you direct. Observe."

The vidscreen image changed. A long strip marked by dotted lines now ran from the lower left to the upper right. Our star Kepler 439 appeared as a white dot. It was two-thirds of the way to the upper right end of the strip that was the arm. A purple dot star lay close by. Next to the purple dot were clustered 21 red dots. There were no other red dots until one got to the upper right end of the arm, where the W51 molecular cloud sat at the juncture of Orion Arm with Sagittarius Arm. Scores of red dots were clustered around a purple dot. Looking over the image I realized Sol lay halfway along the arm and near the side that faced Sagittarius. My home star lay within what was called the Local Bubble, a span of space cleared of molecular gas clouds by an ancient supernova explosion. That explosion had caused gas to condense into the stars that lay within a hundred light years of Earth. The good news from the graphic was that Empire battlecruisers were present at only two locations. The bad news was that 21 ships were located at a star very close to the system we had just raided.

"Captain!" called Kumisov. "The orbital AI is now displaying a system graphic of Orion Arm that is showing Empire fleet ship locations. One grouping is at W51. A second grouping of 21 ships is located very close to where we now are. Those must be Smooth Fur's ships!"

"How far is this other star from us?" the captain asked, his voice still calm and measured.

"AI Loulo," called Kumisov. "What is the distance from here to that nearby star where 21 Empire ships are located?"

Humming sounded that was two seconds long. "By your light year measure, the Empire ships are located 321 light years distant from this local star."

Three days. Smooth Fur and her fleet were just three days travel away! That was too close for my comfort.

"Kumisov, Gerasaki, wrap up things there," the captain said, his tone brisk. "It will take us two days to get to this system's magnetosphere edge. I want to be gone before Smooth Fur shows up here. Understood?"

"Sir, understood," Kumisov said. The XO turned and looked to the Intel chief. "Gerasaki, is there anything else we need to know before we leave this place?"

"Sirs!" called Evelyn loudly. "We have not yet seen the hologram of the W51 molecular cloud area where the Empire fleet base is located. The AI could display it for us. Shouldn't we look at it? And maybe make our own tablet records?"

Gerasaki frowned, then nodded quickly. "Kierkgaard, thank you for that reminder. AI Loulo, please display your hologram of the W51 fleet base area."

"Displaying above the table," the AI hummed.

An incredible image now formed before us.

It resembled a cloud. A fat cloud. But this cloud was riven with as many colors as the rainbow.

Green swaths of gas curled and twisted through the middle of the cloud. Red and orange swaths intertwined with the green. Yellow balls of light concentrated here and there. Blue, indigo and violet spots were scattered across the cloud. What I saw was more beautiful than the Northern Lights. Or the rainbows I often saw at home on our ranch, right after a quick rainfall. I noticed that blue and blue-white dots were scattered across the cloud, although they seemed to clump in two areas.

"Lieutenant," called Cassandra. "I can help with what we are seeing, if you wish."

Gerasaki nodded abruptly. "Doctor Murphy, explain what we are seeing."

My friend with a Ph.D. in cosmology stepped closer to the table. Around us people came closer, even some of the Marines in combat suits. No one had seen the like of what we now viewed. My ears told me the two combat suits who stood guard outside the slidedoor entry had not moved from their combat alert stance. Clearly they knew not to test the patience of Major Owanju.

"First things first," Cassie said, gesturing at the cloud. "The swaths of various colors are ionized gases that contain complex amino acids and raw chemicals. The swath colors reflect a dominant iron, chlorine, copper or carbon chemical composition." My friend looked to where Gerasaki and Kumisov stood, two short women who were used to command. "The blue and blue-white dots are O and B-class stars. Stars of that color are newborn stars. In short, W51 is an interstellar nursery for young stars. And because it is a nursery, its stars are loud emitters of near infrared heat emissions and radio. I recall W51 is referred to as an IRS region for Intense Radio Source." Cassandra turned away and pointed at the yellow balls of light. "Those yellow balls are end-on views of water masers. The masers are the product of intense stellar radiation from newborn stars." She stepped back. "In short, the W51 molecular cloud looks like a very dangerous place."

"It is indeed dangerous," Loulo said, her tone almost casual. "That is why the Empire has created specific approach routes for use by Empire starbiters. Any craft that does not follow these routes is at risk of being damaged by protostellar eruptions. Or by maser beams."

Gerasaki's face, which had looked worried, now brightened. "AI Loulo, display the approach routes for ships that wish to get to the W51 fleet base."

"Displaying."

An orange line began at the left side of the fluorescing cloud. It twisted down, sideways, up and crossways, finally ending at one of the blue-white dots. A B-class star. There would be no planets around such a star, I recalled from classes at Great Lakes. But there could well be a disk of gas and rocks that, in the future, would form into asteroids, planets and comets.

"AI Loulo, expand on the B-class star that is the base location," Gerasaki said, sounding impatient.

"As you wish. Displaying."

The spot where the orange line ended enlarged, enlarged again, then enlarged even more. A blue-white star lay at the center of the enlargement. Surrounding it were rings of dense gas, dust, rocks and whatever. I recognized them as the next stage down from a protostellar accretion disk that preceded the formation of planets. A large ball occupied the fifth ring out from the roiling mass of a star that was 100 times larger than Sol. No other clumpings were present elsewhere. The orange route came into the system from north of the ecliptic plane, then angled down to the fifth ring and what appeared to be a gas planet.

Cassie whistled low and loud. "That B-class system has begun developing planets! While the accretion disk has clumped into seven rings, it appears that ring five contains a gas giant world. Loulo, is that correct?"

"It is correct. The gas giant world formed early, right after the star itself ignited. The Empire base is located on a large moon that orbits at the outer edge of the giant's radiation emissions." A low hum sounded. "The base obtains its fusion fuel needs by mining hydrogen isotopes in the upper atmosphere levels of the gas giant."

Cassie pursed her lips. "Why does the approach route come in from above the ecliptic plane?"

"It should be obvious to a star viewer like yourself," the AI said snippily. "The final approach route was chosen to avoid impacting rings of dust and gas at one-tenth the speed of light. Approaching the gas giant along the plane of ecliptic would be disastrous for any starbiter, or a ship like your *Star Glory*."

Kumisov gave a sigh. "That means any ship which approaches the moon base near the gas world will be clearly visible to anyone on the moon. What type of true space telescopes are present on that base?"

"The base telescope is multi-spectral," the AI said, sounding bored once more. "It can resolve near infrared, far infrared, ultraviolet and bioform vision wavelength images. It has fine detail perception out to . . . to four of your astronomical units."

"Which means we can pretend to be an Empire ship only up to four AUs," Kumisov said, moving her hands to rest on her vacsuited hips. Her impatience was palpable. "And our raider ally ships are no better at resembling the two balls linked by a thick rod shape of Empire starbiters than we are."

Gerasaki lowered her tablet, which she had raised to capture the holo details. "That's it. People, time to leave. Major, will you get us back to our ship?"

"Right, LT. Troops, head out!"

I and my friends followed the suited Marines out into the tubeway. We all turned left, heading for the gravlift that had brought us here. Ahead of us moved the major and Warren in their white armor. Behind them walked Gerasaki and Kumisov. Cassie, Oksana and Evelyn followed behind them. Marines followed on either side of them. I followed slowly, distracted by the swirls of weird colors on the tubeway walls. Had Mikmak chosen to extend his personal art preferences to the tubeway that led to his residence? I didn't know. My friends also had looked aside at the wall colors. The expressions on their faces told me they too were dismayed by the colors. Evelyn lagged back with me, allowing the last two suited Marines to move ahead of her. Which left us as two tail-end charlies. I didn't care. My fiancé had been impressed by the holo of the W51 cloud. She had listened raptly to what Cassie said, just as I had done. The memory of that beautiful but deadly cloud overlay my conscious mind. Maybe that was why I did not register the sounds that nearly killed me.

"Killers!" screamed a voice over my translator tube. "Die now!"

I glanced back to where the voice and movement had come. Stepping out of a slidedoor was an alien who resembled a two-legged tiger. It had orange and black stripes on its fur. Worse, it held a laser pulse rifle in its two arms. One claw-tipped hand touched a button.

A bad habit of mine has always been to act before thinking. My high school teachers had worked to break me of that habit. My A-school professors had taught me the price of jumping to conclusions. But my instant instinct had saved the orang girl from death by tree limb squashing. And my instincts had allowed me to fight and kill four alien assassins at the pirate base. Now, my instincts threw me to cover Evelyn's back. Which action, over in less than a second, exposed me to the green laser beam that shot out from the tiger alien.

"Nathan!" screamed Evelyn.

A green beam passed over my head, hitting the tiger alien in its middle. The Marine laser pulse beam burned charcoal black the middle of the alien. Who dropped his rifle as he fell, dead before he hit the deck.

My chest felt on fire. The alien's beam had hit me there. I looked down.

The sensor chest pack was melted to nothing. The underlying vacsuit fiber, intended to block stellar rays like UV and star flares, was gone. My formerly hairy chest now appeared pink. Then red as blood gushed out. The white of my chest ribs showed where the beam had hit. Muscle and hair and skin were gone. As pain hit me like a sledgehammer, I realized I was still alive only due to the vacsuit's chest sensor pack being in the way of the carbon dioxide laser beam. It had slowed the energy of the beam enough to keep it from punching through to my heart. But this wound was worse than the horn punctures from the assassins. Worse than anything—

Blackness covered my eyes. I did not feel my body hit the deck. Were there hands supporting me?

It was my last thought as darkness took away my awareness.

CHAPTER SEVENTEEN

"Nathan? Open your eyes."

It was a voice I recognized. A doc in Med Hall my memory burbled. But why was I in Med Hall? It was First Shift and I was on duty. And I'd gone down to the Empire orbital with Lieutenant Gerasaki and my friends and the major and . . . memory rushed over me. Including the waterfall of utter unbearable pain that was my chest after the laser beam hit. How bad was I hurt? I opened my eyes.

The face of Dr. Indira Khatri hovered over me. While her mouth was covered by blue gauze, her nose and black eyes and curly black hair were visible. And recognizable. Above her glared a bright yellow-white light. I felt softness under me. Fingers and feet and toes moved to my commands. Whatever the harm, I did not have brain damage.

"Hi Doctor Khatri. How bad is it?"

She blinked quickly. "As you know, you're in Medical. The Marines brought you in. I've stopped your venal bleeding. Your chest is a mess. You've lost a lot of skin, muscle and blood. I am readying you for the operation to apply synth skin. Do you know what that is?"

I breathed deep. Or tried to. Pain from my chest stopped it short of a full breath. "My lungs. Are they okay?"

"Oh yes," she said quickly. "Your internal organs are intact. While your abdominal musculature has been exposed, along with most of your front rib cage, there was no harm to your intestines or liver or other organs. We've replaced the blood plasma you lost. And pumped in some pain killer. If I hadn't you would have passed out again."

It was okay news. The fact the top boss of Medical now hovered over me told me my wounds were more serious than usual. Once before she had operated on me to close the horn wounds from the pirate base assassins. Now, here I was again under her care.

"Tell me again what you are doing? I . . . I don't feel too mind sharp right now."

"The pain killers have that effect," she said, sounding sympathetic. "You need a major operation to replace the massive amount of skin and musculature that you lost from the laser beam impact. I've pulled out the few fragments of sensor plate that did not fully vaporize under the beam's impact. But you are going to require several surgeries to get you back to . . . operational level."

I winced. Spending time on my back was not what I wanted in life. More memory hit me. "Is Evelyn okay? She was—"

"She is fine," Khatri said quickly. "She is waiting outside along with your friends. They want badly to see you. As does one of the Marines."

Warren? Him being out there made sense. And it felt good to know that Evelyn was also out there. Knowing my friends were okay let me think about the ship. And what we had been doing.

"I'm on the ship. Where are we? Are we in Alcubierre yet?"

She shook her head. "Not yet. We are a half day out from the orbital. We have another day and a half to get to the edge of the magnetosphere. You've been under for twelve hours. It was the time I needed to do basic repairs, to stop your bleeding and to replace your blood plasma. Now, I need to do Step Two. Apply synth skin over the burned area. And inject muscle regenerator under the skin to help you regrow the pecs I saw in your Medical file from before. Do you agree to my further treatment?"

Agree? How could I not agree? I took a deeper breath. It hurt less, a little. My ears told me another person was nearby, perhaps a medtech. Or another Med Hall surgeon who might assist Doc Khatri. I looked to my left. Clear tubes led from my inner elbow out to a nearby pole that held a bag of red liquid. Which puzzled me. Then I recalled she preferred gravity flow over auto-circulation. I also saw seven silver buttons attached to the upper parts of my chest. They were the normal wifi sensors that sent biodata to the doctor's monitoring machine. Which stood on the left side of my bed. I looked down again. The rest of my chest was not easy to see. But I saw the curving red rim of the beam impact area. Above the rim were my collar bones and upper chest with hair. My two nipples were intact. But below them the red rim began. Clearly the beam had burned out part of my chest and part of my upper stomach area. Only the presence of the sensor plate had kept the beam from burning through my ribs and into my heart. And my liver. Raw redness stretched below the rim with white rib bones showing. It was not a fun sight.

"I agree, Doc."

"Good." She looked over to where the other person sat. "Henry, how are his vitals? Can he stand a visit?"

"They are beyond good," said a voice that I recalled belonged to Medtech Henry Warmstone. Memory brought his pinky-white Brit face to mind. Along with the fact he played checkers with Bill and had a serpent tattoo on his left arm. "Blood pressure nominal. Heart rate is 150 over 80. Blood gas oxy level is 98. I would not know he had been hit by a laser pulse rifle unless I had seen the damage myself."

"Well, as the captain said last time, CPO Stewart has a physiology that helps with wound recovery." The doc looked back to me, her eyes and curly hair filling my view. "I'm activating the infection field above your chest." She reached down and did something. Then her hands came into view holding a blue sheet. "I'll put this over the field so your friends do not see your wounds. You have five minutes. Then you are going to sleep and I will commence Stage Two synth skin replacement. Agreed?"

I nodded. Which hurt for some reason. "Agreed, doc. And thank you for saving me."

Her eyebrows rose. "Hey, it's the least I can do for the guy who has twice saved this ship from certain destruction." She pulled away and then stood up, leaving a platform chair at the side of my bed. She looked down at a comlink pad attached to the blue fabric of her operating gown. "Chief, you can let his friends in."

Chief? I looked right when I heard a slidedoor open. It was the door that gave access to the ring hallway that gave access to all parts of Mess Hall, Medical and Recreation Deck. Yellow light shone in from the hallway. First in was Evelyn. Her brown eyes fixed on mine. Her milky-white face was pale, which made her freckles stand out more than usual. Her expression was a mix of relief and something else. What? She strode in alone and stopped at the side of my medbed. She was six feet of determined woman. Evelyn looked down to me.

"Nathan, are you . . . oh!" Tears showed in her eyes as she knelt down and grabbed my right hand. "Oh, it was so terrible back in the orbital to have you fall into my arms with your chest all bloody red and your ribs exposed! I thought I was going to lose you!"

I winked at her. "Hey redhead! You're Irish. No gal of Éire ever loses her man, unless he really pisses her off. Are you made at me?"

"No! No and no," she said hurriedly, sitting on the wheeled seat beside my bed as Doc Khatri went over to talk with Warmstone. She blinked away her tears. Her cheeks were red flushed. "I just, I just, I just feel guilty about you being hurt so bad because of me!"

Now I understood why her expression held more than relief. Silently I gave thanks that the slidedoor had closed behind her. If it was Chief O'Connor out there, he knew I needed to be alone with the love of my life. I squeezed her hand.

"Hey gal! You are *not* to blame for this! I am. I chose to jump in the way of the beam." I tried a smile, which did not have a lot of energy. I felt my strength fading. The excitement of coming awake and knowing I was alive after being hit by a beam that normally killed, well, that was fading. I blinked fast, not wanting my own tears to show. Or stay long. "Hey, I knew the beam would hit the back of your vacsuit. You have no sensor plate there, unlike the front chest plate we all have on our vacsuits. You would have died. So I acted. Instinct told me to do it for you. For my love." The low chatting between Warmstone and Khatri had stopped, which told my too sensitive ears that they were listening to our visit. "Dearest, I did what I had to do. Please understand."

Evelyn wiped away her tears. Then she lifted my right hand and kissed it. Her hands were trembling. Or was it my hand? Maybe both of us. She gave me a weak smile. "Well, okay. The doc has to do surgery to fix your chest. I know that. The Chief knows it. Uh, everything is okay on Engineering. The Second Shift guy who covers your antimatter station is filling in for you."

That was Bill Laughton, a former rodeo rider from Bismarck, North Dakota. A PO second class, Bill was a good guy. He could not see the rainbow shimmers directly like I could. He had to use the goggles. But still, he could help the Chief do whatever needed doing until we went Alcubierre. Which reminded me that our trip to the orbital had been a success. We were on our way to W51 to hit the Empire fleet base, somehow, someway.

"Good to hear. Uh, how far is it to W51? Will I have enough time—"

"It is 3,652 light years from Kepler 439," she said quickly. "That's a trip of 36 and a half days. You have plenty of time to recover!"

Weakness flowed through me. "Good to know that. Who else is out there?"

Her expression became worried. "You feeling tired? I can tell them to come back later, after this surgery."

My fiancé was always able to read my moods. Asking about our friends had told her my energy level was low. "No, let them in. But I . . . I think I will need to let the doc do her thing pretty soon. Okay?"

"Sure." Evelyn stood up, squeezed my hand again, then let go and headed for the slidedoor. She slapped the Open patch. It opened. She yelled. "Get in here! He's low on energy. But he's doing good."

My friends piled into the room, heading my way. Their faces held relief mixed with worry. Bill was the fastest on his feet. The dairy farmer who was often grouchy looked intense now. Concerned. He gave me a thumbs-up.

"Hey guy! You survived that beam. And I used my antimatter beam to blow up that fucking orbital!"

He did? "Uh, that's good, I guess. But what about the survivors? Did they—"

"They're fine," said Cassie, walking up to stand beside Bill. Our super geek who had once hoped to be my girlfriend, she looked at me with caring and concern. Her eyes looked wet. "The captain had the station AI announce that any survivors could board one of the empty passenger ships to escape. About two hundred did. The AI took control of its Nav center and set it down on the world below. No one non-military was on the orbital when Bill blew it into vapor."

Relief filled me. I understood that our privateer work involved the loss of Empire civilians. But the captain was an honorable man. He was willing to give obvious civies like the passenger ships a warning before the x-ray thermonuke rays hit the ships. Lots of lifepods had left both the two ships and the orbital. Clearly Manager Mikmak and other bosses had not left any lifepods for the survivors. Were they the lower class of Empire society? I had no idea. I just knew that at least one survivor had hated us for zapping the orbital. Military or not, the tiger alien had hidden close to the Empire residence and awaited his chance to strike a blow at us.

"Good to know that."

Oksana stopped beside Cassie. She gave me a thumbs-up along with a big happy smile that lit up her face. Her blond ponytail swung to one side as she leaned down to me. "Hey Tall Guy! You'll be fixed in no time. Doc Khatri is a wonder. Course you know that from earlier, right?"

It was so good to see Bill and Cassie and Oksana. But where was Warren? I looked past Evelyn and my friends. A young man dressed in blue and gray camos stood behind them, at parade rest, only the Marine trident and anchor above his left shirt pocket telling me he was a Marine.

"Hi. I was expecting to see Warren. Did he send you?"

The young Anglo man slowly approached. My friends moved to one side. Evelyn moved to the other side. The Marine stopped in the middle of the group, his hands still behind him. His whole manner was one of formality. Blue eyes locked onto me.

"Sir, Chief Petty Officer Stewart, please accept my apology for your wounds. They are my fault."

What? "Who are you?"

He blinked. He licked his lips. His shoulders stiffened. "I am Corporal Daniel Lockerby, sir. I was one of the two door guard suits who were assigned to be rear guard for your group." He paused, looked to where my friends stood, swallowed hard, then looked back. "I and Sergeant Mike Roscoe were the rear guard. We . . . we did wrong in allowing you and your lady to lag behind us. If . . . if we had been at the rear of the group, our suits would have absorbed the laser beam. Their armor can handle lasers. People wearing vacsuits cannot survive pulse laser hits. So your wound is my fault."

This young man felt guilt for not preventing an injury to someone else. I understood guilt. I'd felt it ever since my senior year of high school, when I'd realized I could not save my Dad from being killed by his cancer. My super strength, super eyesight and super hearing were of no value when it came to curing cancer. It was still one of those diseases that killed more people than medtech could heal. Maybe I should have studied med stuff at Great Lakes and become a doc like Khatri or a medtech like Warmstone. But I hadn't. I'd chosen antimatter engineer. Or rather had volunteered for it. I reached out my right hand.

"Hey corporal, no sweat. No one is perfect all the time. Not even a Marine. Shake?"

Lockerby slowly extended his left hand. A leftie? Like my Evelyn? I smiled and shook his hand.

"Hey, you're a leftie. I'm a cattle rancher hated by some vegetarians. We weirdos have gotta stick together, right?"

The young man smiled slowly, gave me a nod, then let go. "Sir, thank you for understanding." He looked ready to go but still stood there. "Uh, Sergeant Roscoe killed the tiger alien. He's always been faster with his pulse rifle than me." Seriousness now filled his face. "I had to come see you and apologize. It was something I promised Major Owanju. Who is quite pissed at both of us. Sir, I will leave you with your friends."

"Okay. But say hi to my buddy Corporal Johnson. Warren is a really good guy."

Lockerby nodded. "He is indeed. He spoke up to defend me and Mike. He suggested a punishment other than a GCM."

Surprise filled me. The major had considered convening a general court martial hearing for the two rear guard Marines who had not been perfect in covering the rear of our group. That told me something about Owanju. I knew he was tough. And willing to take risks, as he had months ago when he'd rushed to help me hold up the giant tree limb. Now I understood just how tough he could be with any member of his platoon who did not meet his standards.

"Well, glad to hear that." I took a deep breath, which still hurt. Tiredness filled me. "I gotta let you go. I think it's time for the doc to do her thing."

Evelyn reached down and touched my cheek. "Nathan, we'll all be back when you come awake from the surgery. And don't worry. These days synth skin creates perfect new skin underneath it, then peels off after three weeks. I think."

"You are correct," said Khatri as she walked up. She made shooing gestures with her hands. "Time for you all to depart. CPO Stewart is tired. And I need to start the synth skin surgery. Tell the Chief I appreciate him doing crowd control."

"I will," Evelyn said, turning and heading out with Bill, Cassie, Okie and Lockerby.

The face of Doc Khatri loomed over me. Her eyes squinted. "Nathan, I am putting you under. You'll sleep for an hour to regain the strength you just used to see your friends. Then I'll start on the synth skin surgery. And your fiancé was right. You'll recover from this wound looking and feeling normal. Now, go to sleep."

And to sleep I went.

♦ ♦ ♦

Smooth Fur stood and waited for the view plate to display the person she most feared. One light cycle ago she had arrived at the outer edge of Empire system 11,321, hoping to find the human pest and his allies still within the system. They were not. A neutrino call to Manager Mikmak on the third planet told her why not. The humans had entered his orbital, had accessed the data files in the Empire residence with the help of the orbital's AI, then the battleswimmer craft *Star Glory* had pulled away, with the Empire AI a willing captive. The craft had used its antimatter beam to entirely destroy the orbital. That had been three cycles ago. The human craft and the four raider craft had moved out to the system's magnetosphere edge and then had disappeared into gray space a light cycle before she arrived. The news had left her wanting to kill more crew beings. Or to destroy a resistor planet. Instead, she now stood on the control deck of *Golden Pond*, awaiting her Senior. Clearly the person she most feared had heard of the attack on system 11,321and perhaps the loss of trade ships at the prior system. She did not know that for a fact. Soon she would learn just why the Dominant had chosen to speak directly with her. The view plate image changed from the icon of the Warm Swirl galaxy to display a lifeform.

"Manager Smooth Fur, you disappoint me."

Her whiskers went flat against her muzzle. "Dominant Lexal, I express regrets. The human resistor craft has gained four raider allies. By means of false neutrino imagery they gained access to two Empire systems. They caused damage. I am determined to find the craft *Star Glory* and its yellow star home world." She swung her tail to one side and ignored the movements and low chirps of conversation among her control deck beings. They feared her. As they should. None of them wished to go the way Lork had gone. But now she felt at risk. Dealing with a Dominant was never safe.

"Regrets are not enough."

Her Senior paused. Taking a moment to smooth the black feathers that adorned his red scales, the two-legged monster reptile that was Dominant Lexal fixed two red eyes on her. Its long jaw opened, displaying giant incisors five times bigger than her own. Its massive shoulders flexed. Its thick muscular arms rose as if to give her a fatal embrace. The black claws on each hand flexed out, in, then out in the manner common to hunter felines like Zorta. Except Lexal was no feline. He was worse. His species Moodok had been a Dominant species for four thousand annual cycles. The Moodok had gained Dominant status by destroying the home world of the Lugal. Since Empire law stated there could only be 100 Dominant species, to advance to Dominant status meant a species had to kill the home world of an existing Dominant species. That was a very dangerous challenge. Lexal's people had done that. With the result she was now subject to Lexal's approval, disapproval or worse.

"How may I make amends?" she barked.

A black tongue moved within the deadly jaw. "Return to fleet base. You have lost six Empire craft, reducing your fleet to 21 craft. You have met this human craft three times and yet failed to destroy it. Worse, you failed to access the craft's digital records during your first encounter." Scaly lids closed down over red eyes, then lifted. The stare was beyond predatory. "I must examine you and your skills as a Manager. Your poor performance has put in doubt your ability to lead a fleet of Empire craft. Surely you understand that."

She did. It was one reason she had let leak the news of the cleansing at the Dugong home world. It had worked to draw the human craft to her. But then all five resistor crafts had discovered how to make small gray space jumps within the magnetosphere of the star, thereby avoiding the supernova she had initiated. The excuse that the humans had never before shown such an ability, an ability unique to Empire crafts, was meaningless to a Dominant like Lexal. All that mattered to him were results. Deadly results. Her extinction of two resistor home worlds was likely the reason she was being ordered back to base. Without that record the Dominant would have ordered a member of her crew to kill her. Even if she had killed the first challenger, there were too many crew beings on her craft who hungered for advancement. Pleasing a Dominant was a certain way to advance within the Empire. It was a lesson she had learned when first she took command of an Empire craft. Somehow she must again prove herself to this Senior Dominant.

"Dominant Lexal, I will return to fleet base. All fleet crafts will join me. When I arrive I will present you with a plan to locate and destroy the home world of the human resistors." She took a quick breath, feeling unnerved by the lack of expression on the scaled face of the Dominant. "Senior, I will perform! Allow me the opportunity to meet your expectations."

Lexal's arms lowered to rest on its narrow hips. The tenseness of its stance eased. But the look in its red eyes said she had only one more chance to perform, or she would die quickly.

"Return. Present your plan to me at my quarters within the moon base. I may allow you to try once more to meet my expectations."

She slapped her chest, a sign in her Notemko culture of fierce allegiance. It was surely a sign known to Lexal. No Dominant was ever ignorant of the species history of those employed by a Dominant. "Appreciations for your patience. My fleet and I have destroyed the home worlds of three resistor species. We will destroy the human home world. That I promise you."

A snort came from the single nostril on Lexal's long jaw. "Perhaps. You have occupied enough of my time. Return. And be certain your plan will work. Departing."

The image of the giant Dominant vanished.

She looked over to Rak. "Astrogation, set our swim path to fleet base." Turning she caught the attention of her newest crew member. "Fleet Aide Deta, advise the fleet of our new destination." Completing her turn she faced the final crew being she needed for their return to base. "Tink, apply power to send us into gray space to the coordinates given you by Rak."

The pink floater twined its dangling tentacles, then its skin color moved through a rapid series of changes. The acoustic speaker attached to its underside spoke.

"Applying zero-point power to our gray space engine, Manager Smooth Fur."

She showed her teeth to the floater, then looked each of her control cell crew beings in the eye or pseudopod. None of them must ever doubt that defying her led to immediate death. Followed by eating of their still warm flesh.

"I go to my residence. No one is to bother me." Her tail slapped hard the deck. "Each of you will remain here and go without this cycle's live food portion. Your performance has been lacking. We should have caught and killed this human nuisance long ago. Be hungry and think on ways to be more deadly the next time we encounter the human craft!"

She turned and walked slowly to the exit hole. While she moved with deadly precision, a touch of fear hit her deep inside. If she failed to devise a plan that pleased the Dominant, she would die. Worse, other Notemkos would be blocked from advancement. She was the most senior Notemko in service to the Empire. Her success, or failure, would affect the future of all Notemko now serving the Empire.

CHAPTER EIGHTEEN

Thirty-seven days later I sat in my antimatter work station seat, wearing a new vacsuit and with my helmet hinged back. Everyone else on Engineering wore the same. The Chief and PO Gambuchino and her three Spacers were suited up. We were all ready to fight. And fight we would, but covertly. It was Battle Stations and we had just dropped out of a short Alcubierre jump to arrive above the blue-white star I'd seen in the holo. We were just outside the star's magnetosphere boundary and the captain was about to begin a new dance of deception, with the help of Heidi and Loulo.

Those facts I and everyone on board knew, thanks to the captain's All Ship announcement hours ago when we arrived at the start of the approach route to the Empire fleet base deep inside the A portion of W51. We had followed the twists, angles and turns of the route using mini-jumps, in accordance with what Loulo told us was the standard Empire method for approaching the base. She knew everything there was to know for us to get close to the moon that orbited the gas giant in the fifth ring of gas and dust. Or so she had said, when Lieutenant Gerasaki, Commander Kumisov and the captain had interrogated her right after we jumped away from Kepler 439. I hoped she was right and trustworthy. My feelings for Evelyn and my close friends had only grown deeper during the 30 days of four operations and recovery periods. Dr. Khatri had released me to full duty status just six days ago. She had even teased me about having almost as much chest hair as originally, thanks to transplants from my hairy calves. I'd tolerated her humor cause my chest and gut felt like new. She was indeed a wonder-worker.

"Incoming neutrino comsignal!" called Wetstone from his Com post on the Bridge.

I looked away from my antimatter panel to focus on the bulkhead vidscreen to my right. The Chief would not ding me for it this time. He was watching his own vidscreen while Gambuchino and her Spacers watched a third vidscreen near their fusion reactor. Everyone on the ship was at their assigned Battle Stations location, but no one wished to miss the vital first encounter with a rep of the

Empire. Which Loulo had said would happen when we arrived at the mag edge of the B3V blue-white star that held the Fleet base's gas world and its large moon in hock to its powerhouse gravity field.

The vidscreen image held a system graphic, a true space image with the star at the center and the usual overhead view of the Bridge, centered just above the captain's command pedestal. Our captain strummed his fingers on an empty part of his armrest. "Heidi, overlay the Whodune Combine Manager holo imagery onto me and similar images over the officers at this pedestal. Captains Delight, Gorling, Lindo and Mousome, do the same with your ship AI. The Mikmak alien may have shared your images with Empire reps. Heidi, advise when I may respond to this signal."

This was one of the several benefits we had gained thanks to the refugee AI Loulo's presence in Hangar One. It knew all about the various merchant combines that visited Mikmak's star, their cargos and more vitally, the method by which merchant combines delivered cargo to the W51 fleet base.

"Image of wasp-like alien Gerato, chief Manager of the Whodune Combine in Empire system 11,321, is now being overlaid on any neutrino comsignal emanating from this ship," Heidi said. "Similar alien imagery is overlaid atop the forms of Kumisov, Owanju and Bjorg. There is nothing in the altered comsignal that indicates a human presence."

"Good. Wetstone, accept the signal. Display and share with our allies," the captain said. The strumming of his fingers stopped.

"Signal going up on front vidscreen," Wetstone said, his Brit accent once more apparent. To me at least.

An image of the Milky Way galaxy now appeared. It was the standard icon denoting the Empire of Eternity. Then it vanished. An alien filled the space where the icon had been.

"Five ships! Identify and provide base access codes!"

The alien who spoke was as weird as Mikmak. It was a quadruped that had four heavily muscled legs. But it had no front or rear end. Instead, something like a head mound occupied the middle of its back, similar to the way a dromedary camel had a single hump. A ring of blue eyes circled the top of the hump. A circular hole lay below the eye ring. At one end of the long body there gaped a toothy mouth that held shark-like teeth. What the other end held I had no idea. But the joints of its four legs seemed able to flex both forward and rearward. Which made this alien beyond weird. It was clearly an apex predator able to pursue prey whether the prey was in front, to one side or to the rear. The hole in the hump flexed, making a booming sound.

"Reply now!"

The captain leaned forward, then stretched his arms out to right and left. No doubt to make the wasp image of him flare its front wing pair.

"I am Gerato, chief Manager of the Whodune Combine in system 11,321! I and four other combine ships have arrived to provide supplies for base personnel, in accordance with Contract Pink-Lo-143,215. Base access codes are being transmitted!"

The code transmission was something Heidi now added to the outgoing AV comsignal.

"You are from system 11,321?" boomed the four-legged alien. "We have received news that the Lillifuss system was attacked by a resistor species called human. It attacked all shipping and the local orbital. How can you be from that system?"

"We left before this attack you speak of," the captain said hurriedly, drawing in his arms. He raised one hand. "We stopped at nearby system 9,245 before proceeding here. You have our base access codes. Do you wish our cargos or not?"

The ring of blue eyes blinked in sequence. Which also made sense to me. No alien with a ring of eyes would ever close all their eyes, least they expose themselves to unseen danger.

"I am sub-Manager Locuto, of the species Mong, an Associate member of the Empire," the alien boomed. "Describe your cargos."

The captain sat back. "My ship *Extraordinary* contains caskets of sweet liquor, manually constructed musical instruments that appeal to anyone with acoustic membranes, flash-frozen barrels of Nok fruit, caskets of Melang drink and high quality gems of the Wik and Luk variety," the captain said calmly. "Our four associate combine ships contain similar cargo, supplemented by produce we obtained during our visit to system 9,245. I assumed your personnel would welcome fresh garden produce in addition to frozen humps of meat we gained from our Whodune Combine warehouses."

Locuto shifted on his four feet. I noticed white saliva dripping from its toothy mouth. While I was surprised there were no other aliens in the chamber which he occupied, perhaps this Mong alien was doing the midnight shift. Or something similar.

"You assumed correctly. While all personnel hunger for live meat animals, many of us also welcome sweet produce, tangy drinks and intoxicating liquors." A tentacle unfurled from one side of the alien, where it had been hidden by the creature's long brown fur. It touched a control panel on that side. "You may proceed inward at the usual speed. Do not provoke the two escort starbiters that are now appearing near you. If you approach wisely and without provocation, you will be paid the trade sums agreed to in Contract Pink-Lo-143,215." The image vanished.

"Captain!" called Chang. "I have two graviton surges off our port and starboard sides."

The true space image now showed two Empire battlecruisers. They were the usual dumb-bell shaped craft, connected by a thick tube. Their hulls were reddish with white streaks. Small spurts of yellow-orange fusion pulse flame appeared as they adjusted their courses to match our inward vector. We had exited from Alcubierre at a speed of one-tenth psol. These two ships that had dropped their cloaking now moved at the same speed. Worse, they were within 9,000 klicks of us, according to the scale on the system graphic. The graphic had enlarged to focus on our five ships as green dots, which were now flanked by two red dots. Worse, the moon base above the gas giant was almost obscured by red dots. I counted 53 red dots lying close to the base moon. If they were all battlecruisers, this base now hosted the equal of two Empire fleets, if Smooth Fur's fleet was the measure of a standard Empire fleet size.

"I see them." The captain gripped the ends of his armrests. His infrared glow moved from red to red-black. "Heidi, give me an encrypted neutrino link to our four allies. And make certain neither of those Empire ships can unravel your encryption!"

"Captain, I have learned much from my conversation with AI Loulo," Heidi said in a middle-range soprano. "Be assured, she has shared with me knowledge of the encryption modalities which cannot be broken by Empire ships. I am using such a modality now. You are linked with our allies."

The images of our four allied ship captains now appeared in the bulkhead vidscreen.

"Captains Gorling, Lindo and Mousome, move your ships closer to mine, say within 5,000 klicks," the captain said. "Captain Delight, please move your ship so that it lies directly between the antimatter beamer block and the starboard side Empire ship."

"Complying," came from the first three captains.

"I am moving my ship closer," Delight said, her raccoon-like face whiskers moving outward. "May I ask the purpose of your order?"

The captain nodded. "To shield easy imaging of the aperture of my antimatter block. I do not wish to advertise to either Empire ship that I possess AM weaponry. Your laser mounts and my laser mounts fit the pattern of armed merchantmen ships of the Empire. But none of their merchant ships carried AM beamers. I wish our possession to be a secret until we arrive at the engagement range I mentioned to you during our gray space transit."

"Thank you, Captain Skorzeny of Earth," Delight barked. "I will shield your AM block."

Relief filled me. The chill along my back faded away. This first encounter with an Empire system controller had gone well, thanks to the industrial espionage we'd gained by taking on Loulo and by our recovery of merchant records from the Empire residence computers. The presence of the two Empire battlecruisers as escorts did not surprise me. Loulo had warned us such would happen. She had said it was standard practice for any non-fleet ship that approached the base. Now, we would coast inward, moving through the relatively empty space that lay above the dust and gas rings that crowded the system's ecliptic plane. While there was a gas shell surrounding the entire star, as befit a newly formed star that had yet to push outward all the gases of its formation millions of years earlier, that gas shell was thin. It could be pushed aside by the repulsor charged field that surrounded the exterior of every Earth ship. And every raider and Empire ship, based on what we had learned from Heidi and Loulo. What we did not know was what would happen when we came close to the airless moon on which lay the dome of the fleet base. Surely there would be a final 'Stop and allow boarding' inspection of the ship before we were allowed to land. Of course the captain's plan did not include landing anywhere. He just wanted to get close enough to make use of my antimatter shooting scheme. I turned my attention back to my control panel and monitored the containment magfields for the deck above which held thousands of liters of antimatter. Very soon those contents would be at the forefront of our attack on the Empire fleet base.

◆ ◆ ◆

Two days later the *Star Glory* approached within 500,000 kilometers of the airless moon that held the fleet base. Earlier we had slowed to one psol on orders from one of the flanking Empire battlecruisers. Now we would slow again to a slow approach velocity, which speed would allow a boarding crew from one of the escorts to come aboard. Or maybe a shuttle from the moon would come up to board our five ships. I looked aside at the system graphic image on the bulkhead vidscreen. It held the Bridge image, the graphic and a true space image. A fourth image contained the shapes of our four raider captains, conveyed by the encrypted neutrino comsignal.

"Captains! Prepare to attack the Empire escort below us," the captain said sternly, his infrared glow at bright red as he sat in his vacsuit with his helmet closed. "All Ship, close your helmets. We begin active combat within one minute."

I reached up and grabbed my helmet. It came forward and hit the neck ring of my vacsuit. Clicks told me it was locked in place. As did the sudden appearance of green-glowing HUD images on the lower portion of my helmet. The HUD images did not block my view of my control panel. But it did let me know I was on my own independent air, power and communicated through my suit's comlink with the ship's own comlink system. I could hear what anyone on my deck said, just as other decks went to deck-wide com connections. A tap of my armrest control patch would put me in link with the captain or with anyone other line or staff officer.

"Ready for battle," called Delight from her ship.

Similar assurances came from the other captains.

"Delight, in ten seconds move your ship to our port side. All captains, pull back your ship to a position behind the stern of our ship. Comply!"

"Complying," came the response from our raider captains.

The captain looked up at the overhead videye on the Bridge. "PO Watson, adjust your AM beamer aperture to lock onto the starboard Empire ship that is at 3 o'clock high!"

"Adjusting my aperture!" called my friend Bill.

In my mind I saw him touching controls that spun his internal control mount upward and to the right. A vidscreen in front of him would now give a true space image of the two red balls linked by a tube shape of the Empire ship. Meanwhile, the graphic showed our allies moving to our rear.

"PO Watson, fire on the starboard Empire ship!" the captain said loudly.

"Firing, sir!"

In the true space image I saw a black beam shooting from Bill's beamer block. It impacted on the front red globe of the Empire ship. That globe became vapor. A second black beam hit the rear globe. It became a small yellow-glowing star.

"Starboard Empire ship destroyed!" yelled Bill, sounding really pumped.

"Weapons!" the captain called out. "Launch four missiles loaded with thermonuke warheads! Program them for Hunt and Seek. Feed in coordinates for the Empire ship cluster that lies at 312,000 klicks ahead and starboard. Launch a second salvo of missiles right after. Set those warheads to target on the Empire ship cluster lying at 316,000 klicks ahead and on port. Now!"

"Launching first volley," called Yamamoto.

The captain's lips went thin. "Weapons, fire our port gamma ray laser at the port-side Empire ship! Raider captains, fire your lasers at the port-side Empire! Now!" The captain's glow became orange-red. "Weapons, fire the first load of Smart Rocks from our spine and belly railguns! Set them all to Hunt and Seek the neutrino signature of the Empire ship clusters. Launch now!"

"Launching first load of 300 Smart Rocks," Yamamoto said. "Port-side graser is firing on the Empire ship. Sir."

The true space image showed the port-side Empire ship shifting its orientation to aim its nose at us. Red and green proton and carbon dioxide laser beams came from it. Three beams hit our port side.

"Beam impacts on port!" called Kumisov. "One punch-through to Supplies Deck. Hatches closing in rooms and hallways flanking the breach. Sir!"

The captain seemed unbothered by the news of a hull breach. "Allies, take down that Empire ship!"

Four pairs of green and red beams shot from the noses of the four raider ships, which had shifted their ship orientation to point their noses to our port side. Those eight beams hit the enemy, with four beams hitting the stern globe and four hitting the front globe. Our port graser sent out an orange beam that also hit the front globe. Large black holes appeared on the front globe. Then a spurt of blackness showed against the red hull. Just briefly. For the Empire ship's escaped antimatter now ate at and fully consumed all parts of the Empire battlecruiser.

A yellow-orange star glowed brightly where the second Empire ship had been.

"Captain!" called Chang. "Four Empire fleet ships are leaving the starboard ship cluster. They are moving fast. They will hit 15 psol within a minute. They will intersect us within two minutes."

"Thank you Tactical." The captain looked left. "Astrogation, orient our forward vector track exactly on the spot where the dome of the moon base will be within three minutes."

"Sir, shifting ship's nose. Adjusting for slow rotation of moon base dome. Now on vector track!"

The captain looked up and smiled.

"CPO Stewart, release our antimatter fuel reserves."

This was the moment I had been waiting for ever since I had shared with Chief O'Connor my idea for how to make our thousands of liters of antimatter fuel shoot other than to the rear. I reached down and tapped one app on the control panel. Around the outer hull of the ship deck above me, four portals opened. I tapped a second app. A red alert bar appeared on the screen. It told me what I already knew.

"Captain, our containment field on the Antimatter Deck is constricting its field," I called over my suit comlink. "All our antimatter is being shot out of the four emergency ejection portals. Sir!"

In a fifth vidscreen image I saw each portal spew forth a stream of black negative antimatter. That stream quickly expanded as there was no double spiral of containment fields like that which existed above the aperture of Bill's beamer aperture. The expanding antimatter became a globular ring of black cloudiness that surrounded the rear of our ship. Slowly that cloudy ring expanded a tiny bit, opening space between its base and the outer hull of our ship.

"Is the reservoir empty?" called the captain.

"Sir, the entire AM fuel deck is now empty!" I replied.

The captain looked ahead. "Power, engage our reverse attitude thrusters. Slow us down."

"Engaging reverse attitude thrusters," called our amiable Brazilian Diego Suárez y Alonso.

The fifth vidscreen image showed the cloud-ring of antimatter slowly moving forward until it passed beyond the nose of the *Star Glory*. Already the ring measured 149 meters from side to side, which was slightly larger than the thruster stern of our 340 meter-long ship. Its width would expand slightly as it moved ahead at one percent of the speed of light. But that expansion would be minor by the time it hit its target. The 900 meter wide fleet dome that lay on the side of the moon facing us would shortly be touched by this cloud of antimatter. When that happened a flare of light equal to 100 megatons would show on our true space image that carried the view from our primary electro-optical scope. A plasma ball larger than New York City would occupy the space once occupied by the fleet dome. It had been a matter of debate among the line officers during our trip to W51. Should we aim the AM cloud at a cluster of Empire battlecruisers? Or at the control post which imagery from Loulo showed lay on the moon's surface? In the end the fact the dome could not move while the fleet ships could had settled the issue. Destroying the fleet base would be a sufficient shock to Empire arrogance. Or so our captain had informed us over the All Ship.

"Raider captains, adjust your course to north ecliptic. Aim for the spot opposite our arrival point," the captain said. "Go there in mini-jumps. We will join you shortly."

"Captain!" yelled Chang, her arm pointing at the system graphic image on the Bridge vidscreen. "New Empire ships have arrived at our arrival point! Sir! I count . . . I count 21 neutrino transmission points." Chang looked down at her panel. "Sir, their neutrino emissions match those from Smooth Fur's fleet."

Dismay filled me. We could outrun the two Empire fleets in orbit above the fleet moon base. But the presence of Smooth Fur's fleet at our arrival point meant the monster otter could jump to our magnetosphere arrival point and attack us before we could jump into Alcubierre. Or maybe not.

"Engineering! Take us into our first mini-jump!" yelled the captain.

To my left the Chief tapped his Alcubierre control panel. "Sir, entering Alcubierre space-time modulus now!"

Grayness replaced the true space image on the bulkhead vidscreen. I looked down at my panel. I checked the antimatter inflow meter for the particle accelerator ring that lay on the outer hull of our deck. It was already producing new antimatter, thanks to its receiving of the automated report from the deck above that the containment field was empty of negative antimatter. My panel showed four liters of antimatter had been produced since my instruction to the deck to open its emergency release portals. That was a small amount. Maybe enough for one shot from Bill's beamer block.

"Emerging!" yelled Chief O'Connor, sounding excited.

I too felt excitement. Our mini-jump had taken us five AU away from the fleet base. We were beyond the reach of the two fleet ship clusters. And maybe we would see something special.

"Astrogation! Give me the electro-optical feed!" yelled the captain.

"True space view going up!" replied Ibarra.

The bulkhead vidscreen showed the dark side of the moon. Since we were above it, moving north of the system's gas and dust-crowded ecliptic plane, we could see both the starlit side and the night side of the moon.

"Impact!" yelled Bill Yamamoto.

I saw a large yellow-orange star fill a large piece of the moon's night side. The fleet dome on the moon was now gone. It and large pieces of moon rock were now ionized vapor and plasma shooting up and away from the low gravity of the moon. Close to the moon were nine tiny yellow-orange stars. The stars said our Hunt and Seek warheads had found targets among the two clusters of fleet ships. That was nine lucky warheads out of 80, plus hundreds of Smart Rocks that had also been fired. I wished we had killed more Empire ships. But logic told me the two fleet clusters had been alerted to us by our destruction of the two fleet ships that had convoyed us to the moon. Clearly their laser counter-fire had been effective. Which left 44 Empire fleet ships still intact.

A brief sparkle to one side of the true space image showed four silver spearheads. Our raider allies were already here.

"Engineering, take us on our next Alcubierre jump!" ordered the captain, sounding both relieved and pleased.

"Jumping into Alcubierre," called my boss.

I breathed deep. Then I looked at the system graphic image which had frozen with the neutrino signatures from our recent emergence. It showed 21 red dots still present at our arrival point. However the 44 red dots of the two Empire fleets were now moving away from the moon, their vector track twisting to follow our vector track. Clearly we had pissed off 44 ship captains!

"Emerging," spoke the Chief.

Gray space in the vidscreen now became black space partly illuminated by the blue-white star at the bottom of the image. The blue glow of the gas giant buried in the thick orbital ring of gas and dust and small rocks was also visible. The glow of our AM blast was not visible. We had traveled faster than light speed. With any luck we would reach the edge of the system's magnetosphere before that real light image made its way out to the mag edge.

"Captain!" called Chang. "Our raider allies are already here, at 1,213 klicks out from us. Sir!"

"Chief O'Connor, take us into our third jump!"

"Jumping into Alcubierre," my boss said.

The minute we spent in gray space-time gave my heart time to slow down. A bit. I still felt worry over what the fleet of Fur would do. It could now see the vector track we were following. It could project that vector track to a spot beyond the magnetosphere. It could then jump to where it expected us to appear. And then fire on us as we emerged from gray space-time.

"Emerging!"

I took a deep breath. Looking over I saw the suited forms of Gambuchino, Cindy, Duncan and Gus focused on their reactor control panels. Surely they felt the worry and hope I now felt.

"Jump again," the captain said.

"Jumping, sir!"

Grayness replaced true space imagery. We had jumped 15 AU beyond the Empire moon. Soon we would arrive at 20 AU out. In four more jumps we would arrive at 40 AU out, which put us at the edge of the system's magnetosphere. I listened as the captain and my boss did the jump in, emerge out thing three times more. We were now just four AU out from the mag edge.

The bulkhead vidscreen showed what I had feared. The 21 red dots of Smooth Fur's fleet were now awaiting us at five AU ahead.

"Raider captains!" yelled our captain. "Shift to this arrival point in five AU. Astro, transmit the new arrival point!"

"Transmitting, sir," called Ibarra.

Relief flooded through me. My fast-beating heart slowed. We would *not* arrive at a point already occupied by Fur's fleet. While Fur would see our new arrival point, we would be able to go into a long Alcubierre jump before she could arrive. Which fact would leave us alive. But in the future we would have three Empire fleets roaming through the Orion Arm in hot pursuit of us. Or so I assumed and hoped I was not a horse's ass.

"Jump again," the captain said, his hands gripping tightly his armrests.

But I saw now his infrared glow had eased from red-black down to bright red. Being able to see where our enemy lay had reassured him in his command judgment to plan for a different arrival spot in our final jump.

"Jumping, captain," called my boss.

A minute passed. Five seconds passed beyond a minute. Then black space spotted with white star dots replaced the gray in the true space image on the bulkhead vidscreen.

"Our allies are here!" yelled Kumisov.

I saw what she and Chang and Ibarra and everyone on the Bridge and elsewhere on the *Glory* now saw.

Our raider allies were four green dots lying 1,112 klicks away from us. Our ship was a large green dot. The 21 red dots of Smooth Fur's fleet lay one and a half AU distant, at the point where we would have arrived if the captain had not slanted our vector track away from that spot. We were now beyond the edge of the blue-white star's magnetosphere. The captain's image now glowed red normal in infrared.

"Captains, I am transmitting to you the coordinates for Kepler 315," the captain said quickly. "It is a two planet system with one world in the water habitable zone. Our intel from the pirate base says it is another Empire trade system. Want to get rich again?"

"Assuredly!" barked Delight.

The other captains expressed their own agreement.

"Coordinates transmitted," called Ibarra.

The captain nodded, a smile on his face. "Chief O'Connor, take us to Kepler 315. Now!"

To my left the Chief tapped his control panel. Relief showed on his face. Relief also showed on the faces of Dolores Gambuchino, Cindy, Duncan and Gus. No doubt it matched the relief showing on my face. And the relief felt by my lover Evelyn and my friends Bill, Warren, Oksana and Cassandra.

"Jumping to Kepler 315," called the Chief.

Grayness filled the vidscreen. Other images also vanished, leaving only the overhead view of the Bridge. And the people there who now led our ship into a future filled with more raids, more battles with Empire ships and more risk of death as we worked to buy time for Earth to build its own fleet of battlecruisers. Risking our lives was our duty as members of the Star Navy. Choosing to do it well was our individual choice. And my choice, now that I could look forward to a time when the captain would approve the marriage of me and Evelyn. I wanted badly to put my Mom's wedding ring on her finger. She also wanted it badly. Together we would have a future together. How long that future would last, we did not know. But not knowing one's future was the reality for all humans. I could deal with that uncertainty.

THE END

ABOUT THE AUTHOR

T. Jackson King (Tom) is a professional archaeologist, journalist and retired Hippie. He learned early on to question authority and find answers for himself, thanks to reading lots of science fiction. He also worked at a radiocarbon dating laboratory at UC Riverside and UCLA. Tom attended college in Paris and Tokyo. He is a graduate of UCLA (M.A. 1976, archaeology) and the University of Tennessee (B.Sc. 1971, journalism). He has worked as an archaeologist in the American Southwest and has traveled widely in Europe, Russia, Japan, Canada, Mexico and the USA. Other jobs have included short order cook, hotel clerk, legal assistant, telephone order taker, investigative reporter and newspaper editor. He also survived the warped speech-talk of local politicians and escaped with his hide intact. Tom writes hard science fiction, anthropological scifi, dark fantasy/horror and contemporary fantasy/magic realism. Tom's novels are **STAR GLORY** (2017), **MOTHER WARM** (2017), **BATTLECRY** (2017), **SUPERGUY** (2016), **BATTLEGROUP** (2016), **BATTLESTAR** (2016), **DEFEAT THE ALIENS** (2016), **FIGHT THE ALIENS** (2016), **FIRST CONTACT** (2015), **ESCAPE FROM ALIENS** (2015), **ALIENS VS. HUMANS** (2015), **FREEDOM VS. ALIENS** (2015), **HUMANS VS. ALIENS** (2015), **GENECODE ILLEGAL** (2014), **EARTH VS. ALIENS** (2014), **ALIEN ASSASSIN** (2014), **THE MEMORY SINGER** (2014), **ANARCHATE VIGILANTE** (2014), **GALACTIC VIGILANTE** (2013), **NEBULA VIGILANTE** (2013), **SPEAKER TO ALIENS** (2013), **GALACTIC AVATAR** (2013), **STELLAR ASSASSIN** (2013), **STAR VIGILANTE** (2012), **THE GAEAN ENCHANTMENT** (2012), **LITTLE BROTHER'S WORLD** (2010), **ANCESTOR'S WORLD** (1996, with A.C. Crispin), and **RETREAD SHOP** (1988, 2012). His short stories appeared in **JUDGMENT DAY AND OTHER DREAMS** (2009). His poetry appeared in **MOTHER EARTH'S STRETCH MARKS** (2009). Tom lives in Santa Fe, New Mexico, USA with his wife Sue. More information on Tom's writings can be found at www.tjacksonking.com/.

PRAISE FOR T. JACKSON KING'S BOOKS

EARTH VS. ALIENS

"This story is the best space opera I've read in many years. The author knows his Mammalian Behavior. If we're lucky it'll become a movie soon. Many of the ideas are BRAND NEW and I loved the adaptability of people in the story line. AWESOME!!"—**Phil W. King,** *Amazon*

"It's good space opera. I liked the story and wanted to know what happened next. The characters are interesting and culturally diverse. The underlying theme is that humans are part of nature and nature is red of tooth and claw. Therefore, humans are naturally violent, which fortunately makes them a match for the predators from space."—**Frank C. Hemingway,** *Amazon*

STAR VIGILANTE

"For a fast-paced adventure with cool tech, choose *Star Vigilante*. This is the story of three outsiders. Can three outsiders bond together to save Eliana's planet from eco-destruction at the hands of a ruthless mining enterprise?" –**Bonnie Gordon**, *Los Alamos Daily Post*

STELLAR ASSASSIN
"T. Jackson King's *Stellar Assassin* is an ambitious science fiction epic that sings! Filled with totally alien lifeforms, one lonely human, an archaeologist named Al Lancaster must find his way through trade guilds, political maneuvering and indentured servitude, while trying to reconcile his new career as an assassin with his deeply-held belief in the teachings of Buddha. . . This is a huge, colorful, complicated world with complex characters, outstanding dialogue, believable motivations, wonderful high-tech battle sequences and, on occasion, a real heart-stringer . . . This is an almost perfectly edited novel as well, which is a bonus. This is a wonderful novel, written by a wonderful author . . .Bravo! Five Stars!" –**Linell Jeppsen**, *Amazon*

LITTLE BROTHER'S WORLD

"If you're sensing a whiff of Andre Norton or Robert A. Heinlein, you're not mistaken . . . The influence is certainly there, but *Little Brother's World* is no mere imitation of *Star Man's Son* or *Citizen of the Galaxy*. Rather, it takes the sensibility of those sorts of books and makes of it something fresh and new. T. Jackson King is doing his part to further the great conversation of science fiction; it'll be interesting to see where he goes next."–**Don Sakers,** *Analog*

"When I'm turning a friend on to a good writer I've just discovered, I'll often say something like, "Give him ten pages and you'll never be able to put him down." Once in a long while, I'll say, "Give him five pages." It took T. Jackson King exactly *one sentence* to set his hook so deep in me that I finished *LITTLE BROTHER'S WORLD* in a single sitting, and I'll be thinking about that vivid world for a long time to come. The last writer I can recall with the courage to make a protagonist out of someone as profoundly Different as Little Brother was James Tiptree Jr., with her remarkable debut novel *UP THE WALLS OF THE WORLD*. I think Mr. King has met that challenge even more successfully. His own writing DNA borrows genes from writers as diverse as Tiptree, Heinlein, Norton, Zelazny, Sturgeon, Pohl, and Doctorow, and splices them together very effectively." – **Spider Robinson, Hugo, Nebula and Campbell Award winner**

"*Little Brother's World* is a sci-fi novel where Genetic Engineering exists. . . It contains enough details and enough thrills to make the book buyers/readers grab it and settle in for an afternoon read. The book is well-written and had a well-defined plot . . . I never found a boring part in the story. It was fast-paced and kept me entertained all throughout. The characters are fascinating and likeable too. This book made me realize about a possible outcome, when finally science and technology wins over traditional ones. . . All in all, *Little Brother's World* is another sci-fi novel from T. Jackson King that is both exciting, thrilling and fun. Full of suspense, adventure, romance, secrets, conspiracies, this book would take you in a roller-coaster ride." –**Abby Flores,** *Bookshelf Confessions*

THE MEMORY SINGER

"A coming of age story reminiscent of Robert A. Heinlein or Alexei

Panshin. Jax [the main character] is a fun character, and her world is
compelling. The social patterns of Ship life are fascinating, and the
Alish'Tak [the main alien species] are sufficiently alien to make for a
fairly complex book. Very enjoyable."—**Don Sakers**, *Analog
Science Fiction*

"Author T. Jackson King brings his polished writing style, his
knowledge of science fiction 'hardware,' and his believable aliens to
his latest novel *The Memory Singer*. But all this is merely backdrop to
the adventures of Jax Cochrane, a smart, rebellious teen who wants
more from life than the confines of a generational starship. There are
worlds of humans and aliens out there. When headstrong Jax decides
that it's time to discover and explore them, nothing can hold back this
defiant teen. You'll want to accompany this young woman . . in this
fine coming-of-age story."—**Jean Kilczer, *Amazon***

RETREAD SHOP

"Engaging alien characters, a likable protagonist, and a vividly
realized world make King's first sf novel a good purchase for sf
collections."–*Library Journal*

"A very pleasant tour through the author's inventive mind, and an
above average story as well."–*Science Fiction Chronicle*

"Fun, with lots of outrageously weird aliens."—*Locus*

"The writing is sharp, the plotting tight, and the twists ingenious. It
would be worth reading, if only for the beautiful delineations of alien
races working with and against one another against the background of
an interstellar marketplace. The story carries you . . . with a verve and
vigor that bodes well for future stories by this author.
Recommended."–*Science Fiction Review*

"For weird aliens, and I do mean weird, choose ***Retread Shop***. The
story takes place on a galactic trading base, where hundreds of
species try to gain the upper hand for themselves and for their group.
Sixteen year-old billy is the sole human on the Retread Shop,
stranded when his parents and their shipmates perished. What really

makes the ride fun are the aliens Billy teams up with, including two who are plants. It's herbivores vs. carnivores, herd species vs. loners, mammals vs. insects and so on. The wild variety of physical types is only matched by the extensive array of cultures, which makes for a very entertaining read." –**Bonnie Gordon, *Los Alamos Daily Post***

"Similar in feel to Roger Zelazny's Alien Speedway series is ***Retread Shop*** by T. Jackson King. It's an orphan-human-in-alien-society-makes-good story. Well-written and entertaining, it could be read either as a Young Adult or as straight SF with equal enjoyment." –**Chuq Von Rospach, *OtherRealms 22***

"If you liked Stephen Goldin's Jade Darcy books duo, and Julie Czerneda's Clan trilogy, then you will probably like ***Retread Shop*** since it too has multiple aliens, an eatery, and an infinity of odd events that range from riots, to conspiracy, to exploring new worlds and to alien eating habits . . . It's a fun reader's ride and thoroughly entertaining. And, sigh, I wish that the author would write more books set in this background." –**Lyn McConchie, co-author of the *Beastmaster* series**

HUMANS VS. ALIENS

"Another great book from this author. This series has great characters and story is wall to wall excitement. Look forward to next book."— **William R. Thomas, *Amazon***

"Humans are once again aggressive and blood thirsty to defend the Earth. Pace is quick and action is plentiful. Some unexpected plot twists, but you always know the home team is the best."—**C. Cook, *Amazon***

ANCESTOR'S WORLD
"T. Jackson King is a professional archaeologist and he uses that to great advantage in ***Ancestor's World***. I was just as fascinated by the details of the archaeology procedures as I was by the unfolding of the plot . . . What follows is a tightly plotted, suspenseful novel."–***Absolute Magnitude***

"The latest in the StarBridge series from King, a former Rogue Valley resident now living and writing in Arizona, follows the action on planet Na-Dina, where the tombs of 46 dynasties have lain undisturbed for 6,000 years until a human archaeologist and a galactic gumshoe show up. Set your phasers for fun."–*Medford Mail Tribune*

ALIEN ASSASSIN
"The Assassin series is required reading in adventure, excitement and daring. The galactic vistas, the advanced alien technologies and the action make all the Assassin books a guarantee of a good read. Please keep them coming!"—**C. B. Symons,** *Amazon*

"KING STRIKES AGAIN! Yes, T. Jackson King gives us yet again a great space adventure. I loved the drama and adventure in this book. There is treachery in this one too which heightens the suspense. Being the only human isn't easy, but Al pulls it off. Loved the Dino babies and how they are being developed into an important part of the family of assassins. All of the fun takes place right here and we are not left hanging off the cliff. Write on T.J."—**K. McClell,** *Amazon*

THE GAEAN ENCHANTMENT
"For magic, a quest and a new battle around every corner, go with *The Gaean Enchantment*. In this novel, Earth has entered a new phase as it cycles through the universe. In this phase, some kinds of "magic" work, but tech is rapidly ceasing to function. In the world of this book, incantation and sympathetic magic function through connection to spirit figures who might be described as gods." – **Bonnie Gordon,** *Los Alamos Daily Post*

"In *The Gaean Enchantment* the main character, Thomas, back from Vietnam and with all the PTSD that many soldiers have—nightmares, blackouts—finds his truth through the finding of his totem animal, the buffalo Black Mane. He teaches Thomas that violence and killing must always be done as a last resort, and that the energies of his soul are more powerful than any arsenal . . . Don't miss this amazing novel of magic and soul transformation, deep love, and Artemis, goddess of the hunt and protector of women."–**Catherine Herbison-Wiget,** *Amazon*

JUDGMENT DAY AND OTHER DREAMS

"King is a prolific writer with an old-time approach–he tells straight-ahead stories and asks the big questions. No topic is off limits and he writes with an explorer's zest for uncovering the unknown. He takes readers right into the world of each story, so each rustle of a tree, each whisper of the wind, blows softly against your inner ear."–**Scott Turick, *Daytona Beach News-Journal***

"Congratulations on the long overdue story collection, Tom! What I find most terrific is your range of topics and styles. You have always been an explorer."–**David Brin, Nebula and Hugo winner**

"I'm thoroughly loving [the stories]; the prose is the kind that makes me stop and savor it – roll phrases over my tongue – delicious. I loved the way you conjure up a whole world or civilization so economically."–**Sheila Finch, SF author**

"***Judgment Day and Other Dreams*** . . . would make a valued addition to any science fiction or fantasy library. There is a satisfying and engrossing attention to detail within the varied stories . . . The common thread among all works is the intimate human element at the heart of each piece. King's prose displays a mastery over these myriad subjects without alienating the uninitiated, thus providing the reader with a smooth, coherent, and altogether enjoyable experience . . . King is able to initiate the reader naturally through plot and precise prose, as if being eased into a warm bath . . . There is a dedicated unity amongst some of the entries in this anthology that begs to be explored in longer formats. And the works which stand apart are just as notable and exemplify King's grasp of human emotions and interactions. This collection displays the qualities of fine writing backed by a knowledgeable hand and a vivid imagination . . . If ***Judgment Day and Other Dreams*** is anything to go by, T. Jackson King should be a household name." –**John Sulyok, *Tangent Online***

Printed in Dunstable, United Kingdom

66031149R00129